GOING
UNDERGROUND

ALSO BY SUSAN VAUGHT

Stormwitch

Trigger

My Big Fat Manifesto

Exposed

∞

The Oathbreaker saga
with J B Redmond

Part One: Assassin's Apprentice

Part Two: A Prince Among Killers

GOING UNDERGROUND

susan vaught

BLOOMSBURY

NEW YORK   BERLIN   LONDON   SYDNEY

First published in the United States of America in September 2011
by Bloomsbury Books for Young Readers
www.bloomsburyteens.com

For information about permission to reproduce selections from this book, write to
Permissions, Bloomsbury BFYR, 175 Fifth Avenue, New York, New York 10010

Library of Congress Cataloging-in-Publication Data
Vaught, Susan.
Going underground / by Susan Vaught. — 1st U.S. ed.
p.   cm.
Summary: Interest in a new girl and pressure from his parole officer cause seventeen-year-old
Del, a gravedigger, to recall and face the "sexting" incident three years earlier that transformed
him from a straight-A student-athlete into a social outcast and felon.
ISBN 978-1-59990-640-9 (hardcover)
[1. Interpersonal relations—Fiction. 2. Gravediggers—Fiction. 3. Probation—Fiction. 4. Text
messages (Telephone systems)—Fiction. 5. Sex crimes—Fiction.] I. Title.
PZ7.F3133Goi 2011   [Fic]—dc22   2010051028

Book design by Nicole Gastonguay
Typeset by Westchester Book Composition
Printed in the U.S.A. by Quad/Graphics, Fairfield, Pennsylvania
2 4 6 8 10 9 7 5 3 1

For anybody who doesn't know what they want
    to be when they grow up.
For anybody who doesn't know—or care—what
    growing up is supposed to mean.
For Livia, who wanted to see her name in a book.
And for Fred, even though her name is really
    Frank.

Where am I to go, now that I've gone too far?
"Twilight Zone" by Golden Earring

GOING UNDERGROUND

I've Always Wanted to See a Fairy

(Read to the tune of "Twilight Zone"—Golden Earring.)

Dead zones.

Dead zones are places without life, without feeling, without air. I've seen them in pictures of polluted oceans and read about them in descriptions of the cold void of space. Sometimes I think parts of my body have turned silent and dark like those pictures and descriptions. Sometimes I think I've become a dead zone.

I mop sweat off my forehead with a dirty handkerchief, reposition my earbuds and adjust the iPod in my pocket, then pick up my shovel. It's hot, and it's late afternoon, and this is a graveyard. It's a quiet place, down a long country road and sort of in the middle of nowhere, like graveyards people write about in horror stories—only this cemetery isn't creepy, at least not to me. The graveyard is not huge, but it's big enough and full of headstones and plots. My job is to dig the graves, then close them up again, and it's time to move dirt from one spot to another to bury a body that really, truly has become a dead zone. I'm glad for the pine box that hides the sewn eyes and the blank face. Some things just don't need to see the light of day again.

Before I can turn the earth and start filling in the grave, I catch the whisper and flow of movement in the distance and glance up to check what it is.

Oh.

Not much of a thought, but it's hard to be coherent when a sight clubs you square in the eyes and leaves you standing on a pile of dirt, clinging to a shovel like it's some kind of anchor to life and reality and graves that you shouldn't fall into and bust your face. And my second thought is, *She looks like a fairy. All she needs are gossamer wings.*

The music in my ears blasts so loud it seems like it lives in my brain. Something catchy. Something fast. It's all wrong for the girl. She deserves something slow and classical and thoughtful. There's nothing jangly about her. She's my height, or close to it—and my age, or pretty close on that point, too. She has dark hair.

Is she real?

Because she seems like a dream—something out of another world. She walks like she's barely touching the ground, flowing toward a clutch of trees and newer graves, and she's wearing a yellow dress. The fabric makes her skin look tanned and smooth.

For a second, I can see the girl's face. Her dark eyes have a darker glimmer at the center, like she knows, like she really understands how the world works, in all the ways people like us aren't supposed to be old enough to grasp. Her expression seems distant, and it's sad in a way that clubs me all over again, this time in the heart. She's tired. She's worn down. I can see the hopelessness and resignation sketched across her features. It makes my chest ache for her even though I don't know her.

This Fairy Girl, she's sad like me.

I don't think she sees me. Guys who dig graves tend to be invisible to sane, normal people.

My heart's beating too fast and I'm not breathing right.

Stop looking before she sees you. Stop. You just need to stop.

I shiver even though I'm burning up, and I step back, jerk my shovel out of the dirt, and ram it down to pick up a good load. Yeah, that's better. Go back to the digging, get back to the music, and pay attention to the hard, loud beat. It blots away the hot wind and the plink and crumble of my digging. If I play it loud enough, music shuts out everything, even dreamy girls who float through lonely, boring grave-yards. Ignoring her is definitely the right thing to do, because dreams and Fairy Girls, they aren't for me.

Soft, pretty things don't belong in a dead zone.

I Really Don't Think about Shooting People

("Mad World"—Tears for Fears or Adam Lambert from *Idol*. I like Lambert best, but that's me.)

No cell phones.

No text messages.

The room I'm sitting in, it's way too quiet.

I wonder—if I'd never been popular enough to get an e-mail or a text or a buzzing call in my pocket, would I have felt so lonely when every electronic thing I owned went as silent as gravestones, then got taken away from me?

And when I'm not in this too-quiet room, when I'm at Rock Hill, digging in the ground until I can't breathe, when I'm noticing the way my shovel cracks across the caked silence like a bat beating tin, would I be thinking, *Who am I?*

Or, *Why am I here?*

Or, *What's the point?*

Who am I—that's a good place to start. Before I became *that guy who did that awful stuff*, I was just a person. I'm still just a person in my own head, at least. I'm not anybody special. I'm not fat. I'm not thin. I'm not tall or short or famous. I've made mostly As and Bs since my freshman year, no matter what kind of mess was happening in my life. I'm nobody's brother, and lots of times, I don't feel like anybody's son. My parents exist, but they work and go on dates and take trips and make sure "you've got plenty to eat while we're gone, right?" I'm not sure I was really supposed to happen, but I happened, so my folks do their duty, even with all the trouble I've caused them. I always have enough to eat, so that counts for something.

My mother smells like raspberries. My dad's always smelled like the same aftershave. I think he's used it since he was my age. Somebody should tell him he's got way more options now, but maybe he knows that. Maybe my dad remembers the world before life went wireless, and he holds on to that old-smelling stuff just to keep it all clear in his head.

We have a lot of animals—or my parents do. I mostly have Fred. She's a parrot, and she can talk. Her name is Fred because nobody knew she was a girl parrot until she laid an egg, and her name had been Fred for a long time already. She calls herself Fred, and she talks about herself all the time, so I couldn't exactly get her to switch to Frederica or Freddie May just because of the egg.

Fred is only ten years old, and she might live longer than

me. Parrots can live a long, long time, which is why "teenagers should never have them." Because "parrots are a life-
time commitment." And everybody knows teenagers can't
commit, right? We can't be responsible for anything, we
can't understand how big and huge the future is—but we can
be held accountable for our actions no matter what we really
knew or what we really meant. Forever. All across that big
long future we don't understand, and maybe don't even have.

Anyway, Fred is gray and red.

I am not.

Fred has feathers.

I do not.

I own four pairs of jeans, and two have holes in them.

I wear the same pair of sneakers every day. They have
holes in them, too. I could buy more sneakers because I
have a job, but I like the pair I have because they're worn and
comfortable and don't make blisters, so maybe I'm not much
better than Dad with his aftershave.

I don't know why my mother smells—or used to smell—
like raspberries. Maybe I should ask her, but she probably
doesn't know, either.

Why am I here?

Now, that question's harder, and I don't have any answers.
I used to have lots of plans and dreams, but those are trash
now. The best I can come up with is maybe I'm here because
I have to take care of Fred. Or maybe I'm here because Marvin considers me his friend, and Marvin's a good guy, and

he needs friends, because, well, his name is Marvin, and he's never managed to earn a wicked nickname. His middle name is Harold, so all in all, I think he's better sticking with Marvin. Don't get me wrong—Marvin and Harold are good names, and I've got *zero* room to say anything about nut-ball names thanks to the family traditions my parents plastered on my birth certificate, but right now, Marvin and Harold, they're . . . I don't know. Out of style, or something.

Do you ever get sick of reading novels about teenagers who drink, get high all the time, lie, beat people up, save the world, have dark secrets, tell dark secrets, blow up the neighborhood, shoot themselves, or shoot other people?

God, I asked that out loud, didn't I?

"Do you think about shooting people, Del?"

The voice splits into my skull, and even though I'm alone inside, I remember I'm not alone outside, and that I'm supposed to be paying attention.

Obviously, I suck at that. I have for the last three years.

Dr. Mote sounds totally not upset, but I can hear *tense* floating around in her question somewhere. Maybe *wary*. And *worried*.

I see the words in my head in bold black italic, because Dr. Mote has "emotion cards" we work with, about two hundred of them, and these three come up a lot.

I think my fingers have lost all blood flow.

Was the room this cold when I spaced out?

"No, I don't think about shooting people." *Tense.*

"Not ever?" One of Dr. Mote's eyebrows twitches when she asks this, like she believes I've got a long hit list etched deep across my heart, but I'm still thinking about the emotion cards, and now, I'm thinking a little bit about eyebrows, too.

"What?" *Wary.*

She doesn't sigh, but I can tell she wants to. "Shooting people . . ."

Worried.

"Oh yeah. Not ever." I'm wearing one of the pairs of jeans with holes in them. I play with the frayed spot on my left knee, and the threads feel soft. "Before Columbine, nobody asked questions like that. Columbine sucked."

"It did suck, and this is after Columbine, and do you ever think about shooting yourself?" Dr. Mote's voice seems to bounce off the pine paneling and pictures of mountains and trees and beaches. It slides between beanbags and two recliners, and the barrel chair where she usually sits, about five feet away from me. Her sandal presses against a green area rug on the hardwood, mashing down the carpet pile.

What's the point?

That's the question I never have any answer for at all, but it pops up in my head over and over again, and it takes a lot of energy not to ask it out loud every time I think it. This, however, would not be the time or place to get morbid or philosophical. "No, I don't think about shooting myself."

"Don't roll your eyes, Del. You know I have to ask every now and then. It's a doctor thing."

"The doctors on HBO don't ask shit like that. And some of them screw their patients."

<therapist blinking>

<crickets chirping>

<Fred would pick now to say *Freeeeed* in her me-like birdie voice, just to get my attention.>

Maybe I should bring Fred to session with me. She's been invited more than once, and I take her everywhere else that allows birds.

"Doctors who sleep with patients are scum," Dr. Mote says.

Dr. Mote is definitely not scum.

I'm glad for that, since I'm required by law to see her at least every two weeks. We've racked up some hours together in the last three years.

Dr. Mote doesn't have wire-rimmed glasses or a beard like just about every therapist ever in shows and movies. She doesn't look old or pinched and plasticked-out. She's got boobs, and I think they're real, and that's kind of nice, because to me, fake boobs look wrongly perky, and it's hard not to wonder if they'll pop if somebody touches them. Dr. Mote doesn't wear jeans and try to be young, and she doesn't wear suits and try to be stuffy. She just . . . is. She's just . . . there. Like her office, which is in an old historic house with an old historic couch with dents where my ass goes.

My therapist scores on the Dad-aftershave and me-sneakers scale. Maybe we all like familiar things.

"I'm still not certain I like you working at a graveyard." She settles back into her barrel chair, which is greener than the area rug, and adjusts the pillow where she rests her elbow.

"You got other ideas? Even Mickey D's does a background check." I glance away from her, because this kind of stuff isn't as fun as talking about whacked-out shrinks on HBO.

Dr. Mote keeps looking relaxed, but she says, "I know it's not fair."

The shrug's automatic. I couldn't not shrug unless I sliced my shrug muscle in half. "That depends on your perspective."

"You're allowed to be angry about your situation, Del. Sooner or later, you're going to have to let it out. I wish you'd sketch something about your feelings, or blog them privately. Write a poem or an essay or a novel about your life. Something?"

My sigh reflex activates and I don't try to hold back. We've so been here before, and too many times. I don't answer.

Dr. Mote stays quiet for a count of five, then hits me with, "Mr. Branson still wants you to testify this spring at the hearings about changing the juvenile laws. He left your name on the legislative list in case you change your mind, and I hope you do."

Panic doesn't quite cover the blast in my gut. No words for the feeling, unless I call it scared-embarrassed-hopeless-horror-no-way, all crammed together, screaming so loud against my ribs I'm wondering if I'll crack loose and let it all blow right out of my mouth. Sweat beads on my lip, my neck and shoulders, but I'm not yelling, not yet at least, and after a few more seconds, I think I can talk.

"Talking at a bunch of hearings about stupid, bad laws won't do me any good. Being pissed doesn't do me any good, and I don't want to turn my life into some kind of artsy picture or novel or essay or whatever."

I'm breathing way too hard, but Dr. Mote lets me wheeze along and doesn't slow down. "I'm not sure testifying at those hearings would be about helping *you*—more about helping other people so that nobody has to go through what you've been through."

She pauses, but only for a second. "As for you, what *will* help? What *do* you want to do with your life to move on from all this, to reclaim some of what you've lost?"

"I don't know! You're the doctor, aren't you?"

Okay, that was too loud and beyond stupid and a way major cop-out.

Back off, blow off, settle down.

"I'm writing the letters to all the colleges on Branson's

list," I start back, glad Dr. Mote's expression never changes. "I might make his deadline."

"Get a life and future by your eighteenth birthday," she says, reconnecting, and I like her for doing that.

"If I want his good recommendation to the court about ending my probation." Force the smile. Be polite.

"That's several months away." She smiles back, not forced. "Several months to get a life and a future. No pressure there. What are you doing to relax?"

That takes some thinking. I start with, "Digging graves helps a little. It burns energy and it pays good with all the other stuff I do for Harper. Harper never judges me for anything. He's almost as good as Marvin, if you leave off the cheap-ass beer."

Now Dr. Mote's expression does change. She kind of looks like she's got to go to the bathroom, or maybe something's hurting her brain. "You don't have to . . . you know. Handle the dead people, do you?"

"Um, no. They're sealed up by the time we get them."

"Good, because even though you're very mature for seventeen, with everything you've been through, that would just cross a line for me—wait a second." She studies my face like she's pinpointing the exact spot where she can see the whole truth, and nothing but the truth, which she always manages to do. "There's something you're not telling me. Did anything happen with that Goth girl who won't leave you alone—Cherie Blankenship, right?"

"Right, but no." I swallow, hunting the exact right words, coming up with zilch. Crap. I knew this would happen.

Dr. Mote stares at me even harder. "Something new. *Someone* new?"

And here we go.

"Yeah, well. Kind of."

She waits.

I wait, but not to be a dick.

It's hard to wrap my mouth around the words, because I haven't said them since the summer between eighth grade and my freshman year, and figured I'd never say them again, and I know even letting them out in this safe, familiar room could cause a lot of trouble.

"There's this girl."

Dr. Mote's fingers clench in her lap, then relax quick, like she didn't want me to see.

"I know, I know," I jump in before she comes back at me with any questions or warnings. "And no, she's not from here, I don't think. She's coming to a new plot we put in last month, a woman's grave. The woman died young, about twenty-four years old."

"How old is she?" Dr. Mote's question shoots out too fast. She hardly ever does that. "The live girl, I mean."

My teeth grind together, but no way will I say anything ugly to Dr. Mote, because really, she isn't scum, even when I *am*. "My age, maybe more."

"You know I can't recommend this."

"I didn't ask you to. I'm not breaking any rules." This time it's me talking too fast. "There aren't any rules about this, right? It's her decision whether she wants to talk to me or not."

"As long as you tell her. As long as she's making an informed choice. And it's still very, very risky."

If Dr. Mote were my mother, she'd probably hit me with a *you be very, very careful, Cane Delano Hartwick*, but she doesn't have to. *Tense* comes through like she's screaming it with a bullhorn. It's sweet that she worries about me, but it still kind of makes me mad.

"You will tell her, won't you?" Dr. Mote's blinking again, which she only does when she's gearing up not to accept anything but a total, unconditional *yes*.

Barely controlling my shrug and sigh muscles, I manage, "If I ever even talk to her."

Dr. Mote's eyes get small as she studies me some more. "You need to get a life, Del. Branson's right about that part. Some sort of normal, healthy, happy teenage life, even if it's hard, so maybe this isn't all bad. I'm thinking you'll talk to her. Is she pretty?"

"She's . . . she's . . ."

What?

Beautiful doesn't quite cut it.

I think she might be pretty in ways that don't have anything to do with outside looks.

I think she might be like me, and I've never met anyone like me since the bad stuff happened.

I think she might . . . understand.

Just trying to describe her makes me breathe funny all over again. The girl who visits that grave in Rock Hill still reminds me of a fairy, with her long legs and arms, and the way her black hair hangs straight around her face. It flutters in the wind like her loose skirts and shirts, making her seem wispy and flyaway, and I wouldn't be surprised if she did sprout wings and take off into the sky.

"She's special." That's the best I can do.

Dr. Mote nods. After a long few seconds, maybe a whole minute, she says, "Talk to her. Then tell her about yourself and your situation. And don't wait too long."

I lean back on the saggy sofa and blow out a breath. "Could I find out her name first? Seriously, she's never even noticed me."

"She will."

Psychic. Therapist. Sometimes it's hard to figure out exactly what Dr. Mote should call herself.

So you're waiting for it, right? I know you are.

Why am I seeing a therapist? What horrible problem do I have? What rank, lame, rotten thing did I do?

Shame on you.

What if I didn't do anything at all?

Maybe I witnessed a vicious crime. No, wait. "Brutal." When newspeople talk about murder, it's always "brutal."

Brutalmurder should be a new word, since they always get said together, even though they're kind of redundant.

Wait, wait. Maybe I got hit by a drunk driver and have to live in a wheelchair now. That happens to people. It could have happened to me. But I guess that's a crummy thing to joke about, even though I'm not really joking about stuff like my life being wrecked and having no future.

Maybe I have a learning disability and I'm all frustrated by not being able to read, or sit still, or whatever.

Maybe I have real problems I didn't even cause.

See? Now don't you feel guilty?

Good.

Because God knows I do.

Three Years Ago: Dreams in Dreamland

"I like the way your lips taste."

Crap. I wasn't expecting that. My cheeks go hot, but I keep still on the quilt in the park, eyes closed tight so I don't see the blue sky or the drifting clouds, or the way Cory's probably smiling at me because I'm turning red.

She laughs. "You're blushing." She touches my lips with hers again, just a brush, like a whisper without any words. She's right beside me, stretched out, her arm draped across my chest, her head on my shoulder when she's not giving me fast little kisses.

I keep my eyes closed and wonder how exactly my lips do taste.

What did I eat for lunch?

Tacos? Brownies? I can't remember. It's been four hours and a baseball game. My stomach tightens, winding up to rumble, but I tense my muscles to keep it from making some obnoxious noise.

When I open my eyes, all I can think is, *it's summer* and *she's pretty.*

Our phones are turned down low, and we're ignoring them if they don't give our parents' rings. A warm breeze blows against the dirt and mown grass of the infield we're using. Cory's blond hair looks ready to make a break from her ponytail. Her nose has a few freckles on top of her dark softball tan. I'd count them, but she's looking at me with her blue eyes, the same color as the sky, and then she's moving to lie down again.

"You always taste like cinnamon," I tell her as she settles her head on my shoulder.

She lets out a breath, almost a sigh, but more *I'm relaxing* than *I'm ticked about something.* "It's the gum."

I like kissing her.

I mean, I've kissed three or four girls—but nobody like her. I can't believe I didn't notice how kick-ass she was until the end of eighth grade. Weird, how that happens, how you can know people for months or years and then suddenly see them different, like they just stepped off a bus and turned into someone else.

Watching Cory play softball did me in, I guess. She's one wicked-mean underhand pitcher, and she can run like a

track star, and she just—I don't know. Shines in the sun or
something.

We're lying in a lot of it. Sun, I mean. My team, Home
Hardware, is safely in the finals, so we're getting a rest
before tonight's games. Cory and I are three fields over from
the tournament, and the grass is deserted except for Cory and
me. Jason and Randall are playing right now on the Backwater Restaurant team, against Tom and Raulston's team,
Perlman's Law. On the girls' field, Jenna and Lisa are playing
for Sonic Drive-In Team I, and we left Dutch and Marvin
running back and forth between the games, cheering everybody on.

Well, Marvin was eating a bunch of hot dogs, but he'll
cheer between bites, when he's not burping.

"Are you scared about next month?" Cory murmurs, her
lips close enough to my neck that I feel the puff of heat from
her breath.

"No way." I tighten my arm around her, because I know
she's nervous about it, and really, so am I, but I'm not admit-
ting that to anybody, even her. "I'm ready for high school.
We're all ready. And we're tall, so that'll help."

She gives my chest a little punch with the heel of her
hand.

Everybody knows I'm superorganized, and everybody
but Cory hates me for it. I've already got my schedule planned
and the notebooks bought and labeled. Everything's in its
place for school to start, because I'm gonna kick ass with my

grades to keep myself on whatever team I pick, and so I'll have no trouble getting into premed or prelaw. I want all my options open. My parents might have invested their degrees in small-town life and small-town jobs to "be sure you get raised in a place where life is simple and real, Del," but farming and settling for less—absolutely not my plan.

I have dozens of plans. If plan A doesn't work, I'll move to B. If B doesn't work, there's always C.

Who says teenagers don't know what they want? Who says we're not able to set goals and reach them?

Just watch.

"I think I'll take chorus instead of drama, at least for the first year," Cory says.

I keep her as close to me as I can. "You've got a great voice."

She doesn't say anything back. She just snuggles into me and lets me hold her and enjoy how it feels to have her next to me. She smells like cinnamon, too. Cinnamon and vanilla. I think the vanilla comes from her shampoo or lotion.

My eyes float closed, but she rattles me awake a little bit later, answering her phone, then getting up.

"My folks will be at the park in a few," she says as she punches off her phone and slides it back in her pocket, then dusts the wrinkles out of her Coldair Refrigeration uniform. That's her team's sponsor, and their colors are white and red. "We should get back."

I don't budge from the blanket. "What's the big deal? We're not doing anything."

Her smile comes fast as she tucks her shirt back into her red pants. "Fine. I'll just let you explain that to my dad."

Um, yeah. Rather not.

For a second or two, with the way she's looking at me, I'm nervous that Cory does want to do something more than kissing. But she doesn't say anything. She just waits for me to get up, then waits for me to follow her.

When I do, I watch her walk.

She has a great walk, too.

I think maybe she will be the one.

Why shouldn't she be? She's the best girlfriend I've had, and the longest so far, four months and counting. I've known her for lots longer, of course, so some of that time should count toward the "knowing each other really well" part, right?

We're both smart. We know what we want. We'll use protection.

She sees her team getting ready to go warm up on a practice field, so she gives me a wave and runs off to join them. Just about the same moment, the bleachers empty as the afternoon crowd heads for the bathrooms, food, or walking tracks to take a break between games. By the time I turn toward the main field gate, it's open, and Raulston's heading right at me with Tom behind him, grinning like an idiot.

Jason and Randall are heading for the concession stand, looking pissed, so I figure Backwater Restaurant is out of the tournament.

Raulston's even taller than me, and his black hair and dark eyes make him think he's ten kinds of handsome. He waggles his big thick eyebrows at Cory as she heads onto the practice field, then gets close enough to me to smack my shoulder.

"You two been gettin' busy?" Raulston's laughing as he asks the question, and he's making obscene motions with his fingers. It's a perpetual thing with him, the sex obsession. All Raulston thinks about is sex. All he talks about is sex. I don't know how Dutch stands him, but then, she's kind of the same way.

"No." I say it too fast, but he bugs me sometimes, about Cory anyway. "Just resting up to kick your ass next game."

"The man knows how to dream," Tom says. He's got red hair and tons of freckles, but Jenna likes him anyway. "Are the girls done?"

"I don't think so." I glance toward the girls' field, but I can't see the scoreboard from my angle. "Last time we checked, Sonic Team I was winning by eight."

"Ouch," Tom says, looking like he feels sorry for the other team. "I'm too broke for concessions. Let's find Marvin."

"Why?" I ask. "He won't have any food left."

But we're moving in the direction of the girls' field so

Raulston can see Dutch and Tom can see Jenna. Jason's with Lisa, and Randall and Marvin are still wishing. Randall used to be with Lisa, but he's over that now. He likes some girl in Allenby.

Marvin—well, Marvin likes hot dogs. He's into food—fast, slow, gourmet, or greasy—and it doesn't matter how much he eats, because he still looks like a toothpick with big feet. He likes music, too—psycho level with that since his dad took off—and animals, but not as much as my parents. Nobody likes animals as much as my parents do (way past psycho level).

As for me, music kind of gets on my nerves. I like the popular stuff, but I'm not into in-depth studies of singers and songs and types of music like Marvin. I'd rather read about baseball, and I can't read while I'm listening to music. I don't have any pets—of my own, at least—and I don't want any because I'm too busy with baseball and Cory and my friends and, soon, high school, too, even though this one bird my mom rescued from a hoarder is trying to make friends with me. It's a parrot named Fred. Fred doesn't talk like parrots are supposed to do. Mom says lots of parrots don't talk. As for Fred, Mom says Fred hasn't talked for us *yet*. Fred makes good smoke-detector-alert noises, though.

Not much fun when I'm trying to sleep late.

I see Cory's parents coming through the far archway to watch the afternoon game. Her mom, who looks a lot like her, only older, spots me and smiles and waves—again, lots like Cory would do. Her dad gives me a nod. He's got blond hair and blue eyes, too, but he's not like Cory at all. He and Cory's two older brothers look like stone-faced soldier guys, even though they've never been soldiers. Mr. Wentworth is a plumber.

I nod back to him as they move toward the practice field where Cory and her team are warming up, and I'm suddenly glad we came back to the main area when we did. We weren't doing anything, not really, but it might be bad luck to piss off a plumber. *That* plumber, anyway. He's already explained what he could do to me with a pipe wrench if I make him too unhappy. The creepy part was, he smiled while he was talking about it, and I've never seen Mr. Wentworth smile any other time. Ever.

Cory says he's just being a badass for my benefit.

I'm not too sure.

"Marvin!" Raulston yells, and when I look, I see Marvin in the girls' bleachers, wearing the same pair of faded jeans he always seems to wear, and a T-shirt from the refrigerator factory where his mom works. I try to get the boy to pay attention to how he looks, to go through my closet and at least try some of the sharp jeans I've collected, but he blows me off.

The game's still going on, and Dutch is with Marvin. She's got on a fridge factory T-shirt, too, but she looks way better in hers than Marvin does in his. For her, any T-shirt can be a fashion statement.

"I don't see any hot dogs," Tom says, like he seriously had hoped Marvin—hello, this is *Marvin* we're talking about—would have leftovers.

We all jog toward Marvin and Dutch. When I run my tongue across my lower lip, a little bit of cinnamon tingles in my mouth, and I smile.

We'll be playing until late tonight, and I wonder how long I'll be able to taste Cory's kisses, and whether or not I can sneak a few more to keep me going. Without running into the pipe wrench problem, or my folks after they get here, or any coaches who want to have an attitude about "fraternizing with the opposite sex."

I'm thinking a few, maybe, if Cory wins her game and stays in a good mood.

And I'm still smiling.

Nothing's Wrong with Me

("The Only Living Boy in New York"—Simon and Garfunkel. I like old stuff, too. And new stuff, and hard stuff and soft stuff—if it's music, I like.)

She comes back to the graveyard twice more the next week.

No, really, I'm not hiding behind an oak tree and staring at her like some kind of psycho. I was working nearby. I'm just . . . on a break. And stuff.

Fairy Girl isn't the most gorgeous female on the planet, but she really is beautiful, and she seems thoughtful and smart, and she's sad, and every time I see her crying, I think about . . .

Galloping up on a white stallion and asking her what dragon I should slay.

Breaking into a Broadway number to make her laugh.

Stepping into the afternoon sunlight like a gunslinger and tipping my hat.

Offering her a handkerchief. A clean *handkerchief.*

Or . . .

Saying hello would be a start.

Sometimes she sits by the grave she visits and reads. Other times, she has a little notebook with her, and she writes. This afternoon, I think she's sketching.

She has long fingers.

And probably good-enough eyes to notice a dork lurking behind an oak tree.

When I get back to the grave I was working on, my brain is still buzzing. I'd walk it off, but I can't, because my boss, Harper, is sitting on the pile of dirt next to the opening, resting his elbow on the little travel cage where I keep Fred when I'm working. Harper's got stringy gray hair, three days of gray stubble on his chin, a beer, and half a peanut butter sandwich. Fred's crawling across the top of her cage, trying to get a bite of the sandwich or Harper's elbow. When Fred's on the attack, she's not picky.

Harper sees me coming, and he points a hunk of bread crust at me and says, without swallowing, "Something's definitely wrong with you."

"You're just figuring that out?" I hop down into the grave and pick up my shovel.

"Fred," Fred announces brightly, as a way of saying hello to me.

I say hello to Fred, and Harper grumbles, "You're spying on that girl over in Oak Section."

"I'm not spying. I'm . . . studying." I pitch a shovelful of dirt in Harper's general direction. Talking about the girl definitely won't help the brain buzz.

"Whatever you're doing, knock it the hell off. I don't want any trouble in my graveyard." He chews up the rest of the sandwich, swallows it with a swig of beer, and squints in Fairy Girl's direction. "She's pretty, though. What's her name?"

"No idea."

"You haven't talked to her?"

"No."

Harper frowns at me, then shakes his head. "You and me, we should have a long talk about stuff like this, sometime when we ain't got digging to do."

I throw more dirt, barely missing him.

Fred whistles at me.

"My dad and I had that talk," I tell Harper.

"Well, he must have done a piss-poor job." Harper gets up, leaves his beer can next to Fred's cage, and stalks off, muttering, "Ain't even found out the girl's name. Swear to God . . ."

The next day, I'm thinking about asking Fairy Girl her name, but I can't stop seeing Cory's face.

It's been three years.

That's a long time, but I remember Cory like no time

ever passed, like nothing ever changed. I think about her a lot. Probably too much. Sometimes when I think about Cory, I feel things down deep inside—things like steam and tension and sweetness and aching. Things deeper than that, too. Stuff almost forgotten, like it's lost to me forever.

That makes me work to stop thinking about her, to stop thinking about everything. It turns me into flatness and thinness, into a paper-doll person.

If you want to make a paper doll of me, make it regular height with decent muscles, dark brown hair, and a smile. Mom and Dr. Mote say I smile a lot even when I should be really pissed off, that maybe my smiles actually *mean* I'm pissed off, but I don't think it was always that way. Sometimes I think I remember smiling because I was happy—the Cory days—but now, maybe Mom and Dr. Mote are right, so don't forget the smile. Don't forget the little gray parrot with the red tail, either, because Fred's always with me, on my shoulder, my arm, my chest, or my knee—or in her travel cage if I'm outside.

If you make Marvin, he's a little taller than me, more buff, with lighter brown hair, a few freckles, thick eyebrows, and he grins instead of smiles. He wears jeans and vintage T-shirts. Oh, and if he's at my place, he's usually holding Gertrude. Gertrude's a fat cat who drools a lot.

Make a medium-sized paper town for Duke's Ridge, with a complex for G. W. Morton High School (big, square, brown brick, lots of buildings) on the south side. Then make a

paper box for Marvin's house near G. W., and my house
about twenty miles out in the middle of nowhere with nothing nearby except Rock Hill Cemetery, a huge, rambling
collection of gravestones, a little cottage in the back, and the
funeral chapel near the stone front gate. If you want, make
my parents and Marvin's mom, but I wouldn't put them at
the houses. My folks are usually gone doing animal rescue
stuff, and Ms. Brown works all the time at the refrigerator
factory north of Duke's Ridge. (Did you add the factory?
It looks space-age because it's all silver.) Make dozens or
even hundreds of paper people for G. W. and kids downtown
in Duke's Ridge in the park around the square, and people
in Walmart, and people at the little hospital in the middle of
town, and the four-screen movie theater, and at the gas stations and grocery stores and all along the fast-food strip.

You can move your Marvin doll anywhere you want
because he goes lots of places. You can match him up with
some of the other paper people at G. W. or all through
Duke's Ridge. He's friendly. Most people like him, even
though lots of them snicker about his name, and pinhead
Jonas Blankenship, defensive end for the G. W. Eagles, calls
him "the Great Marvolo" just before he slugs him in the arm.

You can move everybody everywhere, except me. I stay
apart from everybody except Marvin. I'm at G. W., Rock
Hill, home, Dr. Mote's office beside the little hospital (twice
a month), and James Branson's office on the square once a
month for my probation meeting and to drop off college

letters and pay off another chunk of my fines. Technically, now that I'm off house arrest and just on probation these last months until I turn eighteen, I could go more places as long as I'm home by ten o'clock curfew, but I'm used to my routine, and I don't have a car and can't get a driver's license until after I'm off probation, so I stay in my regular spots. When Marvin gets an itch to drive somewhere else for a few, or go talk to people, I get nervous and stay quiet, so then my paper doll would look like invisible lines in the passenger seat. Nobody seems to see me, they don't talk to me, and that's fine.

So, I'm invisible, or separate, or removed, or whatever you want to call it. I'm at home, at school, at therapy, at probation, or digging graves, but always sort of . . . I don't know, lost in space, or secretly made out of paper, meant to get a little older, fade, then just blow away. Doesn't seem like much point to thinking about the future, because I can't really do anything I had planned, and I can't figure out anything I'd rather do, so here I am.

Lost in space, without the robots.

That's my life. Any questions?

Oh. Right. *That* question.

Which I'm not answering yet—but, like in Dr. Mote's office, I'm not trying to be a dick. I just don't have the words rehearsed, or know how to explain everything, or even if you'll let me finish. If I start in the wrong place, you'll walk away before you hear everything and you'll just think I'm a shit. Maybe I am a shit, but I try not to be.

It's late September now, and I'm in Duke's Ridge, in
G. W., sitting with Marvin.

I watch Marvin pull out the books for his next class,
drop half of them, grin, and pick them up before he shuts
his locker.

"It's mind-blowing how you never get mad at anything," I tell him. "I wish I was like that."

"I get mad." Marvin gets a better hold on the books he
snatched off the green tile floor. His jeans are the same black
color as the book on top, only not as shiny, and he's wearing
a vintage KISS T-shirt that looks like it's really forty years
old. The air in the hallway's five different kinds of hot and
stinky, but I'm not really paying attention to anything else
in the hall but Marvin. No point, really. Nothing in the hall
pays attention to me, other than him.

I shift my grip on my backpack strap. "Name one time
you've gotten mad. Just once."

Marvin's big thick eyebrows bunch like his brain's cramp-
ing as he thinks. "This year, or since I've known you?"

"See, that kind of makes my point." I push him away
from the locker and into the blurry crowd of people clogging
the halls between us and fifth period.

"You don't get mad at anything, even all the shit that
should make you furious, so why're you busting *my* balls?"
He elbows through people, but he smiles at them before
he bumps them out of the way.

I don't bother with the smiling part. "I get mad all the

time. Like, every day, two or three times a day. I just don't
say anything."

"That's your problem." Marvin shuts up long enough to
smile at five more people before we turn the last corner
toward class. "That's why your PO stays up your ass and
your therapist always asks you if you're about to turn serial
killer. They know one day, the wrong thing's gonna hit you,
and you're gonna blow like Vesuvius."

My stomach does a nervous weird thing inside, and it's
time to move on to new topics. "When was the last time
Vesuvius erupted, anyway?"

Marvin snickers. "This year, or since I've known you?"

"Hey."

The female voice makes me jump, and two seconds later,
I process who it belongs to and have to work not to groan.

"Hi, Cherie," Marvin says as she comes up from behind
us before we can get to the classroom, because he's always
polite. It's natural to him, like being a giant dork and not
caring at all. Only the slight flush of red under his freckles
gives away the fact he's not really happy about her sneaking
up on us.

My eyes move like they're on autopilot, double-
checking to be sure that King Kong Jonas is nowhere nearby
to be pissed off that I'm jawing with his baby sister. Though,
really, nothing about her looks like a baby. Cherie's dressed
in her school best—black skirt, black shirt, black bag and
shoes to match her black hair. She can't do weird nails

and makeup at school, but she'd do it if she thought she could get away with it.

Cherie ignores Marvin and keeps her eyes on me. "Are you working today?"

"Uh—I—um, probably. But Harper doesn't want you—I mean, he doesn't want me to talk to people while I'm digging." I stop at the door to class. Probably should go inside, but that feels too, I don't know. Abrupt or something.

Cherie stares at the ceiling for a second before staring at me again. "It's just graves. You can talk and shovel dirt."

"Not a good idea." Marvin edges through the door, but Cherie doesn't take the hint because she never does. In the hallway behind us, I notice a few faces turning in our direction, probably because it's weird to see me talking to anybody besides Marvin.

Cherie acts like Marvin didn't even speak. "I want to see you, Del. It's been like days. A week. Maybe almost two."

Damn. I'm smiling. I wish I wouldn't do that, because people probably take it wrong, especially Cherie. "You don't need to spend time with me. You're not my girlfriend. I'm not your boyfriend. We don't have any reason to spend time together."

You think that was rude, right? Right? I know you do.

That's because you're normal.

Cherie is not.

No matter what I say to her or how I say it, she never takes it bad—even when I want her to.

She gives me a soft punch in the belly. "Don't be like that. You know I just want to talk."

"But he doesn't want to talk to you," Marvin tells her.

She turns her back on him completely.

"How many different ways do we have to explain this to you?" Marvin asks. "Not wanted. Not welcome. Don't bug Del at work."

Hmm. Marvin actually does sound a little irritated. I'd forgotten Cherie could get to him so totally. Maybe he *is* more regular than Vesuvius.

"I'll come by Rock Hill as soon as I can," Cherie says, demonstrating whole new meanings for the word *oblivion*. Her smile is fast and bright, and it seems real enough, which always catches me off guard.

She punches me in the belly again, a little harder this time, and then she's gone, running off down the hall as first bell rings.

Marvin and I stand in the door, matching big dorks, watching her fly away like a skinny little bat.

"She doesn't get it," he says.

"She doesn't want to get it."

We have to move to let somebody in, so we go sit down.

Both of us are sure Cherie will show up at Rock Hill, if not tonight, then tomorrow night, or soon enough, and she really, really, really needs to stop that.

I Hate Peeing in Cups

("Keep on Tryin'"—Poco. Mellow music is good, especially when I'm not feeling mellow.)

Fate chooses to smile on us, and Cherie's not waiting at the graveyard when Marvin and I get there. I don't have to worry about her or pissing off her gigantor brother, at least not this afternoon. All I have to do is stand in the sunlight under a cloudless sky next to Marvin, trying to dig a good grave. To make him happy, I leave the iPod off and I try not to hum stuff and drive him nuts.

In front of me, hanging from a shade tree branch in her travel cage, Fred fluffs out her feathers, yawns obnoxiously loud (no, parrots don't really yawn like that, it's one of her sounds), then sighs and smacks her beak together.

"Quit complaining." I jam my shovel into the ground and flip a load of dirt onto the tarp on the right side of the grave, careful not to hit the neatly stacked squares of grass I cut out before I started digging. I'm about a foot down, with my perfect rectangle already forming. "It's not that cold yet. Wait until winter. I'll have to put a heater under your cage."

"Fred," she says, in a tone that means, *Yeah, right, are you finished yet, and where's my damned apple?*

"It creeps me out when you talk to that bird like she's human." Marvin's sitting on top of the first foot of dirt I piled on the tarp, holding Gertrude the fat drooling cat and eating a burrito. He's wearing some of the burrito, too, smeared across the crinkled KISS logo on his shirt.

"Fred talks better than a lot of humans I know." I dig. I need to get at least two graves done before Saturday, because we have three burials on Sunday, all before noon. I've got a lot of work to do to get everything ready, and Harper's already halfway sloshed. He won't be much help, but Marvin will pitch in after he finishes his bag of burritos.

"It's still creepy," Marvin says. "Why does she have to talk in your voice?"

"Fred," Fred says to Marvin in my voice, then makes a perfectly pitched fart noise and laughs about it.

Marvin shakes his head. "That's just messed up."

"Fred," Fred says in Marvin's voice, because she can talk like him and Dad and Mom, too, if she wants. She doesn't blink at Marvin like Dr. Mote would, because parrots don't really exactly blink, at least not as much as people, even though they can close their eyes.

When Marvin doesn't say anything, Fred burps like she's sucked down a case of ginger ale.

Parrots don't really burp, either. It's just a sound she makes, like the yawning and sighing and farting. I guess she learned most of them from me, which I suppose doesn't say much for my personal habits. At least I usually don't wear burrito juice. Just fresh grave dirt, and I wash that off as soon as I get home.

Marvin burps back at Fred, shifts the cat in his lap, and digs in his greasy white paper sack for another burrito. He feeds the first bite to Gertrude, who is supposed to belong to my mother. Mom rescued her after her owner died, and Gertrude's got a chewed ear and cataracts. I've mentioned she's kind of fat, and she's a little clumsy. She's also gray like Fred, and she hangs out in my room whenever Marvin's around, and usually follows us the mile and a half down my rural road to Rock Hill. I think she likes Marvin better than me or Mom and Dad, who are attending a fund-raiser at the next county's animal shelter tonight.

All the animals at my house got rescued from one big disaster or another. There's some cats other than Gertrude— six right now, I think. I lose count of those, since they come and go after they get better and adoptable. We've got three dogs confiscated from drug dealers, and I've got Fred, who blew into some guy's garage during a storm four years ago, then ended up at the hoarder's house where Mom found her, and Dad's working on a chicken. It's a rooster with one eye that got used for fighting, and most of the time, the Humane Society just "humanely euthanizes" fighting roosters, but Dad's gotten to be some kind of rooster whisperer or something. He keeps the one-eyed rooster in a way-fancy coop in the backyard, and it crows every morning and every evening, so Fred's learning to crow.

As if she's reading my mind, she crows for Marvin a few times, then barks for good measure.

Marvin hugs Gertrude a little closer, like maybe she'll protect him. He might need protection from Fred. When she's out of her cage, Fred likes to attack Marvin's shoes and bite big hunks out of the soles.

"That bird is possessed by the devil, Del. Really. Seriously."

I keep digging.

Maybe Marvin counts as a rescue, since he started being my best friend in fifth grade after his dad ditched him and he and his mom had no place to live. They stayed with us for a while, but now they have their own place over on Backdrop Road, which isn't out in the sticks like our house. We kind of have to live in the sticks, since my parents can't stop rescuing things.

I wonder if Marvin thinks I'm a rescue. That would fit, probably for lots of reasons. He didn't ditch me like everybody else did when all the shit came down three years ago.

There wasn't any big fight or huge divorce from my old friends or anything. We were all just about to start high school, so we were going in lots of directions—me trying out for baseball, and Raulston, Tom, and Randall looking at freshman football, and Jason and Dutch had joined ROTC. Jenna and Lisa were going out for softball, and Cory wanted to sing in the chorus. She really did have a beautiful voice.

She still has a beautiful voice, I guess, but I don't know. She doesn't live here anymore. None of them do. Jason, Tom, and Randall went to Chicago. Their families figured they'd stick out less in a bigger city. Raulston's family took him back to California. Jenna and Lisa and Dutch all went west, too, but not as far—Arizona and Colorado and New Mexico. Some big towns, some little towns. Anywhere but Duke's Ridge and the prying, interfering eyes of District Attorney William Kaison.

My folks figured we'd be better off here, where people knew me and knew our family, since my charges were more serious than everybody else's. Plus, they would have had to get permission from the court for us to move, and go through a lot of hassle, and we've had enough hassle for a while.

When it was all said and done, Marvin wasn't charged, but other than him, Cory was the only one Kaison didn't tear to pieces. I'm glad for that at least. I'm not sure where she went, and I'm not sure if I'm allowed to ask, but I'd really like to know how she's doing. She's e-mailed me a few times to ask about how I'm getting along, always from anonymous untraceable addresses, but I delete the e-mails. I'm too chickenshit to answer her. Digging graves for a job is one thing. Digging graves for myself to fall into in real life— thanks, that's okay. Been there, done that, put my face in the dictionary next to the definition. Kaison's out of office now, but who the hell knows about the woman who replaced him? She could be just as bad, or maybe even worse. I'm not taking any chances.

About an hour later, Marvin's still churning burrito farts, but we're through with the first grave. He pitches his shovel out and hoists himself back to level ground. "I still think it's weird we don't have to dig six feet down."

"Eighteen inches." I get out behind him and rub dirt off my lips. "Weird, how some stuff doesn't have to go as deep as you think, right? But the plague was a long time ago, and nobody much robs graves anymore. Eighteen inches of dirt on top of what you're burying, that's the law here, but Harper says most states don't even have laws about it anymore. He thinks four feet is plenty, as long as the casket's normal size— and in the winter, four feet will be hard enough."

Marvin stretches out the kinks from digging, ignores Fred's rendition of bombs whistling down and exploding on impact, and asks, "What's the difference between a casket and a coffin?"

"No idea." I put down my shovel and stretch, too. Too bad Marvin ate all those burritos. It's probably getting close to noon and I'm hungry now, but I'm betting Harper ate the rest of his peanut butter and bread yesterday. Probably no point in going to the small one-bedroom house he has at the back corner of the cemetery. Maybe later today, Marvin will make a grocery run for Harper.

"If Harper sold caskets or coffins or whatever, he'd make a lot of money," Marvin says.

"Hello, bird," Fred adds, just to get me to look at her, which I do, and I blow her a quick kiss.

"The funeral homes do all the sales stuff and handle the funerals," I say. "Harper's job is Rock Hill, and I think it's a lot more complicated. Mowing, digging, pruning, trimming, cleaning, polishing, chasing off weirdos, helping all the sad people—he stays busy."

"*You* stay busy, Del. Harper mostly stays passed out. The whole funeral thing, that's a racket, man. Cremation's the best way for the planet."

"Harper says that until World War II, people mostly handled their dead at home, themselves. They'd clean them up, keep them around for a couple of days while the pine box got made by family members, then bring them to his father to be buried here, or just plant them in the backyard. Then the whole funeral industry started and everything changed. Maybe death made more sense before that, or felt more real."

Marvin's face is totally straight when he says, "Or a lot more gross and creepy. Two more to dig?"

"Yeah. I got the turf cut off over there, third from the road. The tarp for the dirt's already down." I climb out of the grave and catch myself staring at the section of the cemetery where Fairy Girl usually visits.

Stop.

I look back at Marvin and try to sound casual when I ask, "You still following your dating rules?"

"Of course. No dating. I don't date." He sounds smug, like he's got it all under control, like his body never bothers to react to girls like mine does. I use music and digging to block it all out, make it go away—but Marvin doesn't seem to have that problem.

The way Marvin figures it, if he's eighteen, and he cards the girl (and probably makes a copy of her ID) and she's eighteen, nobody can say anything to them about doing anything. If he waits until he's an adult and his life is nobody's business, he won't have any trouble like we had before.

I'm not sure that logic works, but it's a big deal to him, and with Marvin, it's better not to mess with his big deals.

Marvin's smug expression fades, and I realize he's starting to stare at me. "Why'd you ask about dating?"

I shrug. It's what I do best. "No reason."

The lines of Marvin's body get tense. I can tell he's thinking about standing and facing me. Maybe even getting in my face. "You interested in somebody?"

Dangerous ground. Definitely entering Marvin-thinks-this-is-a-big deal territory. "No."

He does stand, but he doesn't get in my face. "You wouldn't lie to me, right? Not about something like that."

"I'm not lying to you about anything." My calm tone usually works with Marvin. He blinks at me like he's weighing the words, maybe measuring my tone.

"Fred," Fred says.

And Marvin says, "Okay."

He's easy like that. It's why he's still my best friend. Anybody hard would have ditched me a long time ago.

Marvin glances at the sky as he sits down again. "What if it rains tonight? Will the graves fill up?"

"Nah, I'd use a gazebo tent to cover them—we've got ten of those—but it's not supposed to rain until Wednesday." After we finish digging, I'll need to cover the dirt and turf with more tarps, and before Sunday, I have to mow, then put up gazebo tents and arrange foldout chairs under them for the first services. The funeral home will cover the chairs with their velvet drapes, to make the mourners more comfortable and to make sure everybody sees their logo. That's it. Rain's no big deal.

"Fall's usually dry," Marvin mumbles, as much to himself as me.

See? Talking about the weather. He's easy. We move on to the next grave.

I start digging. After the graves get filled and covered, I

won't have to hurry putting the turf back in place, then moving the extra dirt to the back of the fifty acres Harper tends. The ten acres farthest to the west hasn't been divided into plots and sold because the land is still too rough. We're using the fill dirt and Harper's ancient red Ford tractor with its barely functioning spreader to smooth out the ground. Eventually, Harper will be able to lay turf and make a profit off those acres, too.

"Harper should get a backhoe," Marvin says as he digs up a shovelful from the bare patch third from the road while I stop long enough to move Fred's cage to a shady spot on the branch of a maple tree.

"Even if he could afford a piece of machinery like that, he'd blow it off." I give Fred's beak a quick stroke through the cage bars, then head toward Marvin and grab my shovel again. "He says it's disrespectful, and his father and grandfather who started this place would haunt him."

"Maybe his family wouldn't haunt him if he drank less skanky beer."

"None of my business." I start digging near Marvin, but I have to nudge Gertrude with the shovel so she'll move enough to let me drop my first load on the tarp. Harper leaves us alone to do our work. He knows his drinking is a problem, so it's up to him to fix it, or not. He pays me to do the crap he blows off and he never shorts me a dime.

Fred amuses herself by singing "Twinkle, Twinkle Little Star" off-key, mostly in Mom's voice.

"Well, when it's my turn to get planted," Marvin says without even looking in Fred's direction, "I'm putting in my will that I want a lot more than eighteen inches of dirt over me if I don't get cremated." Then, "Hope you gotta piss, because Branson's here."

I dig out another chunk before I glance at the road. Branson's black Jeep is slowing to a stop at the top of the small hill on the way to the entrance, and a few seconds later, he gets out. He's got silver hair cut close to his dark skin, he's wearing jeans and a University of Indiana sweatshirt, and he's carrying a shoulder bag in one hand and a white sample bag in the other. Branson's dedicated. Ex-military, now a retired cop who does juvenile probation. He makes random checks on me to do drug tests, but never at school. He's good about keeping the humiliation to a minimum.

"I'll go start on the third grave if the turf's cut," Marvin says.

I point to a spot in front of where we're standing, three rows up, first from the road, with the turf cut and stacked and the tarp spread to receive the dirt. Marvin takes his shovel and heads off with Gertrude walking every step beside him.

Branson reaches the second grave and hands me a sample cup while Fred greets him with a burp, a fart, and the sound of a telephone ringing.

"What's up, Fred," Branson says as I get clear of the grave, drop my shovel, turn my back, and oblige him with the sample he's wanting. "And hello to you, too, Del."

"Hello," I say back, but not until I've got my pants zipped and the plastic lid twisted tight. It's hard to be conversational while pissing in a cup. I just hope I didn't get any dirt in the sample.

"Marvin looks busy. Do you pay him to help out?"

I hand Branson the sample cup and go for my shovel. "I keep him in burritos so he can stink up the place."

"Is that the stench? I was afraid it was—you know. The dead guys."

"Or girls," I point out. "But no. Embalming and coffins and caskets and vaults and dirt take care of the dead-guy-smell problem."

"Fred," Fred says, eyeing Branson with her feathers poofed out, which is parrot for, *Maybe I like you and maybe I'll bite off your face. Want to take your chances?*

Branson keeps his distance from Fred's cage as he seals my sample into the white bag. "I'm assuming this will be clean. And assuming you're working on your applications and letters. Did you keep your appointments with Dr. Mote?"

"Yes, yes, and yes." The shovel bites into the dirt as I push it hard, trying to get a good start on this section.

"One, two . . . four," Fred says.

I correct her automatically. "One, two, *three*, four."

Fred starts beeping like an answering machine, or a bull-dozer about to back right over Branson.

Branson puts the sealed white sample into his shoulder pouch and pulls out a packet of brochures bound up with rubber bands. He hands these to me, but I lay them down beside the grave and keep digging. I know what they are. I know they won't make any difference and so does he, but he wants me to keep "making an effort."

"Those are mostly community colleges," Branson says. "Ones that don't turn away felons on the front end. You'll still have to tell them and write your explanation letter, but you'll have better luck starting there than a four-year."

I stare at my shovel and keep digging. There's a smile on my face and I feel like laughing, but not because I'm thinking any of this is funny or bright or a real possibility.

"You've got good grades and a good record of community service," Branson tries again. "It's not hopeless, if you'd just put a little feeling into those letters. A little bit of the real Del. You *can* win people over if you try."

Here we go. He's about to get to wanting me to testify at the juvenile sex offender laws hearings, and I don't want to hear it.

Keep digging.

That's to myself, not him. He's trying. I know that.

"Fred," Fred says, and she's trying, too, probably feeling the waves of *tense* and *wary* coming off me all of a sudden.

"Del, if you really make an effort tell your story— *especially* if you tell it at the hearings—somebody will look past the felony convictions and see you as a person. Somebody will give you a chance."

"I'm not testifying," I tell him.

Branson's rolling now, so he won't stop even though I've said no—again. "The press is all over this, accusing senators who support the bill of going soft on the worst types of crimes and criminals. If we don't put a human face on this nightmare, if they can't see the real cost to real people, I'm not sure the law has a chance of passing." His eyes have a gleam when he gets all wrapped up in this, and I'm not bothering to say anything to him now because he won't hear it, and my opinion doesn't matter. "You could help a lot of people by doing this, a lot of kids just like you. This could be a new start. The moment where you move forward again instead of just treading water. Maybe the moment where you convince a college or even a university to give you the opportunity to prove yourself."

Before he finishes getting out the *prove yourself* part, Marvin says to Branson, "You're a nice guy and all, but you're dreaming about schools giving him a chance." He's back with his shovel and Gertrude, maybe figuring I need extra support. "Kaison took away all of Del's chances."

"His record will be sealed at eighteen." Branson frowns at Marvin, who steps into the grave rectangle and starts to dig beside me. "That's a first step."

Marvin doesn't smile at bad times like I do. When he gets *tense* and *wary*, he looks it. "Wherever he goes, he still has to register as a criminal. He'll still get shut out of everything. Why are you setting him up for shit by asking him to go public all over again? Wasn't it hell enough the first time?"

Branson comes back with "Yeah" a little too loud, when he's usually in control. "That's—that's why I brought those." He points to the brochures. "And I'm still hoping you'll change your mind about the hearings, Del."

I'm not smiling anymore, but in my case, that's probably good, like the digging and digging and digging that's keeping my hands busy. Branson's a good guy. He doesn't want it to be over for me, even though really, it is.

When I was little I wanted to be a doctor, or maybe a vet (parental obsessions can be contagious). Now I think off and on about being an avian vet. There are never enough of those. But even if I get into school and graduate with perfect scores, manage to get residencies and fellowships and pass those with perfect scores, too—even if I turn out to be the Messiah of Avian Medicine, I still can't get licensed in any state I've researched. So I'd have the skills and the degree, but I wouldn't be allowed to practice. At least I'd be able to keep Fred healthy, and if Dad ends up with a broken rooster farm, I wouldn't be useless.

"The hearings—well, if they pass the Romeo and Juliet law, things could get a lot better for you." Branson brings this up like it's new, but we've covered it before.

"I'll be fifty before all that's settled," I remind him.

"There isn't any miracle do-over for poor Romeo, dead before the laws take effect."

Branson lets out a breath, half sigh and half grumble. "Kaison's long gone and you can't make a living digging graves."

"I'll figure something out."

"What?" he asks, like he and Dr. Mote have been comparing notes, which come to think of it, they probably do. "And when?"

You've got ten months before you're through with all this.

He doesn't say that because he knows he doesn't have to, but you never know about people. That's one lesson I've learned, and I'll never forget it. Branson might sell me down the river at the final hearing to close out my probation, but I hope not.

And . . .

And . . .

I stop hoping. Stop thinking. Stop existing in the same reality as everyone else.

She's drifting past Branson, behind him, about a hundred yards from where we were standing.

Fairy Girl.

Can't breathe.

Her dark hair's down, sleek and shining in the bright sunlight as it hides her face. She's wearing a light blue skirt with a matching shirt and light-looking sweater, more angel than fairy today, and every nerve ending in my body reacts to her existence.

Not normal. I'm not okay. Harper's right, something's definitely wrong with me.

I realize I'm blinking at Branson, and since I can't fire up my music to make my brain and body act right, I think about ice cubes, my great-grandmother, Mom, dad's one-eyed rooster, and the time I did real damage falling straddle-legged on a sawhorse. Fresh sweat breaks across my forehead, streaking the dirt on my cheeks and neck as it trickles slowly downward.

Marvin's not digging, either. He's just leaning forward watching the girl go by, because really, when she's in the universe, what else can you do?

Branson glances from me to Marvin, turns, and goes very still when he sees her. It's like the three of us, me, Marvin, and Branson, are caught in some web-spell of silence, wrapped up tight and glued in place, unable to speak or move or do anything to save ourselves.

Fred, always aware of the exact wrong thing to do, cuts loose with a whistle that would put any construction worker to shame. Then she follows it with the loud "HEY!" I use to warn the dogs off dad's chicken lot if the gate's open.

I jump so hard I almost slip into the grave. Gertrude hisses, and Marvin pitches forward, hitting himself in the teeth with the shovel handle. Branson jumps, too, swearing to himself, then glares at me and realizes I didn't do it.

"Parrot," I mutter.

Branson rolls his eyes.

I'm burning hot from top to bottom as the girl pauses and turns her head to where the three of us are just standing like giant, grave-digging idiots.

She studies each of us for a few seconds, too far away for me to make out the details of her face. Marvin points back toward Branson, who points at me, so I point at Fred's cage. I can't say anything. It's Marvin who forces out a quick, "Sorry. That was Del's parrot. Her name is Fred, and he takes her everywhere even though she doesn't know how to behave."

Fairy Girl seems to appraise Fred, squinting toward the tree where the cage is hanging. Then she looks from Marvin to Gertrude, who's bathing her front paw and drooling into the dirt piled next to the second grave.

"Gertrude," Marvin calls to her. "That's the cat's name." Then he says "Sorry" again, like that'll help anything.

The girl waits another few seconds, like she might be wondering if Branson is going to speak, or maybe me.

Fred says, "Fred," then counts to four, making *three* the loudest, just like I do when I correct her.

The girl laughs.

It's a sound like all the music I enjoy, rolled into a few bright, happy notes. Then she gives us a wave and heads on toward her usual destination, in the Oak Section, one of Rock Hill's more recently dug areas.

It's Branson who talks first, and all he can say is, "She's—uh."

I get the shovel moving again. "Yeah."

Branson's not finished. "She's probably a bad idea, Del."

"Yeah."

"I mean, there's nothing saying you can't have girl-friends, but if I were you, I'd wait until all this is over."

"Yeah."

Marvin and I dig. He's giving me a half-ticked look now and then, and I can tell he's wondering if this is why I asked him about dating.

Branson stands there, staring in the direction the girl went. Then he looks at the college brochures I still haven't touched. "Then again, on second thought, it might be good for you. Give you a little something to look forward to, maybe a little motivation. If I talk to your parents—wait, I could talk to her parents, and—"

"No." I choke the shovel. God, that would make me want to die. "Thanks, though."

Keep digging. Just keep digging, and burn off the steam, and maybe Branson won't get back to the stupid hearings and the laws that'll come way too late to help me.

Branson looks disappointed, but also like he probably understands. For a while, he doesn't say anything. Then he gives us a nod, and a few minutes later, he leaves. His Jeep engine makes a growly noise when it starts up, but it's smooth and quiet as he guides it out of Rock Hill.

"My lip's bleeding from where I hit it on the shovel," Marvin complains, then fouls the air with a new round of burrito farts.

I'm trying to dig, to pay attention to squaring my corners, but I'm thinking about Fairy Girl. If Marvin weren't here, I might slip over to the Oak Section, just to look at her again for a few seconds.

"She doesn't go to G. W.," Marvin says over Fred's flurry of whistles, clicks, and other bird noises, the crow sound being her best. "She's got to be new to Duke's Ridge. I would have noticed her before if she'd been anywhere in town."

Duh.

I mess up my corner and have to back off, glare at it awhile, and start over fresh.

"Are you going to talk to her?"

"No." My shovelful of dirt splatters on the college brochures, but Marvin reaches over, shakes the dirt off them, and moves them next to Gertrude.

He waits a few seconds. "Mind if I talk to her?"

I jam my shovel double-hard into the ground. "Yes."

"Okay." Marvin looks triumphant, like he has the answers to all his questions. He's not mad that I can tell, or even interested in talking about the weather, because he's easy, and I'm way glad. Marvin burrito-farts, and he digs, and I dig, and Fred sings a garbled verse of "Baa, Baa Black Sheep." If I really believed in God, like a traditional fatherlike God in the sky, I'd think he sent Fred to stick pins in my brain right when I need to be stuck.

I'm not sure what I think about God, or what God thinks about me, but I'm sure that whoever Fairy Girl is, she's sad because somebody important to her died. That makes me double-sure that the last thing she needs is the biggest black sheep in Duke's Ridge interrupting her peace at the cemetery.

Three Years Ago: In My Dreams

"It's not like having sex." Cory's voice sounds whispery through the phone, and I know she's probably under her covers with her door locked and her lights off, because it's midnight. If we get caught talking, we'll be so fried.

It's amazing.

Cory's way amazing.

The picture she texted me—I can't stop staring at it. She's so beautiful, clothes off or on, doesn't matter. I don't want to tell her that the only naked women I've seen before are porn pictures on the Internet and some movies and magazines, but if I did tell her, I'd be sure to say she's prettier.

She is.

She looks real, and soft, and the light on her skin is

perfect. One day, when I do touch her naked, I want it to be in a bed with nice sheets like she has in the picture, and candlelight. Or maybe in a hot tub with the water slowly moving around both of us. Or maybe outside on a blanket in the moonlight, somewhere quiet and private and just right. I want it all to be pretty, like she is.

The thought of touching her makes my body ache. It makes my brain burn. I've joked about wanting this or that, or this girl or that one before—but I didn't know what *want* even meant. Now I know, and it's hard to think.

"It's not like sex," I tell her through the speaker-phone, keeping my voice low as I stare at the picture. "But it kinda is."

"Can't get pregnant from it." Her laugh makes me feel watery inside, like I don't have as many bones as I'm supposed to.

"I want to see you," she says. Quiet. To the point.

My face goes hot, but she's not asking to see my face. She doesn't keep at me about it, and I know she won't, not tonight anyway, but it's something she wants from me, and I like giving Cory what she wants.

But taking a picture of myself?

That feels stupid.

Sort of a rush, but stupid, too.

I'll be embarrassed as all get-out. And I'm sure a guy's body won't look as good as a girl's in a picture like that, especially when the girl is Cory, but—

But what the hell.

Really, it's not sex, and you can't get pregnant from it, like she said. And I trust Cory not to get all movie-whack-job and pass the picture around if she gets pissed at me. Besides, we're not putting our faces on pictures, even if Cory's little rose tattoo beside her belly button gives her away. Her dad so doesn't know about that tattoo, but her mom thought it was okay.

I make sure I'm stretched out as best I can under the covers, and that stuff's . . . you know . . . arranged as much as it can be, and make sure I'm not too close or touching anything, and I snap the picture.

From the speakerphone, I hear a soft giggle, and then, "Did you take it?"

I get the phone back up high enough to say, "Yeah."

Then I check the picture out.

Okay, that is *so* not something I want to stare at for very long. I click Save, then start a message to Cory.

"Let me see," she says, all happy sounding, which makes my face go even hotter.

"Just a sec." I'm aching all over, getting tense—in lots of ways—needing some relief. This isn't a huge deal, but it feels like a huge deal.

My finger hovers over Send, and I can't help wondering stupid crap like, has she seen bigger ones? Better ones?

How many has she seen?

Whose?

Don't go there.

But seriously, how am I supposed to know if my junk, uh, looks good, or whatever?

Worrying about how I look makes everything . . . deflate a little bit. That's probably good.

"It's me," Cory tells me like she's reading my mind. "You know I'll like it."

She doesn't say, *I showed you mine, now show me yours*, but she could, and she'd be right. I didn't exactly say *no* when she told me what she was doing under her covers.

I close my eyes and press the button, and it's gone.

Now I'm so hot I have to come out from under the covers, but I wiggle all around and leave my head under so the light from the phone doesn't spill into the room and maybe sneak under my door to bust me to my parents. I don't think they're up, but who knows. Rescued animals vomit a lot, so Mom and Dad are always washing sheets in the middle of the night.

This is taking forever.

Has she seen it yet?

She should have seen it by now.

I can't breathe.

Totally stupid. Why did I send that? She'll think I'm stupid when she sees it. I don't feel like art, like the picture of her that she sent me.

Her breathing echoes into the phone, then stops, then starts back.

"What?" Damn. Too loud. Take a breath.

I take a breath.

Cory says, "I think you're hot."

I'm definitely hot, as in inferno, but the other meaning? "Guys aren't supposed to be hot. Are we?"

"Yes, you are too supposed to be, and you are."

I manage not to cough or choke or puke like one of Mom's rescued animals, so that's good, even if I can't manage to say anything that makes any sense.

Cory's voice drops, like her mouth is closer to the phone. "One day, I want to look in person. One day soon."

When I swallow, I feel like I've got sand in my throat, but I get "Okay" out without sounding like I need a gallon of water to talk right.

"I want to see you because you're hot."

She's teasing me now, only not really.

I start to smile. "Stop saying that."

"No," she whispers. Then quick, but not panicked. "I have to go. Love you."

And she's gone.

"Love you, too," I tell my phone, even though it's telling me what time the call ended, and I'm getting a little more sure. Cory really will be the one, and I'll find some way to make it pretty. I think that's my job, if I like her a lot, to make our first time together something special for her, and I do like her a lot.

But . . . will I know what to do?

I know all about protection, and babies are definitely

not in *any* of my plans until after my career's up and going, and I'm through with professional sports. That part's not an issue.

It's . . . the rest of it.

The actual sex.

I've watched it in movies. I've talked to my dad about it, though not in details like how-to or ways to make Cory the happiest. (Dad would croak on the spot if I asked him something like that.)

I'd call Marvin, but he doesn't know any more than me, and he won't hear his phone because he'll have his headphones in like he always does at night. I don't know how anybody can listen to music all the time. All that background noise would make my brain rattle—and when does he have time to think?

I think when I listen to music, he always tells me, *I just don't think about bad things.*

From down in the laundry room, I hear a smoke-detector screech noise and barely hold back a groan.

It's that parrot.

The thing won't even eat unless I'm around, and Mom's saying the parrot thinks I'm its person.

I'm not. Definitely not.

I don't know why anybody would want a parrot. If the parrot did learn to talk, or if it made noises all time, when would *I* get time to think? You know, about Cory and stuff. About how it will be. And where. And when.

Something like this will probably take lots of thinking and some whole new plans, if I'm going to get it right, and I definitely want to get it right. With no Marvin or music or parrots or Dad or anything like that, and definitely no plumbers with pipe wrenches.

"Shut up," I mutter at my door as the parrot makes another smoke-detector screech. "No parrots allowed."

No parrots. No pipe wrenches.

Yep.

Lots of thinking to do. Lots of plans to make.

Always Never Lasts Forever

("Use Somebody"—Kings of Leon. Great name. If I had a band, I'd call it Gravehound. Or maybe Eighteen Inches.)

Dear Sir or Madam:

I am writing to request permission to apply to Mission Heights Community College. I have a felony conviction that occurred when I was fourteen years old, but I am almost eighteen now, and much has changed in my life . . .

Dear Ann Smith:

I am writing to you in your capacity as Director of Admissions of Blue Sky Community College to request permission to apply. Per your brochure, people with felony convictions may offer an application with permission from you and your board, following a comprehensive letter of explanation . . .

Dear Dean Johnson:

I would like to request permission to submit an application to West Mountain Community College. Enclosed, please find the required letter of explanation concerning my felony conviction, along with a recommendation statement from my probation officer . . .

Now, really, how bad do my letters suck?

Go on. You can say it. They totally blow.

If you were a Sir or a Madam or a Director of Admissions or a Dean of Admissions, would you bother to give me a chance?

No.

Really puts weight on that *What's the point?* question.

But Branson has his requirements and his deadlines, and the big clock of the universe is ticking away toward my birthday next August, so I keep writing and getting turned down or ignored. The rest of the time I bust my ass at school, then out here at Rock Hill. And I've been trying hard not to spy on Fairy Girl.

Trying.

Not . . . always succeeding.

Maybe Rock Hill's not the best place to spend my time, but other than home, Rock Hill is my only place. I learn a lot just by being here. For example, I've learned this: four kinds of people come to cemeteries.

First, obviously, there's the dead kind.

Second, there's people like Harper and me and the funeral home reps and the headstone carvers and setters who work in graveyards for a living. We're supposed to be there. We've got important stuff to do, and respect for the environment we're supposed to do it in, and even though we're sort of wrapped up in a fog of everybody else's sadness, we keep seeing clearly, and we get our jobs done.

Next, you've got the people who are burying loved ones and visiting loved ones and grieving loved ones—like Fairy Girl. They've got important stuff to do, too. They stand or sit, they cross arms and clench fists or touch gravestones, they keep stone faces or cry, and sometimes, they talk with Harper and me when we're digging or covering graves or doing other duties around Rock Hill.

So, dead people, working people, and grieving people aren't really an issue, because we're all supposed to be in the cemetery. It's the fourth kind of people found in graveyards who cause problems. Freaks and weirdos. These are the assholes who graffiti headstones; the jerk-offs who sit in groups with candles and tell ghost stories and leave beer bottles and roaches tossed everywhere; the nut jobs who think graves are special places to make out with their girlfriends; and the morbid goofballs who think they're vampires, or going to find vampires, or just want to think about death and be around death all the time.

Cherie Blankenship, the one and only younger sister of Jonas the pinhead football player who hits Marvin for a hobby, the girl who cannot comprehend simple phrases like *no* or *hell no* or *blow off*, the girl who redefines *oblivion* on a daily basis, has morbid goofball written all over her. When she's out of school, she wears Goth clothes and makeup, but not because she understands the Goth philosophy or feels it or believes it. She thinks all the black looks good. She likes that the trippy makeup upsets her parents and bugs the pinhead. She thinks maybe I'll find her mysterious or irresistible or some shit, so she slathers on the persona and shows up graveside to irritate the hell out of me at least once a week.

"Fifteen'll get you twenty," Harper tells me like he always does when he sees Vampirella pulling up in her little green hybrid that her parents got her for her birthday.

I grunt like I always do when he says that, then remember the song where the line came from—Jimmy Buffett's "Livingston Saturday Night." Marvin gave me my entire Buffett collection the week I got home from Juvenile.

Music to chill by, he called it.

Cherie, who is probably constitutionally incapable of chilling, is actually sixteen and a year behind me in school. She's driving slow on the main road through Rock Hill, and I know she's looking for me.

Great.

It's Wednesday night and Harper's foggy breath smells like beer and the fresh peanut butter Marvin dropped off before he split. We're hollowing out a larger-than-usual grave for an extra-large casket coming from two counties over for a burial Thursday morning. What's left of Harper's six-pack is in the grave behind us, but I never touch the stuff. Drinking would screw my probation big-time, and besides, I have an aversion to drinking anything that smells that much like cow piss. Marvin's at work at Duke's Ridge Mall, which hopefully doesn't smell like cow piss, but you never know. He's selling cookies. ("Great way to meet chicks, you should try it—chocolate, man. Gets 'em every time. . . .")

In her travel cage next to the dirt pile, Fred quits playing in her water dish, poofs out her feathers, and makes an ear-splitting smoke-detector screech in Cherie's direction.

Harper runs a sun-spotted, knotty hand through his sweaty gray hair and glares over the edge of the grave we're standing inside, propped on our shovels as Cherie swoops down on our location. He's about an inch shorter than me, so I've got a better view of Cherie's long black skirt and lacey long-sleeved black shirt. She's got her dyed-black hair pulled back and fixed with some kind of chopstick-looking things, and her eye-shadow and lipstick, freshly applied because no black makeup is allowed at school, glisten in the late afternoon sun.

She's not ugly—don't get me wrong on that point. The girl is fine. Some people would consider her beautiful, even in the Halloween getup with all the dangling metal jewelry. It's not that I don't notice her, or care about her a little, even, like a big brother might care about a kid sister. It's just that I don't know her, like I keep trying to tell her, and she doesn't know me.

Because she's not real.

And I'm not real.

I mean, I'm not what she thinks I am, this tortured and dangerous dark prince who can save her from the boredom that hangs around her like a shroud. She doesn't see me. She just sees the character she wants me to play. I can't explain it any better than that. Marvin doesn't quite get it when I try to tell him how I feel about Cherie, but even he thinks she's too far gone from normal to rehabilitate.

"Hello, little birdie," Cherie says to Fred, who gives her another ear popper of a smoke-detector screech. That's a special noise for Fred. She only makes it when she's scared, in real trouble, or face-to-face with somebody she really despises. Cherie sits down next to Fred's cage, anyway, and Fred plasters her little gray parrot body against the bars, doing her best to snap through the metal and get out to assault Cherie's big black clodhoppers, or maybe tear into all that lace and black cotton.

As usual, Cherie doesn't notice Fred's less than favorable response to her. "So who is this grave for?"

"He's not from around here," I say, because Harper's scowling too much to talk. He hates digging oversized graves, anyway, and adding Cherie to the equation means he's jabbing his shovel with a lot of extra force.

"Pretty big guy, huh?" Cherie's eyes go wide and bright as she mentally measures the hole we're working on. She knows the drill—and all the usual dimensions. "Wonder if he had a heart attack, or maybe a stroke?" She teases out the ends of her long curly hair with black-tipped nails she has to take on and off, because black nail polish isn't allowed at our school, either. "Obesity is a big risk factor for all kinds of diseases."

I don't say a word, and neither does Harper. The man we're digging a grave for died in a car wreck, but if we say that, Cherie will want details that will make us both sick.

"How was your day?" she asks me, more or less ignoring Harper, which is fine, because he strains brain muscles ignoring her, too.

"Busy." I'm smiling, but Cherie's never figured out that's bad. "Had tests in first and second period."

She blinks her too-thick mascara at me and gives me a little pout. "I didn't see you at lunch today. Again."

Because I saw you first. Out loud, my answer is, "Yeah. Marvin and I had stuff to do for Advanced Math."

"Advanced Math, AP English, Physics—I don't know why you wear yourself out with such hard classes." She laughs and it sounds real instead of all fakey, at least. "Is it just because Marvin does? It's not like you can go to Notre Dame with him, right? They're way too Catholic for you. My dad says sex offenders can't go to college at all."

I wish she'd go away. Anywhere but here would be just fine.

"It's your senior year," she goes on, just like she'd go on even if I told her to shut up. "Have some fun. I plan to party next year, only you won't be there."

Marvin's a witness, and so is Harper, and so are you. I really have tried being direct with Cherie, in addition to lying to her. Besides what we told her earlier today, I've said I'm not interested, that she's sweet but not my type—all of that. She doesn't care. She says I need friends, especially girl friends (who could turn into girlfriends). So, I revert to the standards.

Got to work.

Have to study.

It's against my probation and I'll go to prison.

Not everybody has that last excuse. Cherie is a special person, to make a guy glad he's got *that* shit hanging over his head.

Fred abandons her plan to eat through her travel cage to destroy Cherie, lowers her parrot head, and buzzes her wings in menacing I-will-obliterate-you fashion.

Cherie asks, "Want to go to the game next Friday?"

I cram my shovel into the deepening grave. "Thanks, but I don't go to games."

"Why? Are football games against your probation like everything else?"

I go tongue-tied, but Harper steps up for me. "Crowds." He shrugs and spits, pulls a toothpick out of his dirty shirt pocket, and crams it between his teeth. "Underage kids. And besides, the game would run past his legal curfew."

This turns down the chatter, and there's nothing but the sound of our digging, the plop of dirt, and the bumble-bee buzzing of Fred's wings. The grave's smelling more and more like moldy water and beer. I'm hot from digging despite the cool air, so that makes me want to retch.

Cherie leans back against the grave dirt, then stretches out on it and folds her hands over her belly like she's a vampire princess taking her daytime respite. To the sky, she says, "Are you allowed to be here in the graveyard after curfew? If you're working, I mean?"

"Yes," I say at the same time Harper says, "No."

We look at each other, and then go back to digging, fast. I'm allowed to be on school property for designated functions even after curfew, because the judge decided that when my parents sued to get me allowed back in school. I'm also allowed to be at work if Harper's here to supervise me. Harper's trying to protect me from Cherie, and I'm doing my level damnedest to screw it up.

Think fast.

"What Harper means is, I have to get prior approval from Branson, and he'd probably check up on me."

"Your life is so hard, Del. I don't know how you stand it."

Harper quits digging, leans his shovel against the grave wall, and gives me a look like he'd offer me a beer if I were twenty-one. I give him a look like, I'd take it if I were over-age and Cherie was here and wouldn't go away. He pops a metal top and sucks down about half of the can, then lodges it in the farthest grave wall and goes back to digging.

A few minutes later, as it finally starts getting dark, head-lights sweep over Vampirella as she rests atop her grave dirt, driving my parrot beyond the boundaries of sanity.

"My folks are here," I tell Harper, and he nods that it's okay for me to leave, that he can get the site finished before tomorrow's funeral, especially since my leaving means he'll get rid of Cherie, too.

I think about telling him to go easy on the beer, but it won't do any good, so I don't. I just climb out of the grave on the opposite side from Cherie, slip around and collect Fred, and say, "Bye."

"Bye, Del." Cherie gives a dramatic wave. "I'll see you tomorrow."

Not if I see you first.

"Okay."

I brush off dirt with one hand and carry Fred and her cage in the other. When I get to my parents' car, another hybrid, blue, older than Cherie's, I slip Fred into the back-seat before I climb in beside her.

My parents look alike. They're tall and kind of scrawny like me. They both have brown eyes and brown hair like me, though Mom's is a little on the red side. They both wear jeans and Humane Society T-shirts when they're not at work. (They both work in patient accounts at Duke's Ridge Hospital.) Dad's voice is way deeper than Mom's, though, and it's his baritone I hear as I shut the door behind me and the car starts rolling down Rock Hill's main road.

"Dear God. What *is* that girl's damage?"

"Jonas Blankenship is her brother," I say. "That's enough to make anybody soft in the head."

"I thought you told her you weren't interested." Mom adjusts the small blue animal carrier in her lap. She switches on the dome light in the car to check whatever she's got inside it.

"That didn't compute in her brain, but no worries." I'm smiling, but try not to, because my parents do know that's not always a good thing. "I'm really not interested."

In her.

"Harper stays right there whenever she's around," I add, to make them both feel better.

When he's not drunk off his ass.

"Has she ever—you know, offered?" Mom's voice sounds definitely tense.

"No."

Yes. Repeatedly. And in some very creative ways.

"Fred," Fred says in Mom's voice, like she doesn't approve of my minor mangling of the truth. I'm not sure I approve, either, but I don't want Mom or Dad worrying for nothing.

"What would you do if she did?" Dad asks, sounding sort of official, asking his I-have-to-do-this parent stuff.

Lie and tell her dating and having sex would violate my probation. Give her Branson's card. He's met Cherie. He'll totally back me up.

"I'd just come home," I say. "You know, get away from her."

My parents relax, and mom shifts the carrier on her lap again. The creature inside it—cat, I'm presuming—lets out a motion-sick wail. Mom speaks softly to the cat, stroking it through the slats in the carrier.

I remember sitting in a holding cell at the Duke's Ridge jail with Mom outside, gripping my hand through the bars.

It's a mistake, Del. It's got to be. We'll get this taken care of. We'll get this fixed.

I close my eyes to shut out that image.

"Fred." This time, Fred's almost whispering, and when I open my eyes, I see she's staring out of her travel cage at me, the yellow sections of her eyes wide and the little black dots in the center boring into me. She considers me her parrot mate, so if I let her out, she'd probably crawl all over me, nipping and grooming until I got out of feeling-weird mode.

But I do feel weird. I mean, maybe I should be 100 percent honest with my parents all the time because they've been so totally great through all this, but I just don't want them to worry anymore. I can handle Vampirella. She's irritating, but harmless.

Maybe Cherie's trying to look tough and crazy and fearless to her friends, hanging out with the most dangerous guy in Duke's Ridge. Maybe she's looking to save me or rescue me or something. Maybe my folks should get her involved with the Humane Society so she could rescue truly helpless things, and leave me the hell alone.

Women write Manson in prison and offer to marry him, Marvin told me once. *The Menendez brothers have fan clubs. The felony thing—chicks dig it. Well, weird chicks, anyway.*

An hour or so later, I've "had enough to eat" and I've taken a shower. I'm in my room, which is nothing special—just a bed, some dressers, a desk, a chair, and a TV I don't get to watch much. The only thing I spend money on is retro cereal sheets, because they make me laugh. I've got Count Chocula and Cocoa Puffs and Corn Flakes, but right now I'm sitting on a too-green Lucky Charms bedspread with Fred on my shoulder, staring at a stack of blank paper and holding a pen. I don't have my own computer, because I'm not allowed to own or have unrestricted access to a personal computer or even a cell phone with text capacity or Internet access. There's a computer in the living room, but my parents have to keep software on it that blocks sites that might have certain kinds of content. The software doesn't work so well, so it blocks just about everything. We have a family blog that we update, with comments disabled to keep assholes from leaving us hate mail because of what happened with me, but otherwise, we've kind of given up on the computer thing for a while.

But, Dr. Mote wants me to write stuff down or draw stuff or whatever, and Branson wants me to do better with my explanations in my letters to colleges, so I'm trying this the old-fashioned way.

I don't know why I'm bothering.

Nothing ever comes out, even though I do try, just like this, lots of nights. I want to tell everybody the real truth about the real me, but I always freeze up because I know I won't even get the chance to finish. People hear the words, the labels, and they're done with me, no questions asked.

"Once upon a time," I tell Fred, "there was this girl named Cory, and she had blond hair and cute freckles and blue eyes, and she was, you know—built and stuff. She was funny and smart, and she liked watching me play baseball, and I came to her softball games, and we had a bunch of friends who all ran together at Duke's Ridge Park, especially during the summer league games."

I stop because I'm feeling something. Something slow and warm and a little tingly. Emotion, sensation—but also memory. I'm remembering what it feels like to . . . feel. Without analyzing it, thinking about it, or trying to kill it.

Fred gives my earlobe a love bite and clicks her beak together, like she's trying to get me to keep going.

The pen twitches in my fingers, but I don't start writing.

I see Cory's happy, smiling face too sharply in my head, and now I'm feeling more, and what I'm feeling is, it hurts.

Cory was a few months younger than me. The summer before high school started, she was thirteen, and I was fourteen. Everybody else was fourteen, too, except for Raulston, who turned fifteen the first week of summer vacation. The night Cory and I sent each other pictures of ourselves, I had decided to plan some special date for her birthday, only we never got to have that date. We became the "Duke's Ridge Eight"—ten, minus Marvin, and also minus Cory because the reporters weren't allowed to say much about her—before I could give her the flowers I wanted to buy her, or the bracelet I put on layaway, or the card I tore up and burned a few months later, because I thought setting something on fire might make me feel better.

It said, *You're my best. You're my perfect. You're my always.*

I made it myself, using this site on the Internet, and I decorated it with roses like her tattoo, and I didn't know it wasn't true. I wanted to give it to her and make her happy. I wasn't even planning to have sex with her, because I'd decided we should wait longer. Maybe until we were both fifteen. There was other stuff we could do—but the sex part could wait.

I hate remembering.

I really hate trying to talk about it, or explain it, or write it down.

How can it make any sense to anybody if they don't

know everything? I can't explain it right. I can't ever say enough. I don't even want to try now. People just judge. I bet that happens to Raulston and Tom and Randall and Jason, too. Maybe even the girls, but please, God, if there really is a God and you really do listen to me, not Cory, okay? Don't let people blow Cory off.

I slam down the pen, which doesn't make me feel better, because nothing does when I try to go digging up this damned moldy grave in my life. Branson's insane if he thinks I'm testifying about sex offender laws. Dr. Mote's more insane. She should know better.

There is no way.

No. Way.

"I can't do this," I tell Fred, and she answers by nipping at the top of my ear not so lovingly.

Then she bites hard and says "*Ow*" before I can do it.

"*Ow*," I agree, rubbing my bitten ear.

A few minutes later, I crank back on the bed with my headphones on, listening to my *Hallelujah* mix on the iPod. Fred's on my chest with her beak down, letting me scratch the tiny pearl-gray feathers on top of her head, which are so smooth and layered they're almost like soft scales.

Not much of a social life, but it's what I've got, and it's safe. For now, I'd rather have safe than warm and tingly and always in the end, painful.

Three Years Ago: Party in the USA

"Lockdown!" the coaches yell, and everybody laughs and cheers as the city league gym doors slam shut and the chains get thrown over the bars. They aren't really locked because of fire code, but if somebody tries to sneak out of the inside campground, everybody'll hear all the rattling.

Who would want to escape, though?

We've got burgers and hot dogs, all the punch and water and soda anybody could drink, already toasted s'mores, candy, chips, cakes—the food's endless. The tents are all pitched on the rubber basketball floor cover, and they're cranking up the rented DVDs on the giant-screen television that the coaches rolled under one of the pulled-up basketball goals.

Everything smells like chocolate or meat or sleeping bags and popcorn. Everything looks great.

It's Good-bye Night for city league baseball and softball—about a hundred of us, ten coaches, a bunch of parent volunteers—and my folks and Cory's folks and even Marvin's mom blew it off this year.

We're on our own.

Cory snuggles next to me in front of the giant television, her beanbag touching mine, her head on my shoulder. I'd rather her be in my lap or on my beanbag, but I'd also rather not get popped in the head by one of the coaches. My belly's so full I'd probably fall off and roll across the rubber floor until I hit the nearest wall.

From my left, Raulston lets out a raunchy belch, bringing a chorus of *boos* and *grosses* from everybody else.

The horror flick is stupid, so we're mostly talking in the semidarkness, and Cory whispers in my ear, "Did you like it last night?"

All the hamburgers I ate bang against each other as I get a vivid picture of what she's talking about, from the field out behind my house. It involved one of mom's quilts and not a lot of clothes.

"Yeah." I know my face is changing colors, and I hate that. When will that stop? Will I have to be fifty years old before I stop turning purple every time Cory says something sweet—or hot?

"Do you want to do it again?" she asks, so quiet only I can hear her.

"Here?" My voice comes out too loud, and it cracks a little, and I feel stupid.

In the flickering light from the television, her smile gives me that water-in-my-bones feeling, but I say, "I don't think that's a good idea."

Really, there's nowhere to hide or sneak away, and if there are any hiding spots, other people have probably already found them.

But when she keeps looking at me, I want to find one for us. I really like looking at her. Putting my hands on her. She touches me, too, but we just use our hands. We've done that three times. She wants us to use our mouths, but then stop there. She agrees we need to wait for real sex. I'm fine with that.

"Not here," she murmurs, sounding disappointed, but also like she gets it. "I know. But soon."

"Soon," I agree, watching people kiss on television and thinking they're lucky.

"No way." I'm looking at Raulston and Tom while Randall and Jason laugh their nuts off and Marvin eats a bag of Oreos. He's got one white iPod earbud in his left ear, but he's listening to us with his right ear. It's after lights-out, but there's a little glow coming through our tent from the gym safety lights.

Raulston pulls out his phone and whispers, "Want me to prove it?"

"Dutch will beat your ass with a bat, man," Marvin says around a mouthful of cookies. "If you say she sent you some sizzling pictures, we believe you."

"I've got some of my own," Randall brags. "Past and present." He lifts up his phone and rocks it back and forth. I can't see the details of his face, but I can tell he's grinning. He makes a motion like he's slicking back his hair.

"Screw you," Jason says, because Randall's "past" would be Lisa, and—oops. "She never sent you anything."

"Did she send you something?" Randall asks Jason.

"Hell, yes. And we've done a lot more than pictures. Want to see?" Jason pulls out his phone and acts like he's about to slide it open and show us an amateur porn video.

Marvin swallows really loud, then grumbles, "Don't. If Coach sees all these lights and has to tell us to put up and shut up again, he'll crack our skulls."

"Eat your cookies," Tom says, holding up his phone and waving around a picture. "I've got three of Jenna."

I try not to look straight at it, but I see enough to know there's lots of skin.

She's not Cory, though, so I'm not interested.

I glance at my phone, cue up her picture, and smile at it,

but I don't show it off. I keep my phone tight in my fist so nobody can grab it. I'm definitely not sharing Cory's picture with anybody. She'd never show mine.

Would she?

A bad image pops into my head, of her and Dutch and Lisa and Jenna, huddled around their phones in their tents. They've gotten hollered at a few times, so I know they're still up, too.

My phone buzzes with a message, and I jam it under the edge of my sleeping bag to read the text from Cory.

Luv u.

Luv u 2, I type back and send it.

"Cookies are better," Marvin says as Raulston's phone buzzes with a text, no doubt from Dutch.

Tom's phone goes off next, with a big loud blast of Aerosmith's "Walk This Way," and we all start carping at him about putting it on mute, but it takes Coach like six seconds to be in our tent door.

Well, Coach's arm, anyway.

"Hand 'em over," he demands from the tent doorway, sticking his big hand inside and waiting for us to fill it with phones.

We all groan and grumble, but we do it.

And a few seconds later, all the coaches are going into all the tents and confiscating all the cell phones until the morning.

"Get some sleep!" one of them yells as Coach zips up our flap and gives it a thump with his phone-filled hand.

We all flop back on our sleeping bags except Marvin, who's still eating.

"Way to go, asshole," Raulston mutters to Tom.

"Dickwad," Randall says.

Jason adds, "Moron."

"Want a cookie?" Marvin whispers to me before I can think of any name to call Tom, who's busy telling everybody to shut up, and I end up eating half the rest of the Oreos with Marvin, wishing I could talk to Cory, or text her, but we'll be back to normal tomorrow night, except for high school starting in like, two days.

There are probably lots of private places in high schools, though.

That thought makes me smile around the cookie crumbs on my teeth.

Maybe high school will rock as much as baseball and city league and the field behind my house, and just about everything else in my life right now, except for that noisy parrot.

I push the Oreo bag back at Marvin and it crinkles, and he laughs as he shoves in his second earbud and closes out the universe.

I laugh.

"Shut up," Tom growls again, but that only makes us laugh harder, until cookie stuff gets up my nose.

"Hallelujah" and Burrito Farts, Not Necessarily Related

("Hallelujah"—the Willie Nelson version. Yeah. Laugh. Dude is old and twangy, but he can *sing*.)

I could write some kind of research paper on the song "Hallelujah" by Leonard Cohen. I listened to it over and over again during lockup, and any time I had to come face-to-face with the minion of Satan known as William Kaison, with his black suit and narrow, mean eyes—never mind the bad comb-over. Maybe there's no such thing as the devil, but if the king of hell does exist, no doubt he's got more style than Kaison.

Now I've heard there was a secret chord that David played, and it pleased the Lord, but you don't really care for music, do you?

Yeah.

Or, from the Jeff Buckley version, *Well maybe there's a*

God above, but all I've ever learned from love was how to shoot somebody who outdrew ya.

Those two lines just about sum up Kaison. Well, that, and the comb-over, and the belief that it was his divine right and electoral mandate to "teach young people how to act." When he was in office, he picked targets and "made examples out of little hoods," he admitted to a reporter later, after he left office due to some marital scandal. "If you force one teenager to pay a price, the rest sit up and take notice."

"And if you bankrupt one teenager permanently, if you ruin one child's future, what does that teach the rest?" Mom had asked when she read that article. "Go ahead and try, but life's hopeless, anyway?"

Dad had taken the newspaper away from her and quietly thrown it away. Then he telephoned the *Duke's Ridge Daily* and told them if they ran one more story about that bastard, he'd cancel his subscription. We could have been mad at the coaches who turned us in, I guess, but that never made any sense. They were just following rules, and they could have lost their jobs and gone to jail if they hadn't done what they were supposed to do. It was Kaison who made it all crazy and miserable.

I've seen him a few times on the local news. He never acknowledges getting run out of office for being such a hypocrite, and usually babbles about some mix of God, country, and drawing lines in the sand to keep everybody and everything under control. I try really hard not to let that asshole bother how I think about God or the Lord or whatever you want to call Him or Her or whatever. But that's not easy. Even now, years later, when I close my eyes and make some attempt to pray, I have to stop, because it's Kaison's face I see in my head. I can't even conjure up some ancient white long-bearded grandfather like I used to see when I was little and thought about God.

I hate that.

But, I don't hate my "Hallelujah" mix.

I've got fourteen versions—the original, of course, with Cohen's whispery, murmuring I-so-need-Prozac voice. Hard to beat that, but Jeff Buckley sort of does, if you ignore the heavy breathing and weird chords at the beginning. I like Willie Nelson's take, the one I'm playing in my head while I try not to fall asleep at the end of first period, and Allison Crowe's cover is awesome—the arrangement and her voice and everything. Except it's on a holiday album, which is just totally weird. "Hallelujah" is about as close to "Christmas song" as somebody cutting up virgins with chainsaws.

The prettiest version is probably the one by Mary Angels, but my favorite is Brandi Carlile's Live at KCRW.com version. It's raw and pissed and sweet, and sometimes I just can't stop listening to it.

Also, Brandi Carlile is hot.

That definitely does not impair my enjoyment of the song.

"I can hear the music," Marvin whispers, bringing him and the classroom back into focus. "You're gonna get busted if you don't knock it off."

I pull out my one ear bud and slide it into my shirt pocket. The iPod's tucked in my jeans pocket.

"Have a good Thursday," Mr. McCash announces, closing his teacher's copy of our physics book, and I get a grip on the fact that I totally forgot I'm in class, and that I've got no idea what he's been saying for the last half hour.

Concentration. Sucks.

I wish that would stop happening. I thought the music in one ear would help, not make it worse.

I glance at Marvin's notes, but instead of formulas, I see the name *Lee Ann* sketched in big fat graffiti letters, underlined, with flames coming off the top. Guess Marvin has his own reasons to be distracted, and I'm betting his reasons are more fun than mine.

"I was listening to 'Hallelujah,'" I tell him.

"I don't want to talk songs or music theory."

"You're the one who got me hooked on all this stuff."

"I'm not that guy anymore." Marvin gestures to the classroom around us as people jam out the door. "When you start talking about all the different versions of 'Hallelujah,' I zone out like a big dog. It's boring if I'm not right in your head listening to it with you. There's a world outside your earbuds, you know that, right?"

"Music's better."

"In moderation," he says, doing his best straight-out impression of our health teacher from last year. "All things in moderation. You should try giving it a rest sometimes."

He lets out a wide, long yawn before he stands and packs up his stuff. We wait for the rest of the class to get out before we head into the hall to get to Advanced Math, because we don't have that far to walk. I glance left and right, making sure I'm keeping my distance from everybody, even though it's second nature now, and I'm too old-news to stare at.

When I first got out of Juvenile, I had to go to alternative school and wear white T-shirts and black jeans every day, and ignore the bastards who liked to yell and fight and poke people with pencils—bunch of dill weeds. With "good behavior," I earned out of there and back to real school in four months—hard, since I'm not supposed to live, work, or attend events within a thousand feet of "anywhere children congregate." My parents had to sue so I could go to school, then Branson hammered out permission for me to do stuff like go to movies and community events as long as I'm not alone.

About school—yeah, I took some shit from a few people when I came back, but overall nowhere near what I expected. Everybody at G. W. had read about the case, or heard about it day after day for months. Lots of the other students felt sorry for me, even if they didn't want to hang around and be my new best buddies. A few parents protested me going back to regular classes even though I'd done my time and gotten probation. My parents and I knew they had been ginned up by Kaison, but his big affair scandal hit the news and he left office, and the conscientious objectors who didn't want me near their pure little angels got blown off by all the people on the school board who just wanted to settle the lawsuit and stop the news coverage.

After that, it was like I made some twisted peace treaty with everybody at G. W. without even knowing I did it. The agreement seems to be that I'll get a few grumbles here and there, but mostly I'll get totally ignored in exchange for not trying to talk to or stand next to or even look in the general direction of anyone else, or take part in any aspect of "real life" as far as high school's concerned.

Except hanging with Marvin, of course. He's never much paid attention to the "everybody's doing it" thing. My hero. Seriously. Everybody in the world should be more like Marvin.

When we get to Advanced Math, he's talking about some girl who hung out at the cookie counter last night. "She had red hair, long, down to here." He slaps his chest, then gives a quick whistle he learned from Fred. "Perfect. And she likes action, so we're probably going to see the new *DrugRunner Chronicle* tomorrow night if I can get tickets before they sell out."

"Is her name Lee Ann?" I ask as we wedge through the door.

He looks amazed. "How'd you know?"

"You're going to go out with her?"

"It's not really a date. It's just a movie. I don't date."

"You're not on probation, Marvin. That's me." We've been here before, and I know he'll blow me off—which he does, just by rolling his eyes.

"Eighteen." He plops into his desk chair. "Not before. I'm not doing anything there might be a law against."

I'm still standing up, blocking the aisle. There's only a few people here, and we're not paying attention to the people coming in behind us, so we don't see him.

Where's Fred and her smoke-alarm screech when you need it?

"It's the Great Marvolo," comes the line that announces Jonas Blankenship's arrival, right before he sucker punches Marvin and knocks him halfway out of the desk where he's sitting.

Marvin smiles and shakes his head. He pulls himself back into the desk, but he doesn't rub his shoulder even though it probably hurts. Marvin's never been a fighter, so he gets by on charm and friendliness. He says, "Jonas," with a quick nod, then glances at the posse Jonas must have towed through the door behind him. Three guys, easily as big as Jonas, stand there looking bored. I know their names but I never talk to them. The four of them don't take this class, and

probably don't even know what it is. They just make a matching set with their jeans, football jerseys, blond hair, throw-
back scalp-cuts, and tans. One guy's hands are bigger than
my face.

"Cherie says she hung with you last night." Jonas smiles
at me with big white teeth. We have that in common, smiling when we'd rather say a bunch of stuff I shouldn't put on
paper. "I thought I told you to stay away from my little
sister."

"Trust me, I do whenever I can, but she won't stay away
from me." I keep my arms perfectly still at my sides. It's not
that I couldn't defend myself if pinhead jumps on me. He's
big, but I'm fast and strong from digging. I'd probably hold
my own, or maybe even take him. Only, he'd get griped at
and sent to detention while I'd face violation of probation,
maybe new charges because of my record, and going straight
back to Juvenile and on to prison after I turn eighteen. Definitely not a fair fight, and besides, Jonas isn't that much of a
fighter. He's just a pinhead.

"Hartwick—" he starts, frowning, but I interrupt his
dramatic lather-up by lifting my books and dropping them
hard on the desk beside Marvin's. The crack of the impact
makes the five or six people already in the room for class
look up and stare at us.

"Cherie's safe, Jonas." My arms go still again. "You take
real good care of her, and I respect that. I'll never lay a hand
on her, no matter what. I swear it." I'm not imitating his

cadence and style on purpose, but it happens whenever I deal with him. Something instinctive on my part, I guess. Maybe it puts him more at ease. "Want me to swear it on the Bible, or my mother's life? Name it."

Jonas's frown eases. "Nah." His muscles relax, and his three buddies look more bored than ever. "Cherie's a little mixed up, that's all."

One of the buddies snickers, and Marvin goes to add a few words to that opinion, but stops when he sees the warning look on my face.

"Is she still showing up at the graveyard a lot, like last night?" Jonas asks.

"Three or four times per week. Harper's told her not to, but she's—"

"Stubborn. Like me." He sounds proud, but also worried. "Tell Harper I'll talk to my folks again."

"Will do."

Jonas and his buddies make their exit as the rest of the class wanders in, and I don't really feel relieved or weak-kneed or anything. I've read a ton of "young adult" books, too. Guys like Jonas are supposed to be brain-dead zombie hulks who bully everyone weaker than themselves. Every story's got to have some sneering jerk called (insert tough thug name of your choice, fantasy or contemporary—your call). To tell the total truth, I met guys like that in Juvenile, and a few in alternative school, but mostly, G. W. doesn't have zombie bullies, or at least I haven't run into any, maybe because I'm just made out of paper, or I don't really live on the same planet.

There are few natural zombie-bully targets like me, and some of the scrawny or "different" guys or girls in each class year, but we don't get mowed down on a daily basis. As for the football team and the other jocks (not thinking about baseball, not thinking about baseball), some are thick, some are pinheads like Jonas, and some are smart and on the honor roll. Some of the popular girls are mean as hell, and some are sweet and kind to everybody. It's just not that black-and-white around here, in what passes for my real world. I might get glared at or snickered at or, as previously noted, thoroughly ignored, but that's about the worst of it.

Marvin and I sit and take out our math books. He pulls a few sheets of paper from a folder and lays them next to his book, then says, "Jonas is cranking up on you and Cherie."

I get out my paper, but I don't arrange it neatly like Marvin's. "He won't do anything."

I'm not just blowing smoke. I really don't think pinhead's any kind of threat, but when I close my eyes for a long blink, I flash on Cory's smile and Kaison's comb-over, and I hear a few strands of "Hallelujah"-like ghost mutterings in the back of my brain.

Meaning clear, message received, no problem. Okay, universe, I surrender and admit the following: it's hard to say what will and won't be a threat, and what will and won't be a problem. Satisfied?

When I open my eyes, the hateful image of Kaison fades away and the song gets quieter, but I still feel stupid. If anybody should have figured that last part out, about how everything's always an unknown—it's me. In fact, I think I know it. I think I have it memorized, but I keep it a few inches out of my conscious thoughts, so it doesn't turn me into a screaming, head-banging candidate for a straitjacket. I try to breathe through it, but it's too late. My body tightens like something bad's hovering just behind my left shoulder out of sight, where I can't see it or touch it or even be sure when it's going to lunge forward and sink its teeth into my head.

"She needs to quit bugging you at the graveyard," Marvin says.

My teeth clamp together as I go to war with my own anxiety, and I know the rising heat I'm feeling's got nothing to do with Marvin, or the worried-friend thing he's trying to do. No way am I taking any of this out on him, even though he's the one currently setting off the naggity-nag worrying I can get into when I let down my guard. "No argument. I truly do not want Cherie around."

"Seriously, man. I've got a bad feeling about her—well, her anywhere near you." Marvin leans toward me like I'm not hearing him, or not listening to how much he means it. "You and Harper need to put a stop to that shit."

The hot-hot-hot wave rolling through me, it's trying to explode out of my face now, and worse, it wants out of my mouth at Marvin.

Leave me the hell alone.

Don't you think I know everything's a risk for me?

What if I just don't give a shit anymore?

"Let's talk about something else," I say, really careful not to let even an ounce of my inside-crazy touch my voice. "Like, maybe, Lee Ann with the red hair?"

The bell rings, but Ms. Anderson isn't in the room yet, so nobody gets quiet except Marvin, who just keeps staring at me, waiting for some sign that I know how important he thinks this is.

I blow out some air to reduce the boiling in my skull. "Look, I've told her to stay away, I've had Harper run her off, I've lied to her—what else do you want me to do?"

Marvin's face sags. "I don't know. Just—try harder. It's important."

Big deal, big deal, Marvin thinks it's a big deal . . .

What do you say to the only guy on earth who has your back even when he's driving you up a tree?

Screw off?

Quit playing grandma?

Thanks?

I opt for, "You sound like Branson."

Something in my tone gets through to Marvin, and he seems to take in the fact that I get it, that I really, really do get it.

He leans back, and his frown lifts back to a normal Marvin smile. "Branson's okay," he says, then lowers his voice so Ms. Anderson doesn't hear as she passes by. "For a guy who lugs cups of convict piss all over town."

The anxiety leaves me just like that as I cough out a laugh against my will, and turn toward Ms. Anderson.

Marvin's still easy, after all. Thank God. I'm not sure what I'd do without Marvin and Fred, but what's left of my life would really suck if they weren't in it.

As for Cherie, yeah. Marvin's right. Maybe it's time to try harder.

For some reason, my distracted psychobrain offers me an image of Fairy Girl, like she's becoming a piece of this puzzle, even if I'm still too chickenshit to ask her name.

Is there some relationship between getting Cherie to back off and talking to Fairy Girl more up close and personal? Like one has to move out of the picture to make room for the other? That doesn't exactly make sense, but then again, I'm not the best person to judge what makes sense and what doesn't.

The paper under my right wrist moves as I shift in my chair, making a squeaky noise against the desk and bringing me back to right here, right now.

Damn, I'm doing it again. Not paying attention. I pinch one of the Fred bites on my ear, using the quick flash of pain to keep me in the real world, except there's distant music in my mind, whispering,

The baffled king composing hallelujah . . .

When I glance over at Marvin, I see he's starting a new

rendition of *Lee Ann*, this time in fat '70s-groovy letters, complete with little sketched beads hanging off the *L*.

You know, if I'm made of paper, then Marvin's got to be built out of whatever's opposite of paper. If I asked him, he'd probably say cookies. Or maybe burritos and farts. Right now, it kind of feels like nice sturdy wood to me, or maybe rock. As for what Lee Ann is made of, or Fairy Girl, well. Those are mysteries for later, if I want to keep my grade in Advanced Math.

Three Years Ago: Freaky Creep Show

White light. Blazing. I'm blind. Somebody has hold of my shoulder, and the grip hurts like hell.

Flashlight?

"Wake up, son."

I don't know the voice, but it's deep and older and it bangs into my sleepy brain like a fist. The man holding on to me's wearing a uniform, and he's shining a white sun in my face, and I'm in a sleeping bag—

I'm still at Good-bye Night.

My heart's beating and it's hard to breathe and harder to talk. "Who's—what's—"

The police officer pulls on my arm, not hard, but hard enough to make me wince and scramble to push up on my knees, then get my feet under me. "Get up and come with me, quiet like."

Everybody else in my tent is getting rousted, too. Marvin's already outside with Jason and Randall and Tom when the policemen pull me and Raulston out the door.

Raulston's still only half-conscious. He stares at Marvin and blathers, "Dude, did you spike those cookies with something? What the hell?"

"Do you have any drugs or weapons on your person?" the policeman who has hold of me is asking.

"What?" I can't quite understand what he means, or why he's fastening cuffs around my wrists, or why all of us are wearing handcuffs, and a bunch of coaches and Coach are just standing there staring, and I see people staring at us out of their tents, and I hear girls crying and older female voices asking that same question, *drugs or weapons, drugs or weapons*—

"Anything that might surprise me or upset me when I search you?" the policeman who cuffed me explains as Raulston stammers out a denial to the officer patting him down.

"Marvin urped up some Oreos," I say as my officer pats my legs, then my hips and midsection, and my arms. "I got some on my sleeve and it kind of stinks. Sorry."

The officer narrows his eyes at me, and I see a kind of angry hatred I don't expect or understand.

My skin goes cold as he asks, "Are you trying to be funny?"

"N–no, sir."

He turns me toward the front of the gym. The doors are standing open, and the girls are moving toward them with female officers—Cory, Jenna, Lisa, and Dutch. They're all cuffed.

"Why are you taking them?" I ask, wanting to run forward and knock Cory out of that procession so we both can make a break for it. "What did they do? What did we do?"

"You don't want to talk about this here," says the officer with Marvin. We're all walking now, the five of us, and five officers, toward the doors the girls are walking through with their officers.

"I want to call my mom," Marvin says, and he sounds as sick as I feel.

"I want to call my parents, too," I say, trying not to stumble as I move—and am moved—forward.

"Yeah—" Raulston starts, but my officer cuts him off.

"We've already called them. All of your parents are meeting us at the station."

"At the station?" Tom sounds half-crazy. "This isn't a stupid TV show! What are you talking about?"

"I didn't put anything in the cookies," Marvin says. "They were just cookies. I swear."

He starts to cry, and I want to, and I'm not sure why I don't, except I'm afraid Cory will see me and she might need me not to be crying.

"It's okay," I tell Marvin, but I don't know why I'm

saying that, and I don't think I believe it. I'm dizzy and I'm scared I'm going to faint.

What did I do?

How did I do anything while I was asleep?

I've never been in this kind of trouble ever. Never planned on being in this kind of trouble.

"It's okay, Marvin," I say again, like an idiot. "Don't cry. We're going to be okay."

My Life, the "Supermassive Black Hole"

(That song is by Muse. They *have* to be talking about my life. And there is no life outside the earbuds, Marvin.)

A lot of parrot experts advise clipping wings regularly for the safety of the parrot. This involves stretching out the bird's wings and snipping off the ends of some of their flight feathers. Fred, being an African Grey, hates being handled by anyone other than her preferred person, who is me. But, most avian vets—when you can find one—don't recommend that the preferred person hang around when beaks are ground, toenails are trimmed, or wings are clipped. Parrots, especially Fred's kind of parrot, can get ticked and hold grudges for a long time, sometimes forever.

All of this is to say, when I took Fred in to the vet clinic at the local PetSuperhaven on avian day to have her wings clipped a few weeks after I finally surrendered and she officially claimed me as her own (that's how it works with parrots, just so you know—never the other way around), things did not go well. From the waiting area, I heard lots of smoke-alarm noises, the vet swearing several times, and some terrifying phrases, like these:

"Towel over her head now!"

And . . .

"Catch her! Catch her!"

And . . .

"Did that go to the bone?"

By the time Fred came back out, I was freaking. Fred was freaking. The avian vet with the bloody fingers, bitten ears, and scratched face, he was freaking, too, but he tried to pretend he wasn't. He had me hold Fred and comfort her until her heart rate came back to normal and her body temperature lowered out of volcano-drop-dead range. Then he explained to me that when parrots or any bird gets way upset, they really can drop dead.

This did not make me happy.

The fact that Fred's wing feathers looked like somebody had chopped them with a meat cleaver didn't make me happy, either.

The worst part was, when I got her home, she tried to zip from my shoulder to her cage, flapped her clipped wings, and splatted on the floor like a fat, squirming little gray bug with red tail feathers. The way she looked at me, all full of pain and confusion because she couldn't do something so natural to her—it was awful. I got down on my hands and knees and looked her in her bird face and told her how sorry I was, that it might be right for most parrots but I understood it wasn't right for her after all she'd been through, and that I'd never ever do that to her again. I knew what it felt like to be surprised in a nasty way, snatched up and pinioned and restrained, then trapped even though you should be able to fly.

I couldn't believe I'd made such a stupid, stupid decision. I couldn't believe I let somebody hurt her like that.

She pulled out some of the mutilated feathers, but I got her to quit that by soothing her and distracting her, then giving her lots of birdie baths to keep her skin and feathers conditioned. Because Fred had a tough life before she came to me, her belly's bald from feather picking, and those feathers won't grow back. I've always figured if no other part of her ends up naked, I'm making progress.

After the wing-clipping disaster, I read lots of books on parrots. *My Parrot, My Friend: An Owner's Guide to Parrot Behavior* by Bonnie Munro Doane and Thomas Qualkinbush and *African Grey Parrots: Everything about History, Care, Nutrition, Handling, and Behavior (Complete Pet Owner's Manual)* by Maggie Wright were two of the best ones. I've also read *First Aid for Birds: An Owner's Guide to a Happy Healthy Pet* by Julie Rach Mancini and Gary A. Gallerstein. I do Fred's beak and nails myself now, and I've never gotten her wings butchered a second time. She can fly all around the house, but I never let her do it unsupervised, and I'm way neurotic about making sure she's in her travel cage before I take her outside.

Harper doesn't mind when she flies around his little house, so she's out with me right now while we eat peanut butter sandwiches. I've brought him a stack of books I checked out from the library, and I hold up *Caring for the Dead: Your Final Act of Love* by Lisa Carlson. "I always thought you had to take dead people to a funeral home, but this one talks about all the laws about bodies and burials. Marvin's right. Funeral homes aren't necessary, and you could go way greener and less expensive if you do it yourself."

Harper glances at the book I'm holding up, then at the top book on the pile in front of me, which was something about how to "prepare" loved ones for private funerals—meaning, cleaning the deceased and getting them ready for whatever ceremony you're holding. "Families handling their own dead is a lost tradition," he says. "I took care of my father, and he took care of his. It wasn't so bad."

"Most people would vomit or run away screaming," I tell him as Fred flaps past my head and lands on the counter, close to what's left of Harper's sandwich. She won't usually eat after anybody but me, but she has a thing about grape jelly, and so does Harper.

"Taking care of Pop got me past the loss." Harper gives his plate a nudge so the bread crust and blob of grape jelly moves closer to Fred. "But people are a lot lazier now.

Everybody wants stuff neat and clean. Can I keep these books a few days?"

Fred digs into his jelly, getting purple smears all over her black beak. Later, she'll climb up on me and wipe her beak all over my shirt, but that's okay. By the time I go home, the purple will get lost in all the grave dirt.

"Sure." I push the pile of books to Harper. I remember being surprised when I realized how many books Harper reads. His whole bedroom is nothing but bookshelves full of classics and crime novels and Louis L'Amour westerns. He's got old comics mixed in that mess, and a bunch of old *Life* magazines he told me he keeps for their pictures. When I asked him about why he read so much, his answer was simple enough.

Graveyards get boring.

Yeah.

Which is why I spend more and more time obsessing about Fairy Girl and hoping she'll pass by so I can catch a glimpse.

Harper lets Fred finish her tiny bird-sized jelly sandwich, then picks up our plates. I watch him, how matter-of-fact and simple he does stuff, and I think about the day last year when I walked down the road and asked him for a job.

He was digging a grave in the Oak Section when I found him, and he pulled himself up to stare at me, holding on to his badly lettered HELP WANTED sign—just an old board covered with spray paint.

"You live a mile or so west," he'd said, and I'd nodded.

He took the sign away from me and asked, "You one of those kids who got in trouble a few years back? One of the Duke's Ridge Eight?"

Didn't seem to be any point in telling less than the truth, so I'd answered, "Yes."

"Thought so. Worst of the bunch, right? I figured you'd be in jail."

"I was. I'm on probation now." I remember wishing I could hold the sign again, just to have something to do with my hands, but the rest went fast enough.

"Going to school?" he had asked.

"Yes, sir."

"Drink or drug?"

"No, sir."

"Bother you if I like beer?"

"No, sir."

"You're hired. But if you call me *sir* again, you're fired. Go to the shed by my house and get a shovel."

And that was it.

Harper never asked me for the story, or any of the details, which is kind of strange, because of all the people in the world, I don't think it would be hard to tell him. He'd hear me out even through the not-so-good parts, but he's never seemed that interested. All he cares about is how fast I dig, how straight I mow, and whether or not I make the flowers look good when I arrange them on the graves after filling in the dirt from a burial.

"Daylight's wasting," he says, plopping Fred's travel cage onto the counter.

Time to go to work.

I collect my parrot and put her safely in her cage, and the two of us head out to the spot beside Oak Section, just inside Cedar Section, where we need to start digging. We both glance at the front gate, then glance away fast, because we see my parents where they've decided to position themselves to guard me tonight.

They have their cars pulled at angles across the entrance, and they're waiting.

"Fred," Fred says, as if acknowledging I've called out the big guns.

Well?

I couldn't think of anything else to do. Marvin and Branson wouldn't have near the same effect as Mom and Dad and their best grim expressions.

"Let's get the hell out of here," Harper mutters, picking up his pace. "This is gonna be ugly and I don't want to listen."

I don't really want to, either, but graveyards are quiet, even with shovels and parrots around. I brought my oldest iPod, the one Marvin gave me when I was allowed private belongings in Juvenile, so after I get Fred settled on the ground beside the grave-to-be, I pull out the machine, stick it in my pocket, and fit the buds in my ears. Then I crank the playlist I've picked, which is marked "Dig."

Songs to dig graves by.

Thank the universe iTunes isn't something Branson's filters block from our computer—and I bet you don't have a playlist for digging graves, do you? "The Boogie Monster" (Gnarls Barkley), "Hey Mama" (Black Eyed Peas), "Cabaret" (Me First and the Gimme Gimmes' version—nothing better than headbanging showtunes to wake me up), "She Hates Me" (Puddle of Mudd)—it's hours long, but that gives you a taste of mine.

I listen to music and dig, and Harper drinks and digs. Either way, we barely bother the silence of the dead, which seems like the way it should be. When I glance up to Fred's cage to check on her, she's plowing through her parrot pellets and the sprinkling of Cheerios (her favorite treat) I added, stopping only to flutter around in her water dish and sprinkle us with droplets from her wings.

We're about three feet down and "Supermassive Black Hole" (Muse) is what's playing when Harper touches my elbow, gestures toward the front gates, then sits down and lowers his head so he's concealed from easy view behind the dirt we've piled on the grave lip.

Sweat drips down my face, plopping onto my dirty shirt, and for a few moments, I just stand still, listening to the hard spank of the song, not sure I want to pull out my earbuds and hear what's going down outside the grave.

In the end, I sort of have to, even if I'm not sure why.

Fred sees me pop out the buds, silencing Muse's first long "Oooh," and she whistles.

I hold my finger to my lips as I sit beside Harper, and for some reason, Fred turns toward the gates. Her feathers poof out, and she shrills a smoke-alarm sound, then goes ruffledy quiet, glaring into the afternoon sunlight as the voices of Cherie and my parents drift across the silent mounds and headstones.

"I understand you want to see him, but it's just not a good idea." That's Mom, in her kindest, most earnest surrender-the-animal-so-it-can-get-the-care-it-needs voice. People rarely fail to give my mother what she wants when she uses that tone.

"We're—we're just friends," Cherie says with a lot less attitude than I expected. "Doesn't Del need as many friends as he can get?"

"You seem like a wonderful girl, Cherie, but you're younger than he is," Dad says. "You can understand why that makes Del nervous, and us."

Dad's not nearly as convincing as Mom, rooster-whispering skills aside.

"Your parents and brother absolutely do not approve of you coming here to see Del like this," Mom adds. "It could cause a lot of trouble for him. Is that what you want?"

"How do you—did you *call* my parents?" Cherie's tone gets a lot sharper and less respectful. "Did you talk to my *brother?*"

I can imagine her black-lined eyes getting wide and furious. If she's wearing fake fangs tonight, they're probably showing.

My parents don't answer her question, which of course answers her question, and I hear Cherie do some major starts, stops, and muttering it's probably better nobody can understand.

"We're asking you to leave our son alone, and to leave," Dad says, flat and certain. "It's better for everybody if you don't come back here looking for him."

The sound of a car's engine grinds up the main road, distant at first, but coming on fast.

"I can't believe you did this," Cherie calls out, too loud to be talking to my parents.

I keep my head down inside the grave and feel guilty, even though I can't quite figure out why. I can't be friends with Cherie because she wants more. I've told her that.

Guilt.

But, why?

It shouldn't be this hard. Why is it this hard?

"Harper doesn't want to call the authorities, but if you keep trespassing, he won't have any choice," Mom says, though it's getting harder to hear her over the car's engine. "This is a private cemetery, not public land, so he can do that. Take it from us, you don't want to get mixed up in the legal system."

I'm breathing hard and feeling awful, but then I think about Marvin at his cookie stand, probably eating a cookie, maybe talking to fiery-lettered Lee Ann. He'll be glad I did this. He'll feel better.

Will I?

I rub my fingers across my eyes, getting dirt in the corners. I have to blink hard to clear them out.

Shit. Am I actually going to miss Cherie?

"Glaciers melting in the dead of night," my brain says, *"and the superstars sucked into the supermassive . . . supermassive black hole . . ."*

God, my life is pathetic.

I bang my head on the dirt wall behind me. The sound startles Fred, and she flutters as the approaching car stops outside the cemetery.

The engine shuts off.

A few seconds later, I hear pinhead tell his sister, "Your phone's off and Mom wants you back home. Now. Dad's coming home early from work."

Cherie says nothing, and I'm just made of paper, sitting in my supermassive black hole, doing nothing and wondering, really, actually, what did I just do? The right thing? The wrong thing? Is the universe about to pop open and drag me to some kangaroo court where Kaison makes a brand-new list of all my crimes?

Laughing at a kid who was just trying to be nice to you, no matter what her reasons were.

Getting that same kid in serious shit with her brother and her parents.

Hurting her feelings.

Making her know that deep down, maybe the world really does suck, after all.

There's probably no law against those things (though, seriously, you never know), and no set penalties or rules or lists of offenders. If there was a list, I'd climb out of the grave, go over to it, and write down my name in dirt and blood with no argument whatsoever.

Car doors slam, first one, then another.

Somebody peels out bad. Probably Cherie. She burns enough rubber that I see the cloud of dust drift over the open grave like a spirit trying to find its way to its resting place. My mother makes some comment involving the word "reckless," then the other car cranks and moves out—no rubber burning, but at a good speed.

I wait until I can't hear the engines anymore, then make myself stand and give my parents a wave.

"Thanks," I call out to them.

Fred yells, "Hey!" because I yelled. Then she makes a bomb-dropping noise and settles down again.

My parents, dressed for their volunteer hours cleaning cages at the Humane Society tonight, wave back. Dad gives me a thumbs-up before he gets in the car, clearly happy with himself for doing his dadly duty. Mom looks happy with herself, too, and Harper's already digging again, and whistling, which means he's way past thrilled.

I still feel like shit.

Fred seems to sense this. As I'm picking my shovel up, she counts to four carefully, making sure to get the *three* in there, nice and loud.

I answer with, "Five, six, seven, eight, nine, ten," and she hisses like she's exasperated with the tedious demands I place on such a poor, helpless little parrot.

I don't put my earbuds back in, because I'm really not in the mood for music (alert the media, alert the media), and that's why, about half an hour and almost a foot deeper, I hear the voice when it says, "Your name is Fred, right?"

Harper and I both startle.

Fred never lets anybody sneak up on us, and she rarely talks to strangers up close, but instantly, she says "Fred" brightly, like she's answering Fairy Girl.

When I look up into the sunlight, she seems like a dream, standing beside the cage in a flowing blue shirt and skirt, gauzy and wispy just like any good fairy would wear. She's gazing at Fred and smiling. Then she looks down at me, and I wish the sun's glare didn't keep me from seeing the color of her eyes and the shape of her lips, now that she's finally this close to me.

"Sorry. Didn't mean to scare you. I just wanted to meet your bird up close. I've seen her here with you lots of times, but I never knew she could talk. That's . . . she's . . . well. I think she's fascinating."

"Fred," Fred says again, sounding more than proud. Apparently, she doesn't consider Fairy Girl a stranger at all.

Fairy Girl laughs. "She sounds just like a normal person. I had no idea parrots talked so much like people."

"African Greys do." The shovel feels like alien lead in my hand. Was there something I was supposed to do with it? "Some of the other kinds of parrots sound really clear, but not all of them."

"How many words does she know?"

Her voice. I think I could listen to her talk for hours.

I plant the shovel in the ground and rock forward, using the wooden handle to keep myself upright and get a clearer look at Fairy Girl's face. "No idea. I think a rough estimate would be tons. She learns more whenever she wants to."

"Can you teach her words on purpose?"

"Yeah, but I'm not that patient or consistent. I kind of let her learn what she wants."

"You can go on and get out," Harper says, sounding half-irked, and I almost piss myself because I totally forgot he was there, or that he or anyone else in the world even existed. "I can finish this last bit. You cover the dirt after you finish talking to your . . . to the . . . to, uh, her."

"Livia," Fairy Girl says as I'm pulling myself out of the grave, and just like that, I finally have her name. "Livia Mason."

"Livia," I repeat before I can stop myself. I'm facing her now, right in front of her, and she has dark, dark brown eyes, almost black, the same shade as her hair. She really is beautiful, not in some fake movie-star way, but natural and smooth and soft looking. I can't find the right words. I don't want to think about Dr. Mote and all her emotion cards, or the descriptive cards, or any other cards to do with therapy or the weird, dark parts of my life. Not standing here in the sun with a Fairy Girl with a fairy name and such a pretty fairy smile, who wants to talk about my parrot.

A big shovelful of dirt plops beside me, and a rock bites into my ankle. I manage not to swear or hop around, or better yet, fall into the grave and look like a complete dipshit. I suppose I'm lucky. Harper could have hit me in the head with that load if he'd wanted to. I edge off the stretched tarp to reduce his temptation, way too aware of how filthy I am.

"Livia," I stammer for a second time, failing at the whole meet-gorgeous-girl-don't-be-an-idiot thing. "Is that—um, short for Olivia?"

"No. Just Livia." She smiles again, even prettier this time. "I think my parents got it off an old television show. They like names with three syllables, ending with an *a*. My sister's name is—was—Claudia." Her hand gives a little twitch in the direction of the Oak Section, and her smile fades away.

I remember why she usually comes here, and for the second time in one afternoon, I get to feel like shit. "Oh— yeah. That's—?"

Brilliant. I'm just the master of sharp verbiage. My AP English teacher would be stunned at my repartee.

Livia nods. "Claudia's been dead for almost four months—and she wasn't really there for almost a year before that—but I can't get used to her being gone. Really gone."

I want to ask Livia more about her sister, what happened to her, why she wasn't really there for a year, and how Livia felt when her sister died. I want to ask her all of that, and a whole bunch more, too, but I know better. I'd never ask another person to tell their story if they didn't want to, given how I feel about my own.

Instead, I go with, "Do you live nearby?"

She shakes her head. "In town. I drive most of the way, but I park about a mile from here and walk the last bit. It helps me relax so I don't start bawling the minute I get here." She pauses for a moment, then says, "We used to live in Allenby, but we moved to Duke's Ridge a few months ago because my dad took a job at the refrigerator factory. I was glad. It's closer to Claudia, and farther away from the bad memories, too."

Her gaze shifts to Fred. "Duke's Ridge seems a lot more interesting than Allenby."

"It's bigger," I offer, demonstrating yet more of my incomparable brilliance. "I haven't seen you at G. W., though."

Because I so would have noticed you, and probably hurt myself trying to talk to you, along with most of the rest of the male student population.

"I'm homeschooled." She frowns when she says this. It's fast. If I'd blinked, I wouldn't have seen it, but since I did, I know she's not happy about not going to regular school. "Since I turned sixteen—over a year now."

She's seventeen. My age. That's good. Should I ask for ID to be sure?

"Do you work here every day?"

It takes me a few beats to process that she's asked me a question. "Yes. Well, no. Mostly, I work when people die and need graves—except for the weekends. On Saturdays, even if we don't have funerals or graves to dig, I do stuff like mowing and cleaning up, and whatever else Harper needs."

"I don't remember seeing you around when we had Claudia's funeral."

I don't remember being there, so I probably wasn't. "I might have been off, on vacation with my folks or something."

"Fred would have made me feel better, I think." Livia gives Fred a very sweet look, and Fred returns it, her yellow eyes bright with enjoyment.

A few seconds later, Livia tears her gaze from Fred to glance around Rock Hill. "This must be an interesting job."

Interesting?

Most people—even my shrink—come off with creepy, disgusting, scary, morbid, but *interesting*?

Interesting's not bad.

Fred burps, then makes a truly obnoxious Marvin-level fart noise, and I think about burying my head in the mound of grave dirt, but Livia just laughs.

"I can tell she belongs to a guy."

I smile, and for once it's not because I'd rather be snarling. "I belong to her. At least I think that would be Fred's take on it."

"Fred," Fred announces, in a tone that suggests *definitely yes*.

"Well, I better speak to Claudia, then get back to my car." Livia glances at her watch. "My dad might burst an artery if I'm late."

"Yeah. Okay." I rest my hand on Fred's cage. "You can come talk to Fred anytime. She seems to like you, but don't try to pet her. She bites. All parrots do."

"Okay." Livia's smile is so perfect I'm hoping it's for me in addition to the parrot, but that's probably hoping for a lot. "Can I . . . can I have your e-mail address?"

My perfect joy rips straight down the middle. I force my face to stay still, but my insides keep right on sinking.

Here we go with the total loser routine. "I—uh, don't have one. Or a cell phone."

Sorry, but I don't live on your planet.

She looks disappointed for a second, like maybe she thinks I'm lying and just don't want to give out my contact info. Then her smile comes back, just not as bright. "Strict parents?"

I shrug like I'm in the middle of a tough therapy session. "Something like that."

"My parents monitor every e-mail I write and every call I make." Bigger smile now. She's believing me. "I get it."

I wish I could hand her a card with my name and address. Something. Anything to connect me to her. Since I don't have anything like that, I say, "I'm here a lot. So is Fred."

Livia eyes me for a few seconds like she's trying to figure me out.

Yeah. Pathetic moron using a parrot to pick up girls. How sick is that?

"I'm glad," she says. "See you soon."

Whoa.

Did I hear that right? Did she mean that how it sounded?

"One, two, three, four," Fred counts as Livia moves away, matching her steps perfectly and making her laugh.

I really do like that sound.

I watch her until she's at her sister's grave, then I make myself give her privacy and space. When I glance into the new grave, I realize Harper's vamoosed and taken the shovels with him. I didn't even hear him leave. If a tanker truck had exploded and sent a fireball to swallow two-thirds of Rock Hill, I might not have noticed that while I was talking to Livia.

Tarp. Yeah. Cover dirt. That's what I'm supposed to do.

It takes me almost a full minute to remember where Harper keeps the tarps.

"Back in a second," I tell Fred, but I end up wandering around the cemetery for a few minutes so I won't be tempted to go back and stare at Livia.

When I do come back, Livia's not at her sister's grave.

I squint out at the main road, and I see her drifting down the long hill leading back toward town, her skirt and shirt dancing in the light breeze. Her timing's good. It'll be nearly dark when she gets to her car. I need to hit the road, too.

Too bad I'll have to head in the opposite direction.

I manage to control my nonexistent concentration enough to get the dirt covered, secure the tarp, then dust off my hand and pick up Fred's cage.

"Home," I tell her, and turn to head for the gate, only to find Harper standing there looking in the direction Livia went. He must not be too drunk yet if he's moving like a silent graveyard ninja, scaring the crap out of me every few minutes. That's a good thing, I guess.

Harper turns back to me, shaking his head. "You and her, it's natural and all, and she's a looker, for sure. Still, I'd say you were better off following your friend Marvin's rules. All talk, no hands." He points at my face, then lower. "Or any damned thing else."

Fred mumbles a jumbled phrase, like she does when she's trying out new words. It sounds a lot like she's trying to say "Livia."

Which wouldn't be good, especially with Harper holding a shovel and pointing at my man parts.

"Got it," I tell him, even though I'm with Fred in my head, saying Fairy Girl's pretty fairy name over and over, and over again one more time, just because I like the sound of it.

So far, even bastards like Kaison haven't figured out how to arrest people for what they're thinking, right? At least I don't think they have.

Fred makes a bomb-dropping noise as I pass by Harper.

"You keep that boy in line," he says, then heads off toward his house at the back of the graveyard, leaving me to walk home, ignoring Fred as she tries over and over to say Livia's name.

When God Shuffles His Feet, Does He Trip over Angels?

("All The Time in the World"—the subdudes)

Livia drops her bag and crouches beside Fred's cage as I rip out my earbuds and fumble to punch off my iPod. My shovel topples over, flipping dirt across my shoes, but Livia can't see that since I'm thigh-deep in a grave.

She smiles at Fred, then gives me a nervous smile, too. "Am I bothering you?"

"No. No way." The words come out fast-forward, almost squeaky. It's the first of October, and Marvin's at work, and Harper's conked out in his shack, and a cool breeze tickles across the sweat on my forehead. I can't believe I just squeaked at Livia.

She sits back on the tarp beside the grave while Fred offers her a series of impressive whistles.

Livia whistles back at her, making Fred do a happy dance on her perch. When she glances back to me, she doesn't look nervous anymore. More like, determined and interested, and . . . strong, somehow. Maybe she is nervous, but she's refusing to let herself stay that way.

She looks at the tip of my shovel, where it fell on the edge of the squared hole. "Do you like digging graves?"

Now I get to be nervous, first because she's talking to me, and second because I've never really thought of the job as a like-or-not-like situation. "Yes and no. It's like a workout, so it keeps me relaxed—but it gets boring."

"Is that why you always have your headphones?"

"Yes." Oh man. She's been watching me, too. I hope I never scratched my butt or anything.

Her smile's coming back, more natural and twice as pretty. "Audiobooks or music?"

"Music. I'm kind of obsessed." I lean forward on the packed dirt, and when Fred chatters, I slip my finger through her cage bars so she can nibble on my knuckle.

"I used to be obsessed with playing violin," Livia says, her smile slipping away again, "but since Claudia died—I don't know. I just don't want to pick it up." She gestures to the bag beside her on the ground. "I've been writing some in a journal my mom bought for me, and reading some, mostly Claudia's old romance novels. I try to draw sometimes, but everything feels flat."

I don't say anything, but I'm trying to figure out how to

tell her I understand when her cheeks go a little red and she says, "Thanks."

Okay, good, I did something right.

What, for chrissake?

"Thanks for . . ."

Now the sadness I saw that first day she came to Rock Hill washes across Livia's face. "For not telling me everything will get better with time."

"I'm—" *I'm like you. I know better.* "I wouldn't do that."

"I kind of thought you wouldn't be that way." She eyes me, like she's had instincts about how I am as a person, like she's been evaluating me from a distance, just like I've been evaluating her. "Working here, maybe that gives you a better perspective?"

No idea what to say, so I nod. And I wait.

And Livia scuffs one tennis shoe through some dirt and says, "I still like movies, some of them. Not sappy ones." She laughs, and I think she's laughing at herself. "I'll take aliens, spies, anything with lots of action and no sobbing and Kleenexes and stuff."

I keep leaning on the edge of the grave, a few yards away from her, as Fred chatters and sings, filling the silence. I know I should think of something important to say, but talking's hard. I didn't know God made such perfect girls.

Once upon a time I thought Cory was perfect . . . no. Cut it out. Don't think about that.

Livia seems content to keep going, like it's me instead of

Fred holding up the other side of the conversation. "I like cooking, too. A little bit. Sometimes it's hard to eat, but if I fix the food myself, I know I'll like it."

Cooking. Food. This I know. A little bit. "I make a mean peanut butter sandwich, and I'm not too bad with Reubens, either—but they're harder."

Was that lame?

She's not acting like it's lame. She's smiling again, and looking relaxed, maybe even a little less sad, and I didn't even kill any dragons. I just talked about stinky sandwiches with sauerkraut on them. Life can be so strange.

"Fred," Fred announces as if she agrees, with an added, "Hello, bird. Whatcha doing, bird?" My voice, but in a slightly higher pitch, as if she's trying to get in hints of Livia's voice, too.

Livia gives Fred a warm grin. "You're really cute."

Fred basks, her eyes wide and the centers tinier than ever, meaning she's really, really interested and paying attention.

"Well, I should go and let you work." Livia stands as she says this, brushing dirt off her jeans.

Don't. Wait. I really can talk about something more interesting than sandwiches. I can say something better, something funnier than "okay."

Will you come back tomorrow?

But I stand there like I don't have a tongue and she gives me a wave and walks away, and I let myself stare at her until she gets to Oak Section. Then I crank up the music and go back to digging, but I can't stop thinking about her.

Funny isn't the right word for how I feel when she's nearby.

It isn't wrong or right, or excited or nervous, or good or bad—it's sort of all of that, all wadded up together.

I don't need to do this. I don't need to get wrapped up in some girl. It's nothing but stupid and dangerous.

But how do I not feel what I'm feeling? Music's not working. Digging's not working.

"Del?"

The word slides into my brain under all the loud music, and I startle so hard I almost pull a Marvin and bash my mouth with the shovel.

Livia's back, still grinning, cheeks red again.

My palms go sweaty in two seconds, and I do the whole bud-ripping, shutting down the iPod thing again, doing my best to focus on her and nothing but her. If I can't say anything intelligent, I can at least look interested.

"Why don't I bring us dinner tomorrow night?" Livia asks.

My mouth comes open. I could lift Harper's lawn tractor with my pinky before I could squeeze out a single syllable.

She looks even more embarrassed, but then that other look shifts across her face, the one that tells me she's really strong inside, and not willing to let her emotions and worries boss her around. "Come on, my cooking's not that bad."

Oh God. I can't say yes to this. I can't let her cook for me and get all nice with me when she doesn't know. Not okay. Not allowed.

My mouth moves. My voice works. And what I say is, "That sounds great."

Who am I?

Why am I here?

What's the point?

The next day at school, I'm a basket case, and I can't stop going over those questions. You'd think by now, I'd have some solid answers. Every time I think I've got a little piece nailed down, though, something changes.

I'm having dinner in a graveyard with Livia. And after I got home from the little high of actually making—well, accepting—my first sort-of date in three years, I found mail stacked on the table for me. The mail was nothing but generic rejection cards from over half of the community colleges Branson wanted me to try. The other colleges either haven't responded or they're not planning to bother telling me to cram my wannabe applications sideways and rotate in the most painful ways. It's entirely possible that the answer to *Why am I here*? is simply . . . *Nobody cares, so why do you?*

The sort-of date thing and the college crap distract me

worse than ever, so once again, I don't notice minor disasters in the making. The halls of G. W. are almost deserted before fifth period when Cherie stalks me down outside the bathroom closest to class. Marvin sees her coming, but he can't help me. The best he can do is slide past her and stand at the corner scoping for Jonas, who should be headed out to the football field for his extra gym credits practice, but you never know.

I shrug my backpack onto my shoulders so my hands are free to block blows, and I'm ticked because my heart's actually beating faster than it should be.

Cherie marches straight up to me, her black jeans and sweater tight against her curves and her black hair pulled back in a teacher's bun. I catch a whiff of some light perfume, and I notice that her lipstick seems almost ruby. Nice shade on her. She looks sophisticated, if you don't count the *screw-off-and-die* gleam in her eyes.

"You're an asshole, Del," she announces loud enough for most of the people in Duke's Ridge to hear.

"Yeah. No problem. I am." If that's what she thinks and what she needs to think, I'm all for it. I keep my hands relaxed just like I did the most recent time her brother threatened to kick my ass. What was that, last week? "Total asshole, actually."

"Your parents? Shit. That's just—wrong on so many levels." She folds her arms and glares like she's waiting for an explanation.

Sunlight oozes off the yellow-painted walls and the blue-green tile floor, making Cherie way brighter than she should be. I figure if I try to go all high-handed and step around her, she'll slug me, and then I'll have Jonas and teachers and probably the police to deal with, so I agree with her again. "It was wrong. I feel bad about that part, but you won't listen to me. I figured you might hear them."

Her eyes get so narrow I wonder how she can see anything. The faded blue lockers on either side of us seem too close, and I have to fight an urge to try to knock them with my elbows to make more room.

"Is this where you do the I'm-no-good-for-you thing?" Cherie's really red lips pull back like she's about to show me fangs. "Stop trying to protect me. I don't need protecting from you, Del."

Ouch. I *am* an asshole, because I'm not trying to protect her at all. I'm covering my own ass by trying to peel her off me. "I'm not deciding what's good for you. I'm standing up for what's good for me, Cherie."

Marvin's whistling nervously. Kind of quiet. I recognize the tune as the theme song to a really old western—*The Good, The Bad, and the Ugly*. It got played right before people got shot or hung or cut to pieces. I think I'll hit him the next chance I get.

Cherie's eyes stay narrow and her arms pull even tighter against her chest. "How do you know I'm not exactly what you need?"

Ouch again.

God, I don't want to do this, but I need to. I really have to. "You're not what I need."

The words make *my* guts ache.

Cherie's eyes go wide and get sad, and her lower lip trembles, not like a pout, but like she's really sad and hurt.

Asshole. TOTAL asshole.

"Why not?" she asks, and her voice is so quiet it doesn't even sound like her.

Oh, jeez.

"I—I don't know. I just don't have those feelings for you." I lift both my hands, palm up, like I'm begging for her to understand, and maybe I am. I hate hurting her, but I can't pretend I'm interested in her just to keep her from crying, can I?

"I'm just trying to be your friend," she whispers, and that's a lie, but I'm not totally sure she knows that.

"You're trying to be a lot more than that, and it can't happen. Find some friends who appreciate you, who like the same things you do. I'm not who you need."

She looks away from me, and now she's pouting on top of being truly sad. My total-asshole meter drops to mid-range, and my muscles relax a little bit.

"Are you going to testify at those hearings about the juvenile sex offender laws?" she asks me without any hint that she's turning left with the conversation, and I actually startle at the question.

"What?" God, does she eavesdrop on everything about my life?

"The hearings this spring," she says like I'm going more and more stupid the longer she stands in front of me. "The legislative hearings on the law changes—your name's on the schedule. Look it up online. It's public record."

Love to, but all my time online is supervised, and I don't want to get my parents' hopes up by checking out my name on that schedule.

Out loud, I can't say anything, so Cherie keeps talking. "I was going to go, you know. To be there in the audience on your side—and bring some people. Show of support."

Back to full asshole now, I think. Maybe asshole times two or three. Is there such a thing as asshole squared?

"Duke's Ridge is wack. It's like—detached from reality or something. Nobody cares. Nobody really tries." Cherie finally looks at me again, and she's not sad anymore, at least not that I can see. She unfolds her arms and takes a step back like she's about to leave. "You're a pussy if you don't testify—and that'll make you just like everybody else in this waste of a town. But that's just my opinion, which isn't worth anything to you."

Pussy?

Did she just call me a pussy?

"Don't sic your parents on me again," she says, then spins around and stalks away, slamming her shoulder into Marvin as she heads around the corner.

"Don't make me have to," I call after her as Marvin

catches himself on the wall and manages not to fall all over the hallway.

He straightens himself up, glances in the direction Cherie just went, and mutters, "We've got a shot at making it to class before we get detention."

"Sounds good to me."

"She didn't punch you out."

"No. Not yet."

We walk, side by side, and there's maybe three other people in the hallway, and it feels like there's hardly anybody else in the world.

"She called me a pussy," I admit, still kind of impressed by that, and grossed out, too.

For a few seconds, Marvin doesn't say anything, but the corners of his mouth twitch a lot. He finally comes out with, "Well. Are you?"

"I don't think so."

He shrugs.

I was sort of hoping he'd reassure me about the pussy thing, but . . .

Oh, well.

If God Trips Over Angels, Does It Piss Them Off?

("Angel's Doorway"—Suzanne Vega)

Parrots change the way you say "Hello."

Once you hear a parrot say "Hello!" in that tight, perfect little bird voice, you'll say it that way forever.

Parrots also change the way you dance. I should probably never dance in public again. My head would bob, and my feet would jerk up and down like somebody crammed a twelve-hundred-volt plug in the bottom of my spine. If you don't believe me, go to YouTube and look up videos of Snowball, the dancing cockatoo. Fred's not a cockatoo, so she doesn't dance exactly the same way Snowball does, but you'll definitely be able to imagine it.

What you probably won't be able to imagine is Marvin in a cemetery in his red jeans, his red cookie-shaped apron, with his red hat with the big rubber chocolate-chip cookie on top, bouncing up and down next to the grave I'm digging, flapping his arms like a stoned chicken, and trying to teach Fred to say, "I'm a jerk."

It's enough to keep my mind off Livia, at least a few seconds at a time, even though I'm not playing my music.

"I'm a jerk," Marvin crows.

Fred stares at him.

"Jerk. Come on, bird. Jerk. Just say it once."

I won't let Marvin teach Fred swear words, just in case she ever has to live anywhere but with me (parrots who drop endless F-bombs get in lots of trouble in terms of keeping good adoption situations), so Marvin goes for the tamer stuff. "I'm a jerk," he shouts again, dancing his rubber-cookie-head dance while fluffy-feathered Fred keeps right on staring at him like he's a few chocolate chips shy of a full recipe. Gertrude's sitting beside Fred's cage, drooling and looking fat, and also staring at Marvin, but I think she might be waiting for the rubber cookie hat to fall off so she can bite it to see if it's edible.

We're in the very back section of the cemetery, close to Harper's house, about five slots from the main road. Two big pines shade us from the late-day sun, but I've got Fred's cage on the ground next to my dirt pile because the branches seem too far away. I smile at her every time I pop my head up to make sure I'm not dumping rocks and mud on Marvin's feet.

"Is Harper already drunk?" he asks, taking a breather from trying to brainwash my parrot into calling herself names. Whenever he moves, I catch a hint of cookie smell, kind of stale, but still enough to make my stomach growl.

"Probably. I haven't seen him this afternoon."

Hope I don't, because I've got a sort-of date. The thought makes my insides clench and I plop another shovelful near Marvin's shoes.

Should I tell him about the date?

Probably.

He might think it's great. Or he might have a big-deal freak-out, and I just can't go there, because I'm so nervous about eating dinner with Livia that I'd freak, too.

Marvin rubs his hands together because it's a little cool, and Marvin's hands stay cold, anyway. "Harper's gonna end bad, Del. You should say something to him."

I stop digging, thinking about it, but a few seconds later, I shake my head. "I don't feel like it's any of my business. He doesn't give me any crap about my life."

"You're not pickling your organs."

"No, just letting my brain and my big glorious future stagnate, according to Branson and Dr. Mote." I cram my shovel in the dirt hard enough to rattle my own teeth.

Marvin's grin droops at the edges, and his eyes dart toward Fred and Gertrude. We don't talk about this much, the fact he's on track for early acceptance at his dream school,

Notre Dame, where we were both going to go. I know he's noticed I haven't even been bothering with stuff like taking the ACT or doing senior pictures, or even paying for my ring or cap and gown, because I'm not planning to walk in the graduation ceremony, and I'd rather not have jewelry with these dates engraved in gold forever.

"You're right," Marvin says. "Talking to Harper probably wouldn't help, anyway. Why ask for trouble?" He glances down at his watch.

My fingers curl tight around the shovel's handle. "Exactly. That's why it's not happening."

"Good. Well, gotta fly." He sounds relieved, and I don't know if it's about me not talking to Harper about his booze or the fact he's getting to leave.

"Cookies don't fly. Especially cookies with rubber chocolate-chip heads."

Marvin ignores this and tosses me a small can of tuna. "Give Gertrude her special dinner, okay?"

"*Su* kitty *es mi* kitty." I give him a salute with the can. "*Mi* big fat huge drooling kitty."

"*Carapedo*," he calls back as he jogs toward his car, which is parked on Rock Hill's main road.

Carapedo. That's like, what? Oh. Fart face.

I got an A in Spanish and Marvin barely got a B, but he remembers every phrase, name, and swear word we ever heard.

"*Cerote*," I fire back as loud as I can, resting the tuna can on the edge of the grave. That's one of the words for *turd*, and the best I can do on short notice. Marvin wins. Again.

I need to buy a Spanish-English dictionary and look up how to say *Giant Cookie-Headed Bastard-Nose*. Then I'd have a shot at scoring a few points.

"*Cerote*," Fred says brightly, keeping herself fluffed against the cool fall air. "Jerk."

Gertrude's not saying anything, but she's staring at the tuna can like her head might start spinning right before she levitates and spits pea soup vomit everywhere and screeches *OPEN NOW!* in Satan's voice.

I risk cat possession and finish the grave I'm working on first, then climb out next to Fred's cage and dust my hands on my jeans. It takes a few seconds to fight the pop-top lid off Gertrude's tuna, and I dump the juice on my dirty shirt trying—stinky crap. The tuna I pile carefully on the tarp in front of Gertrude, but I don't give her the can, because she'd probably cut her tongue on it trying to get every last drop of tuna water. I cram the lid into the can before I stuff the whole mess in my pocket.

"Fred," Fred says in a mocking tone, and I feel sad that in a month or so, it'll be too cold to bring her with me, and she'll probably sulk and pluck feathers off her belly every afternoon I have to work.

Gas and propane heaters emit exhaust fumes that could hurt her, so I can't use them. I've been wondering, though, if I could find a battery-operated plant grow light that would give off enough heat that I would only have to abandon her during the worst part of winter. The part where Harper and I have to use pickaxes to chop up frozen dirt to get the graves started. Nothing needs to be near us when the pickaxes start flying, anyway.

Somebody's walking through the main gate, and I recognize Livia immediately. She waves at me. I wave back.

Guilt washes through me as I let my hand fall to my side.

What the hell am I feeling guilty about?

Cheating on Cory.

Stupid. Cory's been gone for three years. That's over. No contact. Your choice.

Not telling Marvin about my sort-of date.

Marvin doesn't have to know every detail of my life.

Not telling Livia she shouldn't be having dinner with a sex offender.

Now, there's a reason for guilt.

This afternoon she's wearing jeans and a black sweater, and she looks more like a fashion model than a Fairy Girl, and I'm sweaty and covered with dirt, and I smell like Gertrude's tuna juice.

Great.

I knew I had a sort-of date, and I'm filthy and I stink. No doubt Marvin does much, much better with his rubber cookie head. At least cookies smell good.

Livia has her bag plus a second bag, and she comes up to

the dirt pile separating Fred's cage from Gertrude and me and the fast-disappearing tuna pile, and sits down on the drier part of the dirt next to Fred.

"Poor thing. She looks cold." Livia smiles at the bird, then at me, and I like that a lot.

"She probably is cold, a little." I settle myself about an arm's length away, on another dry patch of clods and rocks, and Livia pulls a small blanket out of one bag and spreads it on the ground between us. "Parrots can stand low temperatures for short periods of time, but she doesn't have all her feathers, so I try to be careful."

"*Cerote*," Fred says.

Livia's eyebrows pull together. "What was that?"

"Nothing." I jam my palm into the dirt and glare at Fred. "Sometimes she mumbles."

"Jerk," Fred says, dancing from foot to foot, obviously happy with herself. "One, two, four, jerk!"

"One, two, *three,* four," I say automatically.

"Three!" Fred shrieks. "Three! One, two, *three,* four!"

"She likes you," I tell Livia as she pulls out two bottles of water, two small bags of chips, then what looks like sandwiches wrapped in foil, one package for me and one for her. "She doesn't talk this much in front of anybody besides my parents and Marvin."

"The cookie guy who helps you dig?" Livia puts her hand up to her forehead to shield her eyes from the low-hanging sun.

"Yeah."

Livia's next smile looks a little secretive and mysterious. "Does he ever bring cookies home from work?"

"Sometimes."

"I need to get to know him better." Her smile gets wider, and I try not to be jealous of Marvin, who isn't even here. Butthead. He *would* get a job that girls appreciate at this level. As a gravedigger, I can offer shovels, dirt, and dead things.

"I kept it simple. Gourmet turkey sandwiches." She pulls out small jars of mustard and mayo and some plastic silverware. "Didn't want to scare you to death this first time."

"I'm not scared."

I'm terrified.

The sandwich is warm and it smells like garlic and other spices toasted into the bread. My stomach growls. I add some mustard, then take a big bite.

"Mmm." That comes out unplanned, and it makes Livia smile.

"Sometimes simple is best," she says.

"Fred," Fred agrees.

"How many more graves do you have to dig tonight?" Livia asks as Gertrude finally finishes her tuna, waddles off a few paces, and plops down in the grass to bathe her face and paws.

"Just this one, and it's done. I don't even need to move the dirt tonight, because the funeral's not until this weekend."

Livia's face brightens to almost glowing in what's left of the sunlight. "Do you need a ride home? I could take you when you're finished."

"I just live down the road." The heat hitting my face probably shows underneath all the dirt, never mind the mustard on my chin. I wipe it off with my sleeve, then realize Livia laid out a napkin for me. "It's better if I just walk. Kind of shakes out the kinks from digging. Besides, I'd get a lot of dirt in your car."

She looks disappointed. I hate that, but she wouldn't feel that way if she knew her car would stink like tuna and sour graves and probably mustard, too, when I got out.

Livia goes silent for a few seconds, eating, swallowing, then taking a slow drink of water. She glances around. "Is Harper here?"

"He's—" I point in the direction of his little house, not sure what to say, because if she wants to talk to him, that won't be totally possible. "He's in there, but I think he's sleeping."

Sleeping it off.

I hope.

Because if he comes staggering out, he'll make a scene about this, I bet.

"He drinks a lot, doesn't he?" The shift in Livia's tone is quick and kind of harsh, and Fred picks up on it, too. She makes shooting noises as Livia waves a hand to dismiss her own question before I finish groping around for an answer.

"You don't have to tell me. I've seen him. I know what drunk people look like. My sister was a drunk. That's what killed her."

I don't have a clue what to say, so I open my chips and keep my mouth shut, but Fred says "Fred" in an anxious, quivery voice.

Livia lays her hand on the travel cage, and I almost lunge toward her to pull her fingers out of danger, but Fred doesn't make any move to bite her.

"Claudia died in a car wreck." Livia stares down at Fred like she's talking to the parrot instead of me, but I know that trick too well to fall for it. "The people she hit died, too. That's why we moved—because everyone in town hated us."

My stomach turns a slow, aching flip, on top of my sandwich and chips, and more heat rises from my middle all the way to my cheeks. "I . . . know that feeling."

Livia takes her hand out of harm's way and rubs her eyes with her fingers, as if she's trying to concentrate or maybe meditate. "I can't believe I just told you about that. I'm not supposed to talk about it."

The few feet of blanket separating us seem like too much, but also not enough as I shrug. "It's okay to tell secrets in a cemetery. Dead people don't run their mouths. Neither do cemetery caretakers. That's kind of in our job description."

"Kids. Two of them. And their pregnant mother." Livia

pushes the rest of her sandwich away from her, then picks up a brown dirt clod and crushes it in her hands, letting the dirt sift down between her feet. "My sister killed three people—four, depending on how you believe about unborn babies." She looks intensely disgusted, but also miserable and sort of sick.

"I think I remember hearing something about that on the news." As soon as I see the extra pain in Livia's face, I wish I hadn't said anything, and I wonder immediately what all she's heard on the news about me, and when she'll remember it. I should just tell her, like now, before she confesses anything else to me that she might regret later.

"The family is suing my parents because the car was in my dad's name." Livia says this fast, like she needs it all out of her, and right now. "He says they'll get everything and we'll have to file for bankruptcy. We're not buying anything new because there's no point. It'll all get sold and given to those people."

Jeez. At least nobody sued us. Nobody wanted to—none of the parents even wanted charges filed, but that was up to Kaison the Evil, not them, and he didn't care about the truth.

It could have been worse.

It could have been worse?

First time I ever considered that possibility.

"I'm sorry," I manage, then stumble around getting the

rest out. "You know, what she did, what Claudia did—that's nothing about you."

"I know that here." Livia taps the side of her very pretty head. "Here," her finger slides to her heart, "it's harder. I wasn't in the car, but I knew she was drunk when she drove off, mad at my dad, as usual."

Yeah, she's definitely been needing to let all this out. I can tell by the way her words are boiling up and spilling over, and I can see the tears filling the corners of her big eyes.

"You can't make somebody stop drinking and drugging." I gesture toward Harper's house. "People do what they're going to do." Kaison with his smug face and bad comb-over flickers through my brain. "Trust me on that."

Livia nods and looks down. Destroys another few dirt clods. She's breathing in quick gasps.

We sit quietly for a while after that, then Livia tells me how many times her parents tried to help her sister. How many times she tried to help. When she cries, I want to put an arm around her shoulder, and finally I scoot closer to her and do put my arm around her, even though I stink like tuna fish, mustard, dirt, and all.

She doesn't gag, and she actually slows down on the tears a little, and leans into me. In the afternoon sun, her dark hair looks like sparkly silk, and she smells so much better than Marvin I don't even have words to describe it.

"It doesn't seem real, any of it." Livia's voice is quieter now, and her words are coming out slower. "The people Claudia killed. Claudia being dead." She glances toward her sister's grave. "It's hard to think about her in a box under the ground. She's my sister, you know?"

I don't know. I can't really imagine how much that hurts, but I can tell from her face that it's hollowing out something way down inside her. That sensation, I totally get. Stuff in my life sucks, too, but for the first time, I'm realizing that the bad stuff, the really bad stuff, it happened three years ago. I've had time to get over the worst of it. Livia hasn't had hardly any time.

"When I'm upset and can't calm down, I listen to music." I slide my arm off her shoulders, reach to the pocket without the tuna can, pull out my iPod, queue up one of my mellow playlists, and offer her an earbud. "Like I told you, I'm obsessed. I've got days of stuff on here, most of it memorized. When I sink into the sound, the words, it keeps me from thinking too much."

She takes the bud and puts it in. A second or so later, she says, "'Hey Jude.' Beatles. I like the Beatles. Claudia thought they were lame."

I let her take the other earbud, then the iPod. She sits, totally still except for the finger she's using to scroll through my collection, which is a lot bigger than Marvin's now. She picks out "Shiny Happy People" by R.E.M. and closes her eyes.

"One, two, four," Fred says into the new silence in the cemetery.

I put my finger to my lips.

Fred bobs her head once, fluffs up as much as possible, and lowers her head in a definite parrot sulk. I'm glad Livia's fingers aren't on the cage anymore, because Fred would abandon her unusually generous behavior and chew one off at the knuckle.

When the song's over, Livia takes out the earbuds and gives me back my iPod. "Thanks. That really did help. Your collection is amazing—and you're a good listener."

"I didn't used to be. I think I've learned it working here."

This time when she smiles at me, I feel twice as awful and twice as guilty, like I did when I sicced my parents on Cherie. Trying to figure out some way to say that, I come up with, "Listen, I don't work here because I'm some morbid jerk-off."

Livia laughs. "I know that, and I know you live close. It probably saves a lot of gas, working just down the road from your house."

Yeah. She's letting me off. I want to go with that, to let it pass, but that would make me a giant shit head, and I don't want to treat Livia that way. "Harper pays more than minimum wage and I get a lot of time to myself—but that's not why I picked this place. Some crappy stuff happened in my life a few years ago. I—I got in trouble."

It wasn't my fault. It wasn't fair.

That wants to fly out next, but I hold it back. How many criminals and convicts cue that tired old refrain every three seconds? I'm not going to be that guy.

Livia looks surprised, but not panicked or like she's considering bolting off the pile of grave dirt. "So, what did you do?"

"I . . . I . . . uh. Okay. That's hard to talk about." The mouth's moving, but my brain and the rest of my body go on total lockdown. My muscles get so tight I wonder if muscles can crack, and I can't say any of it out loud. I've never said it out loud, and here, now, I can't, but I can force out, "Look. You probably don't want to be here talking to me."

It's the best I can manage. I'm such a frigging coward.

To be really sure she gets it, I add, "Other people around here—well, the black mark on me might be sort of contagious."

Her eyes go wide. "Uh, like my sister murdering two kids and a pregnant woman? Come on, Del. What did you do?"

My mouth opens, but my mind is blank, and it's all I can do not to start crying like a total, stupid baby. I clamp my lips shut and try to breathe, digging my fingers into the dirt until some of the pile rains back into the grave.

"It's okay." Livia's voice cuts into my panic, but I'm staring into the grave instead of looking at her. "Just tell me when you're ready. I can wait."

I'll never be ready.

Did I say that out loud? I might as well have, with the look she's probably seeing on my face. "If you don't want to know about me, better not look me up online."

I'm famous. I'm infamous.

"I won't." She looks guarded now, but not upset. "My dad would be watching, anyway. Kind of makes everything complicated."

"*Cerote*," Fred mumbles, still sulking like a rejected toddler.

The sound of her bird voice makes me jerk my head up and look at the cage, then at Livia.

Livia shakes her head. "I wasn't sure before, but now I am. Your parrot's swearing in Spanish. She just called me a turd."

"Me," I say, laughing and hating the tin-can sound of it. "She's calling me a turd, not you. Definitely for me."

The rest, I can't say.

You have no idea.

You don't need to come back here.

You don't need to hang around me.

All the things it's so easy to say to Cherie—with Livia, I can't.

"Don't bother trying to warn me about yourself, okay?" Her smile is better than the reds and pinks of the setting sun. "Just get to know me, and let me get to know you, and I'll make up my own mind."

Yes.

And then my brain points out—this isn't so different from Cherie. I'm telling her not to hang around me, and she's telling me she'll make up her own mind. With Cherie, it all feels horrible, but with Livia . . .

Yes.

Out loud, I force myself to tell the truth. "You probably shouldn't talk to me when you come here." I stare at the dirt pile now because I can't look at her. "Not until I can get my sh—uh, stuff together enough to tell you everything, so you don't regret even knowing me."

She doesn't say anything, but she's smiling that little smile, and giving me the I'm-strong-and-I'm-not-backing-down look.

"You shouldn't come talk to me when you visit your sister," I say again. "I mean that."

"We'll see," she says, and she leaves it at that.

I'm Pretty Sure Angels Laugh at Rooster Whisperers

("Almost Lover"—A Fine Frenzy, who probably never whispered to a rooster.)

Who am I?

Before Good-bye Night, that answer was easy. I would have told you *I'm Del Hartwick, the baseball kid.*

Why am I here?

Before Good-bye Night, I would have said, *to play baseball, to love Cory, to go to college and become a doctor and specialize in sports medicine and see what I can discover.*

What's the point?

Before Good-bye Night, I would have said, *only freaks have to ask a question like that.*

I had all these friends and all these ideas and all these plans. I had all these things I could do, all these places I could go, and all these people to go with me. I was somebody—or at least I thought I was.

Now, if I end up dead, only a few people would notice. Livia made dinner for me, and she's come back every night for a week, just to sit and talk for a few minutes before she goes to her sister's grave. She might miss me. My folks would give a care, and Marvin would get upset. Branson and Dr. Mote would feel weird in some professional way, and Harper would notice for a while at least, until he drank me away.

Cherie.

Jeez.

Cherie would make my death a personal tragedy and set up shrines at my grave (or memorial site if I get cremated), but she'd get tired of that in a few months. She'd move on because she'd have to move on, because people like Cherie have to have . . . I don't know. Something they're obsessed with and attached to. A dead guy wouldn't be enough.

All in all, if I died, I think Fred would have the biggest problem.

When parrots grieve, they stop eating and drinking and molt and stand around with their head and their wings drooping. It'd be hard to keep her alive. I've been writing a bunch of stuff in a notebook I labeled THE BOOK OF FRED—everything she likes and hates—and tucked some recordings of my voice in the pockets to help her and who-ever takes care of her in case something bad happens. I hope

Livia would take Fred, but that might be asking too much of anybody not dedicated to birds.

Plus, I don't think anything bad will happen. Right now I'm living on the theory that the really bad stuff in my life has already happened. No matter how many times Dr. Mote asks, I don't ever think about hurting myself or anyone else. Even though the best life I can have now will be crap compared to my original plans and those dreams I still can't let go of, I'm thinking if I just keep doing "the next right thing" (I got that from Branson), my life might not suck completely.

In fact, I've been writing down some plans for my future to show Branson:

1. *Open my own cemetery. The dead don't care about criminal records.*
2. *Win the lottery and buy a fake college degree off the black market.*
3. *Talk Harper into letting me sell caskets at the funeral chapel on the off days.*
4. *Keep asking to apply to schools until somebody gets sick of reading my mail and lets me in, then make it through vet school, too, and just help birds as a volunteer, like dad.*
5. *Go out with Livia, marry her, and let her support me while I open a bird sanctuary for used and second-hand parrots.*

Well?

You got any better ideas?

I really like the vet school option best, and I'm sure there's room for two rooster whisperers in the world. Only, I think I'll be a parrot whisperer and work on birds of prey as a second specialty. Hawks and eagles are amazing, the way they sail high over everything, wings wide, swooping through the sky like kings of the air. They have all the room and solitude in the world, but they aren't lost in space. They own it.

Unlike chickens, who only own what we give them.

Dad has given his current rooster a sixteen-by-twenty fenced and covered lot just behind our back porch, with a divider down the center so he can close off half the pen and regrow grass on one side or the other every few weeks. Clarence the former fighting rooster also has a hay-lined ten-nest chicken condo, with an insulated green tin roof and a cedar ramp up to the front door that reminds me of a pirate gangplank.

"Come on, big fella." Dad's voice is low and supercalm as he edges through the door of the lot. Dad's carrying a bucket of cracked corn, and he wants Clarence to let him in without attacking him. I'm standing on the porch at a safe distance, watching in case Dad needs any help. It's November now and cool this morning, with almost no clouds in the sky. The air feels sharp and fall-winter, and digging graves won't be such a misery.

The rooster glares at dad with his one good eye, all his feathers puffed out. I'm pretty sure poofy chickens are bad, just like poofy parrots. Feathers all ruffled out are a bird's way of saying, *Back off, you big human monster.*

"How do you think it's going?" I ask Dad, keeping my voice as low and calm as Dad did, even though I'd rather advise my father to run like hell.

"I'm starting to win his trust," Dad murmurs, sticking his hand into the cracked corn and scattering some yellow pieces on the grass at his feet.

The rooster flips his head down and rattles his wings.

Dad spreads a little more corn.

The rooster launches himself straight at Dad's face.

Dad drops the bucket, catches Clarence in mid-flog, holds on to him for a few seconds, and waits until the rooster stops squawking and struggling. Clarence can't hurt Dad that much because Clarence doesn't have any spurs. People who fight roosters usually cut off their real spurs and fasten metal claws on their legs for the fight, so the whole show gets more bloody.

Sick, I know. Clarence has got to be scarred inside and out from all that crap.

"It's okay," Dad tells him, scratching underneath the bird's comb as it makes menacing noises deep in its rooster throat. "We'll keep at it. We'll just try again. Sooner or later you'll figure out that all your wars are over."

The rooster makes a bunch more noises, and if we had a

rooster translating machine handy, I think it would read, *Screw off.*

Dad named Clarence after an old angel in an old movie, hoping to give the bird the idea that it's okay to be a cream puff, that he can just take it easy, that he doesn't have to fight every second of every day.

I don't think Clarence has seen that movie.

But my father is the patron saint of all lost animal causes. If he can't get Clarence calmed down enough to go to some farm and do his roosterly duty, Clarence will end up living behind my house in his high-end chicken condo until he dies a natural, quiet, and spoiled death. Not such a bad way to go, really, except I figure he'll miss some of what it means to be a rooster. That's sad, but it's not Clarence's fault.

Maybe Dad will rescue him some hens soon. That might give Clarence a little motivation to straighten up and strut right.

"Do you ever think you and Mom might be addicted to rescuing animals, Dad?"

"Thought it and acknowledged it." Dad puts Clarence down, dumps the rest of the scratch, and gets out before Clarence can fire up again. "It's definitely an addiction."

Like my music. Only Dad acts like being addicted to animal rescuing is a good thing.

And it is. I guess.

"Are you leaving for work soon?" Dad asks.

"In a few." I stretch and lean against the wooden railing on the porch, watching Clarence dig into the corn. "We only have two graves to prepare for funerals tomorrow, so we're in good shape."

Dad puts his empty bucket next to the fence. "Don't forget to give your mother a kiss."

"I never do."

Especially not since all this crap happened, and the three of us stopped having meals together and hanging out as a group. It's like my family's all still together, but sort of going our own separate ways, too. Maybe that's how it's supposed to be when there's just one kid and that kid's almost grown, and he doesn't really have some big shiny set of goals you're supposed to push him to achieve.

When Dad gets to the porch, he puts his arm around my shoulder and squeezes me to him, then lets me go and glances back at Clarence. "Sooo, this new girl Livia. You spending some time with her?"

His tone's light, but the question is completely serious. "She comes by at work, but we still haven't had—you know. The talk."

"And you're sure she's seventeen." A statement, not a question, but the worry in his voice makes me sad.

"As sure as I can be without seeing her driver's license." When I meet Dad's eyes, I see the ton of nervousness wanting to explode out of his brain. "Okay, fine, I'll ask to see her driver's license."

Dad doesn't tell me not to do it. "Bullet and a target," he says, nodding.

Dad always lets me play my iTunes mixes when we're driving, and he's got a big collection of his own. Sometimes, we end up liking the same stuff, and "Bullet and a Target" is the title of a song we both like by Citizen Cope, a singer Dad calls "the best artist nobody knows."

After he heard it the first time, he thought the same thing I did—that it sounded exactly like what happened to us with Kaison, that we got between a bullet and a target, and there was no way we could get away without getting hit.

But what you've done here is put yourself between a bullet and a target . . .

Now it's become a code between us that means *be careful.* Don't put yourself in a dangerous position, because you know the shooting's going to start sooner or later.

"I'm staying out of the line of fire," I tell him.

"I think I'm happy for you, son." Dad's not looking at me. He's staring up toward the blue fall sky. "I hope she keeps coming around once everything's out in the open. You deserve good things, Del. Do you believe that?"

I focus on the maimed, confused one-eyed rooster pecking at the corn Dad dumped in the chicken lot and I nod, but I'm not sure anybody really deserves anything they get. I don't think life and the world work like jobs and a paycheck—do your duties, get the money you've earned. If it worked that way, then I'd have to figure out what crappy thing I did to earn where I am, and I've tried doing that. I really have.

"I guess so." True enough, but a little lame, and part cop-out.

"Mr. Branson got in touch with us about the hearings again, since they're just what, four or five months from now." Dad's trying to sound offhand, but he's not doing a very good job. "Your mother and I are discussing giving testimony, but we wanted to run it past you. How do you feel about that?"

How do I feel?

About ripping all this shit open and seeing my face on the news and in newspapers again? About hearing what people will call me, and getting the hate mail? About being terrified that Kaison or Kaison's ghost or Kaison's "moral successor" in the DA's office will find something else to charge me with if I open my mouth?

I feel just great about it, Dad. How do you feel?

"I'll be okay with whatever," I say, wondering if I sound like I'm lying, then wondering if I am lying. "You and Mom can do what you want."

Bullet and a target. Bullet and a target. Bang!

Dad's not giving up that easily, because he never does, not on anything, even crippled, hateful old roosters who need psychoanalysis not to bite the hand that feeds them—literally. "But what do *you* want, Del?"

The lump in my throat surprises me, and I find something

else to stare at before Dad sees how much I want to cry. I'm way too old to cry now. What good does that do?

After thinking about it and chewing over lots of different words, I tell the truth again, this time not lame or copping out, but 100 percent truth and nothing else. "I don't want any more bad stuff to happen. That's really it, Dad. No more bad stuff."

Dad waits a second or two, then smiles at me. The smile looks sad. "We can't control everything that happens in life." His voice sounds quiet, and it gives me the shivers like my brain's hearing the words as some kind of creepy prophecy. "Sometimes . . . sometimes the bad stuff just shows up knocking and we have to answer the door."

Picnic in the graveyard.

This is our second one, so maybe it's getting to be a theme with Livia and me.

Livia and me.

I think I like that.

Livia and Del.

God help me, I'm going to be Marvin and start etching her name on everything in fat, sparkly hippie letters. Kill me now.

She shows up with warm baked ham sandwiches, potato wedges she cut and fried herself, apple slices, and brownies she made last night. I spread one of Harper's tarps under a big oak in the rough section of the cemetery, the section with no graves, and cover it with an old quilt. Livia laughs as she pours us sparkling water in plastic cups with stems, and we eat shivering in our coats in the cool, bright sunlight, sometimes talking and sometimes just watching the fall day be beautiful and perfect.

My work's done, Harper's already sleeping it off in his house, and Livia and I are full and sitting next to each other on the blanket. The sun feels warm on my arms and face. For a second, I think about baseball and softball and the days before everything happened.

What's weird is, I'm not thinking about Cory, at least not in the way I used to. I cared about her a lot back then, and probably if I knew her today, we'd still be close— but that was a long time ago. It was all a long, long time ago, and Livia is here, and she's now, and right this second, that's all that matters to me.

"So this music thing you've got," Livia says, pointing toward the iPod poking out of my jeans pocket. "How long have you been cramming songs onto that thing?"

I think I'm smiling, and I'm pretty sure it's real and not just a cover for feeling weird and uncomfortable. "I didn't get into music heavy until I was fourteen, when I got in trouble. When all the bad stuff in my life happened."

That stuff I'm still not explaining. The smile starts feeling stiff on my lips.

But Livia doesn't react like I'm thinking she should. She

scrolls through my mega-gig iPod menu and says, "You're kidding. You collected all this stuff in three years?"

"Marvin's gifted me a lot of songs and my parents give me music credits for my birthday and Christmas. I thought music was fun but no big thing until I really needed it to calm down my thoughts."

"I wish it would work for me like it does for you," Livia says. "Sometimes I want to shut everything off, but sometimes I want to let all my feelings out, too, you know? And they just won't come."

"I had to go through hundreds of songs before I found the ones that started speaking to me the way I wanted them to. Kinda had to match my mood and stuff."

She doesn't look any more hopeful that music might work for her, so I try again. "What's your strongest feeling right now?"

Livia stares at me with her dark fairy eyes, and her face is so close to mine I think I can feel the heat coming off her skin, and I have to keep saying stuff to myself over and over again, *Not now, it's not right, it's not fair.* When that slips in my head a little, I try, *She's in mourning for her sister. She's sorting things out. Don't be a dick and try to kiss her.*

Her voice is nothing but a whisper when she says, "Sad." She blinks. Tears slip down her cheeks, and something burns in my gut when I see them. Her fists clench in her lap, and she starts to shake. "Pissed. God! I can't tell which one I feel more. Sometimes I think I'm going completely insane."

Keep hands to yourself. Keep hands to yourself. Keep hands to yourself.

I know I need to do something, offer her some kind of comfort that's not pervy or bad or wrong, so I cue up one of my shorter mixes:

"I Wouldn't Want to Be Like You"—Alan Parsons Project

"Bird on a Wire"—Leonard Cohen

"Losing Faith"—Audrey Auld

"Ohio"—Crosby, Stills, Nash & Young

"Broken and Ugly"—Beth Hart

"The Ocean"—The Bravery

"Streets of Philadelphia"—the Bettye LaVette version

"I'll Follow You into the Dark"—Death Cab for Cutie

Livia takes the iPod from me and looks at the mix. "I've never heard of most of these."

"Old and new—some covers." I wait for her to put in an earbud and hope the expression on my face is supportive instead of worried that she'll think the songs are lame.

Livia puts in the second bud, closes her eyes and listens. After a few minutes, she leans into me, and I slip my arm around her and just hold her.

"This is working," she says after a while. Then, "This is nice."

How can I argue with that?

I drift away with her, imagining each word in each song. I'm not even paying attention when she turns toward me, but I definitely notice when she kisses me for the first time.

I notice everything from the minty taste on her lips to how soft they are, and the way the music vibrates on her cheeks and mine, even though I can't totally hear it. She's breathing and I'm breathing, and it's so right now, and so real.

Livia.

I touch her hair.

Livia.

Softer than feathers. Softer than air.

I don't ever want her to stop. I don't ever want the kiss to stop.

More than anything, I don't ever want us to stop.

Three Years Ago: Vanishing

The man who drove Marvin and me to the police station was Detective Henning. He wasn't wearing a uniform, just jeans and a white shirt. He looked like he was about as old as my dad, same color hair but less of it, and he probably works out. A lot.

The place where he brought us, it doesn't look like police stations on television, and I'm in a holding cell, and Mom's right outside, and I feel like something heavy's standing on my chest.

One of Marvin's favorite songs keeps running through my head. "Bank Job" by Barenaked Ladies. It's about a bunch of guys who try to rob a bank but screw everything up because when they get there, the bank lobby's all full of nuns, and they can't make themselves pull guns on nuns.

That would be my luck.

But, I'd never rob a bank even without nuns, or do anything even close to robbing a bank, so why is this happening to me? What did I do?

Mom's sitting outside the bars in a folding chair one of the detectives found for her. There's nothing in the cell but a desk and the folding chair—and us.

I don't like the bars. They look too big. Too thick. Too forever. I'm being stupid, yeah, but I *really* don't like the bars, or being inside them. I never thought about how that would feel, because I never planned to be in jail or worried about doing something and going to jail, but here I am, and here are the bars.

The cell smells like piss and bleach and pine cleanser. It's enough to make my eyes water, but that's not why my eyes are watering. I'm sitting on the cell's cot, huddling against the bars, where I can hold Mom's hand, and the metal feels cold on my face and shoulder.

Every few minutes, Mom checks to see what's happening.

Stupid, and a big, big baby.

Holding Mom's hand definitely makes me feel like a dork, but I try to convince myself I'm doing it more for her than for me.

"Marvin didn't steal any cookies," I tell her, not sure

what else to say, but talking helps me breathe a little better. "And we didn't try to leave the gym, or get in any fights—nothing. We were just talking."

Mom squeezes my hand. "Whatever it is, we'll get it sorted out."

She sounds confident, but the corners of her eyes are wet like mine, and her jawline looks way tight, like it does when she's about to ask my father if they can "go somewhere private to discuss this."

I wish I had Marvin's iPod. I wish I had an iPod of my own. I could pick out some music and share the earbuds with Mom, and maybe we could both stay calm.

"How's that parrot?" I ask Mom, still fishing for something to talk about.

Her look of surprise would make a funny poster, but she says, "Lonely, I think. When you're not there, the bird sort of droops, you know?"

The bars pinch against my skin, and I wonder if the parrot likes the bars on its cage any better.

Probably not.

"When I get home, I'll try to take it out some."

Mom blinks at me like she's not really sure I said that. I could make a few more posters from her face. She doesn't answer me. Maybe she's afraid if she says anything, I'll take back my offer to be nice to the bird.

A little while later, Mom goes out to check on things, then comes back in to tell me, "They're through with Cory, but she and her parents are waiting until after the officers have questioned you."

She sits down and grabs my hand, and I let her squeeze my fingers, but I really want to scream, *Why am I having to sit in a cell? Why is nobody else in a cell? Why did that man in charge of the detectives pick me out?*

Mom can't answer any of those questions. You'd think I'd be able to answer them, that if I'm sitting in a jail cell, I'd have a clue what illegal awful thing I did. Can somebody go to jail and never know why? Is that possible?

I notice my breathing is shallow, so I cough to make myself stop.

"Denise is here for Marvin, but I left your dad out there to keep her calm," Mom adds.

"That's good." Marvin's mom has a major temper if she thinks somebody's bothering Marvin. This situation would qualify. Definitely.

A little later, Mom goes out and in again. This time when she sits down, she says, "The officers won't let us talk about it, but I heard one of the detectives tell a social worker that the coaches called, that it was 'mandatory reporting.' Do you know what that means?"

Should I be feeling even more dread now? *Mandatory reporting* sounds like something nasty and awful. "No. Am I supposed to know?"

Mom shakes her head, runs her hand across her chin, then faces me, talking very, very calmly, like Dad does when he's trying to calm down an animal. "If an adult thinks a child has been abused or hurt, or is at risk of being abused or hurt, that adult has a legal obligation to call the police or human services—to be sure the child's protected."

And all I can think is, *What does that have to do with cookies?* And, *I really should have been nicer to that parrot, because it sucks to be in a cage and not know when you're getting out.*

Mom's expression turns terrified, but she's trying to control it. "Del, have you been hurt by anyone?"

"No, ma'am." *I'll be nicer to the parrot, God, I promise. Please. I didn't know about the cage thing.* I need to stop blinking and half crying, or Mom won't believe what I'm saying. "Nobody's done anything to me, I promise. I would have told you."

Mom relaxes, then gets tense all over again. "Has Cory been hurt? Any of your friends?"

"No." The "Bank Job" song's going off in my brain again, louder this time, and I keep seeing nuns in a bank with their hands up, and a bunch of guys with ski masks and guns just standing there with their mouths open. Maybe one of them should have a parrot on his shoulder. "Not that I know of."

Mom settles into her chair and rubs the back of my fingers. "What were you talking about before the police came?"

"Nothing. We were all asleep." The bars make me want to bang my head against them until they bend. *I'm sorry, parrot.*

Out Mom goes, and when she comes back in, it's, "They let Marvin go home. He's okay. Your dad's staying with Cory and her folks for now because Cory's upset."

My breath comes out fast, but easier now. Good. Marvin's gone home. Good. I didn't lie to him about everything being okay. Good. Good.

But Cory—I wish I could see her.

Maybe I'll get questioned soon, and we can leave, and I'll see Cory and talk to Marvin, and everything really will be okay.

Keep breathing.

Yeah, that's it.

Breathing in and out.

I'll be out.

I'll be out of the bars. I'll be home. And I'll go play with that parrot.

Nothing needs to live in a cell.

If I Ever Tried to Pull a Bank Job, There Would Be Nuns

("I Wish It Would Rain Down"—Phil Collins. Not really on the rain part, because it makes graves messy, but the song is great.)

"You've got a *what*?" Marvin slams shut the copy of *War and Peace* he's been trying to read just to be able to tell everybody he did it. He drops the brick-sized book in the dirt.

The graveyard's cool and quiet except for the sudden rasp of his breathing and the music pumping into my left ear from the single earbud I left in place. Before Phil Collins can sing to me about why he wishes it would rain, Marvin gets in my face beside a half-dug grave and yanks the bud out of my ear. "A *date*? What the hell? Is she your girlfriend now? Are you actually stupid enough to have a girlfriend?"

I drop my shovel into the grave so it doesn't get used as a weapon. "We haven't really talked about that part."

She just kissed me, and I kissed her, and she's been back every night this week, and we keep kissing.

Thinking about touching her makes me feel hot inside and out. Thinking about touching her makes me stop thinking about everything else in the universe. My body feels alive and . . . right. Like it's working. Like I want it to work even though I know I shouldn't let it, not with my history, not with everything hanging over my head.

I'm not some sex maniac, Kaison, you dickhead from hell.

Am I?

It's one thing, wanting a knockout girl just because she's pretty—that's normal. It happens to all guys. It happens to me. But it's another thing to let myself actually want a specific girl, a real human being flesh-and-blood girl, not some fantasy or memory. Everything feels stronger and more powerful, and I could almost get drunk from the sensations.

I'm not a freak. I'm not.

"I'm allowed to have a girlfriend." I try to sound confident to Marvin, but I'm probably sucking at that. "She's seventeen. I'm seventeen. It'll—"

"Don't!" Marvin's yelling and his cheeks go crimson. "Don't friggin' tell me it'll be okay."

For a split second, I see him skinnier and smaller and crying at Good-bye Night. It wasn't okay then. How can I tell him anything'll be okay now? I consider another few weak, stupid phrases like, *it just happened,* and *she came after me*—but Marvin's red in the face and snorting like a horse when he turns his back on me and scrubs his hand through his hair.

I'm shaking inside and probably red in the face, too, and all of a sudden I don't feel so strong or alive. I don't feel any sense of excitement about Livia or anything else. I don't know if I'm pissed or scared or both.

"Are you sure she's seventeen?" he asks, blowing out more air. It rises like fog in the cool air.

"Yes." I cram my hands in my pockets so I don't start making fists at my best friend.

"Did you see her license?"

"No. But I believe her."

"You're a total idiot." He turns. Looks at me. I'm glad he's a few yards off now, because he's so red he's nuclear. "This is it. You're screwed. You're going to get busted again, somehow, someway, for something. Aren't you even scared of that?"

My fingers dig into my pockets and my legs, and my face gets as hot as his looks. "Yes."

He waits. I can tell he's trying to calm down, keep himself together. Then, "Have you told her?"

"Yes. No." I kick some dirt. "Sort of."

Marvin shakes his head. "You're an asshole, man."

"Yeah." I don't shrug, which is some kind of miracle. "I'm telling you about her. I thought if I did, I'd get the guts to talk to her about my past."

It's not like I haven't tried. It's not like it's easy.

The red fades out of Marvin's face, and he's looking sad and worried instead of mad. "I'm not going through all this crap again, Del. Not for you, not for anybody."

"I don't blame you." I try to sound calm, but *mad* probably sums me up. I'm just not sure who I'm pissed at. "I don't want you to go through anything. I thought you and Lee Ann—that you were ready, too."

"I am ready. I've been ready." Marvin throws up both hands, like he's pleading to me or God even though neither of us is listening. "Don't you get it? I'm not taking the chance. When I'm legally an adult, and she's legally an adult, and nobody has the right to say anything to us about anything—that's the right time. Not now."

Yeah, I know the rules. They aren't my rules, but I'm breaking them. I look past him, into the nearby woods. The trees look empty and scraggly without their leaves. "I thought I couldn't care about anybody again, you know? Livia's making stuff different. It's not all bad."

This takes Marvin a few seconds to process. He walks toward me a few steps, then stops and shakes his head. "You mean—you thought you couldn't be interested? Like *that*? In sex? Why? Your parts aren't broken or defective or anything."

I can't stop looking at the trees. "Seemed like they were, except here and there—you know, wet dreams and everyday stuff. I stay away from magazines and movies, I'm not allowed on porn sites, I listen to music, I work hard, and that keeps everything under control. It was enough. Until I met her."

He breathes for half a minute, then tries, "Un-meet her."

"I can't do that. I don't want to."

"Then you're stupid." He sighs. Messes up his hair again. "Man, I saw how you were with her, how you look at her and stuff, but I thought you had yourself under control. Do your parents know? Does Branson know?"

"Sort of."

He glances at me, more joking than glaring. "Like she sort of knows about your past?"

My face twitches. My whole body twitches. I look all the way away from him, at the gray fall sky and the few gray clouds gathering over the graveyard.

"I'm sorry," Marvin mutters, and when I do look at him again, I can tell he wants to go back to being easy, but he's not quite getting there, and I don't think I've ever seen that happen before.

It makes me go cold inside. "You're right about everything. I've got to talk to Livia. I keep trying, and either I clam up or she stops me. It's like she doesn't want to know any more than I want to tell her."

He gazes at me straight on, eyes a little wide. "Sooo, she likes you. As in, really likes you."

"I don't know." I stare at the woods a little longer. "I guess so, yeah. But that could change when she finds out everything about me."

Some of Marvin's easiness comes back, sliding over his features like paint on a canvas—or like a mask of who-cares pulled on top of an I-care-about-everything-too-much face. I see him younger again, all about food and sports and music, then crying and scared to death.

I'm not that guy anymore.

He told me that not too long ago. I didn't really listen.

The chill inside me chases away all the heat in my face as I wonder who Marvin is now—and, selfishly, where that leaves me.

"Maybe it won't change." Marvin sounds sort of hopeful. "But you should find out. Like, yesterday."

"Yeah."

"Soon as the moment's right. Promise?"

The shrug comes because I can't stop it, but I say, "I swear."

The rest of the day, I try to talk myself into having a more serious conversation with Livia, and I try to talk myself out of thinking about what it feels like to kiss her.

Her lips taste like mint from toothpaste or gum, or sometimes like cherries or grapes from her lip gloss. She's soft when I hold her, with curves where my hands rest, and when I touch her I think stupid caveman things like, *mine* and *totally mine*—oh yeah, and *all mine.*

Five seconds, and my whole body's humming. I go half-man, half-machine, and my thoughts go straight to touching her more, to how far I want to go, how far she might want to go, and damn, I start to hurt. No amount of music or hard work will fix this. My body's a beast. A beast that's been held back too long.

But she's *not* mine. Not really. I know that. Livia's not even a little bit mine, but guy brain seems to think by itself whenever I get around her.

"You're a thousand miles in the clouds today." Harper pushes half a peanut-butter sandwich across his junk-cluttered counter, knocking me out of my Livia daydream.

I take the sandwich and help myself to a big bite. Apple jelly. My favorite. Food's a sucky substitute for sex, but it'll have to do.

"That girl's been coming around. I've seen you with her." Harper raises both hands when he sees my expression. "No, no, don't go worrying I'm gonna say you can't see her here. I know you ain't got nowhere else to have a life. Hell, I'm the one who told you to find out her name."

"Livia," I try to say around the peanut butter in case he doesn't remember. It comes out sounding like *liver.*

"Fred," Fred corrects from her travel cage on Harper's counter. She's glaring from me to my sandwich, so I slide her a little bit of crust. She picks it up with her delicate little toes and eats it.

Harper clears his throat. "Yeah. Livia. Whatever. You just—you know how to keep your nose clean, right?"

"It's not against the rules for me to have a girlfriend. I

need to see her identification to make sure she's really seventeen, though."

"That'd be hard, carding a chick just to be sure it's legal to kiss her."

I don't like him calling Livia a chick or mentioning kissing her. Guy brain. I might as well beat my chest like Tarzan and go swinging through the trees. Probably bust my face on some big pine branch. This is crazy.

Harper's looking squirmy, and before I know it, he pops out with, "And you know about rubbers, I'm guessing. If you need money for some, I can front you some of your paycheck."

Oh God. I literally choke trying to swallow the peanut butter, coughing twice; Fred coughs three times for good measure, then says, "Excuse me!"

"It's not like that," I tell Harper when I can breathe again.

But it is.

No, it's not.

Christ, hold on, hold on, don't lose it.

I take a long, slow breath, trying to wheeze all the tension out of my body.

It's like that, but I won't let it go where it's not supposed to go, because I'm not some depraved sex maniac. Take that, Kaison, wherever you are. Asshole.

"Thanks," I add as my mind settles down enough to realize Harper was trying to help.

Harper gets himself a beer, sees me looking at it, and frowns. "Something else on your mind?"

Way to stay calm and guard your expression. Good job, Del.

But he did ask, so I take the opening. "You doing okay? Physically, I mean?" I point to the beer. "It's none of my business how much you drink, but I've been worrying maybe it was making you a little sick."

"It does." He shrugs like I always do, then drinks. "I used to go to AA. Probably should go back."

He doesn't say anything else, but his expression does. *Butt out, Del.* I butt out.

"Thanks for the sandwich, Harper."

"You bought the peanut butter."

"Fred," Fred says, and I take her out of Harper's kitchen and head off to work.

"I never thought graveyards could be so peaceful," Livia says. She's stretched out on a quilt with her bare feet in my lap, and the setting sun paints the fall sky gold and red and purple. I rub her toes so they stay warm, and because she seems to love having her feet rubbed.

Del Hartwick, full-service gravedigger.

Every time I run my fingers along her skin, it feels electric. Supercharged. I think about stretching out on top of her, kissing her deep, then deeper, and finding out how far we want to take this.

Can't.

Yes, I could.

Won't.

It's hard.

I'm not a freak. I won't be a freak.

"I did college applications today," she says, staring at the sunset, her arms folded under her head. "I hate that. I mean, I want to go to college, but I just don't know if I want to go the day after high school. What are you going to do?"

"Probably work awhile." Was that a lie? Definitely an omission. I hold her right foot carefully in my hands and get a second's worth of relief as all the desire drains out of me. "Look, the truth is, I probably can't go anytime soon. My folks don't have a lot of money left for college, and I can't get scholarships, and most colleges probably won't take me because of that trouble I got in."

She tenses so fast, so much I literally feel it in her toes. Her dark eyes meet mine for a second. "That doesn't seem fair."

"Livia—"

She wiggles her foot to interrupt me, then goes back to staring at the sky. "I should take my applications more seriously. They're my way out of this town, out of life with my parents. I've always thought I wanted to study art or creative writing. That's probably stupid, though."

"Nothing about you is stupid."

"I don't know. I kind of suck at geometry, even when my mom helps me with the problems."

From the corner of the blanket, in her travel cage wrapped around the bottom with a small blanket to block the breeze, Fred starts whistling a tune. It's soft, hard to make out, but I think it might be "America the Beautiful."

I start rubbing Livia's feet again, noticing how delicate her ankles are, and how fast my body gets tight all over again, wanting more. Needing more. Stuff I can't have. Stuff I probably shouldn't even want, but I really, really do.

"Are you close to your mom?" I ask, because I want to know, but also to keep myself square in reality.

"I used to be." Her feet twitch. Tense, then letting it go. Livia seems good at that. I should take lessons from her. "Mom shut down when my sister died. She doesn't talk much anymore. How about your parents?"

I think about this for a second. My family's hard to explain, but then again, it's pretty easy, too. "My parents rescue animals. With work and school and all they do with the SPCA, I don't see them that much—but we get along."

"That must be nice." Livia slips her feet out of my lap, sits up, and kisses me, leaving her lips on mine for a long, long time. I close my eyes as she presses against me, her leg to my leg, her side to my side, and I feel her softness, her sweetness.

What are we now?

That's the question I want to ask, that I feel like I need

to ask, but when Livia's this close to me, words stop making sense and being important.

When the kiss ends, it's like falling off the edge of the world.

I want more. I want it all. I want her.

"I have to go," she whispers in my ear, her voice as soft as fairy wings. "I'll call you later, if I can."

Because I'm not some sex-crazed maniac, I let her go. Then I watch as she gathers her things, watch as she jogs away toward Claudia's grave. She'll stay a few minutes, then head toward home so she's in before dark, like her father wants. Sometimes I go back to work before she's gone, but usually I sit and watch, waving when she waves, until she's a speck on the road, until I can't see any hint of her in the twilight.

After I get home that night, when the phone rings and I answer it, the first thing Livia says is, "I miss you."

Blood pumps in my throat and ears, and before I can stop myself, I tell her, "I miss you, too."

She goes on for a minute or two about how her family's going to visit relatives for Thanksgiving next week. Then, "I told my cousin about you. She's happy I've got a boyfriend."

Oh. Shit.

Boyfriend.

There's the word.

I am. I know I am. I've been acting like that, wanting that, but hearing it out loud—

"Forgot to ask earlier, how's Marvin?" Livia's voice sounds like little bells, all ringing and happy, and I know I can't get heavy with her, not on the phone.

Marvin's pissed that I'm dating you. "He's hot on a girl named Lee Ann."

"And Harper?"

Working on being drunk straight through the holidays and totally oblivious. "Same as always."

He offered me rubbers.

"Is anything wrong, Del?"

You're not here next to me, and when I'm not looking at you or touching you, nothing makes sense. "No. I just miss you."

She laughs. "Good. Miss me a lot while I'm gone."

"I will," I tell her, and when I hang up, I feel completely lost.

If It Rains Down, It Will Rain on Me

("Penitentiary"—Citizen Cope. He's right. Most penitentiaries are in our minds.)

The Thanksgiving holidays come and go, and Livia's still gone. She can do that, since she's homeschooled. When she called last night, she said they'd probably be back tonight or tomorrow.

It's been strange not having her around—and sort of empty, knowing she won't be coming by Rock Hill for her nightly visits. I want to hear her voice in person again. I want to hold her, talk to her. I really want to make myself do the right thing by Livia, explain every bit of my past, give her the choices I should have given her right from the start.

Even if she doesn't make it easy, even if it's the last thing I want, we have to go there. The next time I see her, we just have to.

At school, the noise in the hallway seems halfway bearable after first period as I try to keep myself distracted from Livia and also research the endless grin on Marvin's face. "Is Lee Ann pretty *and* hot, or just one or the other?"

Marvin grins even bigger as he stops in front of our lockers and opens his door. "Pretty. Hot. And pretty hot. She's got these shorts she has to wear in the Bangles and Stuff booth." He throws his books in the locker and taps the top of his thigh. "You gotta see them to believe them."

I change out my books and ask the big, big question. "So, when's the first date—assuming she's not totally blowing you off?"

"Next weekend."

Figures. After his birthday. "Did you check her driver's license?"

The question comes out automatically, and I swear I'm talking in Dad's voice, just like Fred.

Marvin doesn't seem to care. "She's selling jewelry. Gotta be eighteen to do that at our mall—but yeah, actually, I did check the license. She didn't mind." He starts digging through his locker. "Is Branson still on you about testifying at those hearings at the special session in April?" The question comes out light, almost offhand, but I'm thinking there's an edge to it, which is weird. Marvin has his big-deal moments with me, but he doesn't usually start them.

I feel a flash of nervousness, almost like inner movie

music right before something awful happens, and it makes me shiver.

Marvin doesn't notice.

"Branson's giving it a rest." I clear my throat. "But my parents have started—about themselves, not me—but I think they kind of want me to go."

Marvin stops rooting through the junk covering his books, and without pulling his head out of his locker, he asks, "Are they going to do it?"

That dread-the-disaster feeling in my gut doubles, maybe because when I get a look at Marvin's face, he's frowning big-time. It makes him look serious and older.

"I . . . I think so, yeah."

Marvin closes his locker, leaving his hand on the lock, and that frown keeps right on going. "I wish they'd leave it alone. I wish everybody would just drop it and move on."

"Yeah," I say out loud.

Inside, it comes out, *I wish I could, but I'm the one with the felony conviction.*

For a second or two, I stare at Marvin with his frown. Marvin, who never got charged with anything. Marvin, who's leaving for Notre Dame as soon as he can. Marvin, who really can drop all this, the whole big, awful mess, and move on.

His face shifts, and for another few seconds, it's like I don't know him, or maybe it's just that I don't know the *real* him, like lots of people don't know the real me. Is he going to turn eighteen and change everything in his life—me and my nasty past included?

That's stupid.

I do know Marvin. I know him better than anybody, and he knows me.

Right?

Arms slide around my waist and somebody hugs me from behind.

I jump so hard I smack my head on the locker, then wheel around, pushing myself away from Cherie as she lets me go, laughing and barely dodging the flow of bodies in the middle of the hall.

"You should see your face." She hiccups because she's laughing so hard.

Blind mad. It happens fast and my face feels like it's boiling. "Don't be sneaking up on me and touching me like that."

My voice is loud enough to make me breathe and think and breathe again. Marvin clears his throat from behind me, and when I imagine him, I see that frown. My face stays hot.

"Why?" Cherie teases, winking at me. "You fragile?"

Her *pussy* comment comes floating back to me, and all I can do is glare. She's wearing black jeans today, and another one of her black sweaters. Makeup, hair, nails—perfect and dark. She looks like a vampire doll, and the morning sunlight through the hall doors makes her eyes twinkle. Probably

wearing glitter or something. She's definitely wearing perfume again, but this time it makes my eyes water.

"Go away, Cherie." Marvin bangs his books against his
locker, but Cherie doesn't so much as tell him to screw off
because she's too busy staring at me.

"You miss me, Del?"

God, the things I want to say. I settle for, "No."

Her smile makes her lips look like they're made out of
dark blood. "I'm coming out to the graveyard tonight."

"Don't." I point my finger at her. "I'll call my parents."
Which is a total L-I-E. After last time, I could never do that
again, but maybe she won't call my bluff. "We can't be
friends because your family thinks I suck."

"You don't suck?" Cherie's mocking me, laughing all
over again, and I wish she was hateful instead of sort of nice
and playful and cute. I'm so weirded out I can't even tell
what's fake and what's real.

"Uh, yeah he does suck," Marvin says, still behind me.
"And so do I, so go away."

Cherie moves away from the crowded part of the hall
toward me, her eyes getting more serious even though her
lips are still curving up. "You don't suck, Del."

Christ, what am I supposed to do with a girl like this?
She's the most stubborn person in the universe, and I don't
want to stomp all over her feelings, but she doesn't give me
lots of options. Right now, she's just making me sweat and

making my heart pound, because I'm expecting her brother to show up any second and crack my skull.

"Look—thanks for being so nice to me. For not ignoring me." I suck in a breath and pick my next words as best I can. "I do think that's, I don't know, brave, I guess. You're a very nice person. I just don't need any trouble, okay?"

She's too close to me now, and Marvin's starting to gripe over my shoulder about her backing off.

"There won't be any trouble," she says. "My family doesn't get to run my life."

Marvin steps around me. His head seems to be on a swivel as he watches out for Jonas.

"Don't come to Rock Hill," I tell Cherie, having another one of those not-fun premonition feelings. "We're not friends. We can't be, like I said."

The hall fades away as I study her, and I see it's not sinking in, and Marvin's doing that stranger-frown thing, and it's all just too much. "That's not it," I admit before Cherie starts arguing with me again. "What I'm saying—I mean, it's all true, but there's another reason I don't want you to come."

Cherie's eyebrows come together.

Miracle of miracles, I seem to have her attention.

"There's someone else." My tone is as gentle as I can make it, but the words still sound brutal.

Cherie's smile goes still. Her confident expression melts into something like shock. For once, I've got the advantage

with her. She's finally listening to me, and she'll hear whatever I say next, so I'd better make it good. My hands start
sweating like the rest of me.

"I've got a girlfriend now, Cherie. Whatever you thought
this was between us—that it wasn't . . . it . . . it—isn't.
Okay?"

Way to make it good, asshole.

But I can see she's taking my meaning, because what's in
her eyes now is pain. Damn it. I wish she'd get pissed
instead. Pissed would be way easier to deal with. Her
broken-doll look is half killing me, and it's still killing me
when she spins away from me and runs away down the hall,
pushing people out of her way.

I can't move or say anything.

Marvin's standing beside me like he's made out of concrete, his mouth hanging open.

It's Jonas's heavy punch to my shoulder that jars me back
to reality. I bang into my locker wondering where the hell
he came from, what he heard—what's he going to do?

Lots of witnesses all around us. Nobody's slowing down
to watch, though.

Hands down. Don't react.

But I'm reacting. Fists clenched. Breathing hard. So is
Marvin.

My heart thumps fast enough to make peel-out noises as
Jonas says, "Hartwick, that was cold. Past cold. It was frozen."

My ears buzz like my brain's about to explode. I study

Jonas with his perfect jeans and oh-so-I-look-good long-sleeve jersey, with his blue eyes and blond hair and big square face. My thoughts do stupid things like, *Cherie's prettier than him* and *He reminds me of Marvin's frown* and *I bet Kaison was a lot like this in high school.*

Marvin and I stay flush with our lockers as Jonas and his posse crowd us, but that's all they're doing. Jonas is shaking his head. "Cold," he says again. "But, you did what you had to do."

"Cold," Marvin echoes, staring as Jonas and his big boys move off into the crowd, leaving us behind. "Okay, that was like demented or something. What the hell just happened?"

My heart's still bump-bump-bumping, and my fists crush into my own thighs. "Guess Jonas is leaving it alone. You know, dropping it and moving on."

"Yeah, okay." Marvin's mouth twitches like he wants to frown and be that other guy again, but he smiles instead.

For some reason, that doesn't help the way I'm feeling. I still want to hit something, and I can't figure out why it's Marvin.

He's moving, heading off to class, so I follow, but I feel way past strange, and selfish and stupid, and more lost than ever.

Graveyards can be sad and lonely and cold and quiet, but sometimes, they're just peaceful. Sometimes, they're just right.

It's cool when Fred and I get to Rock Hill, and the sun seems to be lazing in the sky, halfway down, in no hurry to disappear and turn the fall breezes into cold night air. My head's still spinning and buzzing from the day, from Cherie and pinhead and even Marvin, and I wish I could figure out what I'm feeling about all that, but the sensations don't make any sense to me.

"Fred," Fred keeps saying from Harper's countertop. I dig around by the phone, knocking beer cans onto the floor as I look for his ledger that has the list of upcoming funerals and the lots where the graves need to be carved out of the chilled, leaf-covered dirt. Fred sounds kind of nervous, probably because I have the little blanket tucked around even more of her cage to keep the wind from being too cold for her when we go outside. She might be nervous because I feel so weird, and I can't figure out what I should do next, and I don't really mean what I should do next in the graveyard.

"What should I do next with my life?" I ask Fred as I finally find Harper's list, count two graves, and figure out which plots need to be turned.

"One," Fred says. "Two. Four. Four, four, four."

I lay the list on the counter beside her, scribble a note on the back of a milk and peanut butter receipt so I don't forget which plots to dig, and give my parrot the best oh-please look I can muster. "Are you telling me to take it one step at a time?"

"Four," Fred repeats, her eyes bright and fixed directly on mine.

"You're as bad as Dr. Mote—and you missed a step yourself. One, two, *three*, four."

Dr. Mote wouldn't really like what I'm doing now, standing in Harper's junky, stinky house, looking at his mess, knowing that he's passed out in his bed, probably crusted with dirt and booze and whatever else he hasn't washed off in the last week. That doesn't help with all my angst about life, either.

"Sad," I say to Fred, because all I really know for sure about my future is, I don't want to be Harper. Not all of what Harper is, anyway. I don't mind the hard work, and his business is legit, and it's not a business that cares about my past, even a little bit. But can I dig graves for the rest of my life and not slowly go insane and end up where Harper is now?

I so don't want to deal with any of this.

How long can you put it off?

Yeah, that last one was Dr. Mote in my head. Right after that comes Branson's voice.

Sooner or later, you have to have a plan.

Write colleges. Testify at hearings about unjust laws. They say it like it's possible for me to make a plan, like it's possible for me to open doors.

"Four," Fred says again, and I carry her outside without asking her any more questions. Sometimes I get afraid she'll answer me in some major way, and I'll have to add insane bird freak to all the other stupid crap people can say about me.

The plot I need to dig is in Acorn Section—older, lots of trees and bushes, but the spot itself has high green grass washed in so much sunlight it looks almost blue. It smells like bark and dirt, the whole area, but not in a bad way. More fresh and natural.

I hang Fred's cage on a low-hanging branch in a little oak tree, find a shovel, and set the dimensions of the grave. The sun on my face feels perfect, and I try digging without my music even though it feels strange and weird, and I have trouble keeping a rhythm.

Something about the addiction conversation with Dad and the drinking conversation with Harper has stayed with me. I'm thinking maybe my music isn't as good as Dad's animal rescuing, even if I'm not sure why. Except, it keeps me from feeling and thinking, and I'm not sure Dad's animal stuff does that. It's like he's using animals to be part of the world, but I'm using my music to be separate from it. I'm using music more like Harper's using his beer.

That can't be good.

When Livia finds me, I'm thinking more than I'm digging. In fact, I'm just standing in the middle of the Acorn Section grave, leaning on the shovel, letting the sun touch me enough to keep me from freezing, and having a whistling contest with Fred.

Livia doesn't try to interrupt, but of course I stop whistling the second I know she's there, because, well, I'm not a gigantic dork or anything.

She comes around in front of me, where I can see her pretty face and behind her, over her right shoulder, Fred hanging in her cage, fluttering around and acting excited because Livia's there. She kisses me. I kiss her back. She tastes like mint chewing gum and she smells like cinnamon and fresh-baked bread. My body molds to hers like we're made to fit together, and I try to keep my thoughts G-rated, but—damn, it's the last place I need to go, and the first place I get to.

Beast.

"I missed you so much."

We say that at the same time, and I feel goofy even though I shouldn't and warm even though it's cold, and she's here, and suddenly that's all that matters. I can handle the ache. I can stand the frustration. I can hold everything together and control myself forever, as long as she's here with me.

Tame beast.

Livia kisses me again, then pulls back and smiles at me. I make myself smile back, but I guess she can read stuff on my face or in my voice because she says, "Hard day?"

"Yeah," I admit. What I want to say is, *I don't know what to do, and I don't really know how to do it. Do you know what I mean?*

But why would she know?

She's had a lot of tragedy, but she's not in trouble. She feels like she's got marks against her, but she really doesn't, not as far as colleges and jobs and the rest of the world are concerned.

I'm not being fair, am I? Her sister getting killed like that—it was a huge punch. It knocked her off the earth, just like my trouble did to me.

I'm such an ass.

"What are you thinking?" She's closer to me now, and whispering, her lips almost on mine. Her dark eyes seem so huge they take up everything in my brain, pulling my thoughts to her and nobody else.

I hold her around the waist, noticing how soft her blue sweater feels, and this time, I pussy out with, "It's complicated."

I wonder how many other things Cherie's right about? Shitty thought. Totally don't want to go there, either. Lots of places I don't want to go right now.

"I can do complicated," Livia tells me. She's got me at the waist, too, her hands pressing into my sides. It's like we're each trying to make sure the other one doesn't fall right over.

<You have to do this, Del.>

Okay, that was scary, because this time, the mental blog entry's all in my voice, strong and definite and nagging, and I know I'm right. Time to stop being a pussy. "I keep putting off talking to you. I can't do that anymore."

Her smile makes me warm and breaks my heart at the same time. "I told you it was okay."

"It's not okay." I make myself stop touching her because that keeps me from thinking like I need to think to get out the words. "You have to know everything, and I hate talking about it. I keep bullshitting myself, saying I can't figure out where to start, but that's not true. The start is, I got in a lot of trouble when I was fourteen, and it's the kind of trouble that lasts . . . sort of . . . forever."

While I'm taking a breath to get my mouth around the rest of it, she pulls me to her, rests her head against my chest, and says, "Wait."

I hold her, and I want to wait, but I make myself let her go and she looks hurt. The way the sun's shining off her hair, off her cheeks and eyes, she's more fairy than ever, like a dream I'll never get to have again.

"I've been happy since I met you." Her lower lip trembles just enough to stick a dagger directly through my will-power and determination. "I can't stand—I don't want anything to change that. Not yet, okay?"

My neck doesn't want to work, but as the oak leaves dance in the afternoon breeze and Fred's cage bobs up and down, blanket untucking and flapping, I turn my head enough, and enough times for Livia to read, *No. Not okay. Gotta do this.*

Fred whistles, louder and louder each time I don't answer, and I have to figure her bird nose can smell how nervous I am. She's trying to fix it, to help me, but there's no help for this. It's a bank full of nuns and all my plans have gone to hell, and the only way out is telling the truth, no matter what it costs me.

Tears pool in the corners of Livia's eyes, as if she hears what I'm thinking and knows I'm right, like maybe she's got a clue how bad everything might get in that space between what she knows about me and what she doesn't know.

"Later," she says. "I'll listen to everything, I promise, but for now, just kiss me again."

<No fair.>

I don't need to kiss her.

<No . . . fair.>

I don't need to put everything away, just drop it like I drop the shovel when I'm through with a grave.

I don't need to do that, but it's exactly what I do, because holding Livia feels better than anything in my life now, and maybe ever.

"Four," Fred shouts, like she knows something I don't. "Four, four, four!"

After we've snuggled for a few long, perfect minutes, Livia kisses my neck and whispers in my ear, "Are you afraid I'll try to push us?"

The cool night air stings my eyes, probably because I just opened them so wide. "What?"

"That I'll, you know, try to push the sex thing." She kisses my ear.

Chills—the cold kind and the warm kind—break out all over my body. "I . . . um, no?"

Yes?

Who the hell knows?

My arms have gone stiff around her, and she wriggles against me to loosen my grip. "I won't push. I know something's bothering you about that. I can tell. And honestly, since Claudia, and with my father always breathing down my neck—well. It's like with food. Sometimes keeping it simple is better."

She moves back in my slightly more relaxed arms, and she stares into my eyes. I stare back, tongue-tied as usual, but also clueless about what to say or do next. I so didn't expect any of that. She's smart and responsible like I always think I am, like I want to be. I talk about it and think about it. Livia, she just *does* it.

"It's not that I'm not interested." She runs her fingers down my cheek, and the chills double, and a lot of other sensations burn like a sudden fire in the night.

I finally speak, or more like croak, "We should—ah, stop talking about it."

Livia grins. Looks pleased. "Fine. We'll talk about it again soon."

"Not until—"

She puts her fingers on my lips. "Not tonight."

"Not tonight."

"Four," Fred says.

I really am completely lost.

Three Years Ago: Broken Boy Soldier

Detective Henning sits across from me, and light shines bright on the metal table between us. There's a tape recorder. Mom's standing on one side of me while Dad stands at the door. I figure people are watching from behind the dark window I'm looking at, but that's probably crazy.

In between the weird music buzzing through my head, I'm sort of writing my own song, and it's

Did somebody die?

Why am I here?

What do you think I did?

What's going on?

Sucks. Doesn't rhyme. But all those questions want to come out, and I'm scared anything I ask will make me look stupid or guilty or just make everything worse. I'm even starting to wonder if I've secretly gone crazy, maybe done a bunch of stuff I don't remember—somebody would have to be crazy to do stuff they don't remember, right?

The room smells a little like pee and a lot like sweat.

My mom leans over the table, covers my left hand with her right, and starts asking some of my questions. "What's going on, Detective? I think we deserve some answers."

"We'll get to that."

"Sooner rather than later, if you want us to keep cooperating with—with whatever this is," Dad says. He's leaning on the wall beside the door with both arms folded, glaring at the police officer. I'm glad he's not looking at me like that.

Detective Henning doesn't react to Dad and takes his time getting his yellow legal pad exactly where he wants it. Then he makes a few scribbles, turns on the recorder my parents agreed to, says his name and my name and the date and our location.

After that, he asks, "So, how long have you and Cory known each other?"

I can't see what he wrote on the pad, so I stop trying. "A long time."

"But your relationship changed this last year?"

"Yeah."

My mother gives me a fast, sharp look.

"Um, I mean, yes, sir."

"The two of you get along?"

"Yes, sir."

"No fighting and arguing?"

"No, sir."

"You ever threaten her or intimidate her in any way?"

"No!"

"Wait a minute—" Dad starts, and at the same time, Mom says, "Okay, look. Del's not that kind of kid."

Tears beat against the backs of my eyes, but I'm trying not to cry or look like a complete idiot. "Did Cory say I did anything like that? Is she mad at me?"

"Does she have anything to be mad at you about?" Detective Henning asks.

Everything inside me feels like it's crawling. "I don't think so."

The detective waits. The sweat-piss-perfume-cologne smell in the little room seems to get stronger. I don't like the waiting. He makes me wait longer. My parents start shifting around where they're standing, and Mom moves away from the table. I think Dad's starting to pace.

"How close are you and Cory, Del?" The detective doesn't look up from his pad when he asks this, but he does when he adds, "You want me to ask your mom to leave? Sometimes this stuff is easier with just guys."

"No," I tell him at the same time Mom and Dad say it.

Then I'm sitting there listening to myself breathe and listening to my parents breathe, and I wonder if maybe

I should have let the detective tell Mom to step out for a few.

Too late, too late. He's waiting for an answer. "I . . . we . . . we've done some stuff. Not sex, though."

"The pictures on your phones were revealing." He pushes my phone toward me, and oh God, there's Cory naked, and I can't put my hand over the picture before Mom sees it, or Dad. It's just there and they're seeing it.

"Oh," Mom says. Kind of a little squeaky voice. Nothing from Dad, but he turns his head away from the photo.

I put my hand over it. "You shouldn't be looking at that. It's mine. It's private."

Detective Henning's smile looks a little sarcastic. "And you and Cory haven't had sex?"

"No, sir." I'm hot all over. I wish I knew what buttons to push without looking to delete that picture.

"Have you done anything else?" he asks. "What are you calling it these days—almost sex?"

I stare at him.

He stares at me. "Oral?"

"No. Just . . ."

He waits.

I get hotter and squeeze my hand around the phone between us, with naked Cory underneath my palm. "Just our hands."

He nods. Slides the phone away from me. "How many times?"

I ignore my parents and start pretending they don't exist, that they're not really in the room with me so I can answer him. "Three."

Detective Henning makes notes on his pad. "You're sure about that?"

"It's not something I'd forget."

"You're telling me the truth, Del. I know because that's exactly what Cory said. That's good." He fiddles with the tape recorder. "We're almost done."

"I didn't make her do it. She wanted me to. It was her idea." I know I'm sounding nervous, and I look at my parents. "We're not having sex, not even oral. We're being safe. We're waiting."

My parents keep looking at me, but their eyes—strange. Hollow and surprised. Dad seems pissed, but not at me.

This feels like cutting my own guts out and laying them on the table for everybody to stare at and poke and rate on some screwed-up scale. How will I ever look at my parents again after this? How will they ever look at me?

Detective Henning waits for a bit, then seems to realize I'm done. I hope I'm done. Will he let us be done?

"Okay, Del," Detective Henning says as he stands up and starts clearing stuff off the table. "What I need you to do is wait while I get this typed up. You'll read it, then sign that what I type up is right, that it's what happened and what you told me. Your parents will need to look it over, too."

This activates my dad like shoving batteries in his back

and hitting an On switch. He comes off his leaning spot on the wall. "I don't want him signing things. If you want him to sign things, I want to talk to an attorney."

Detective Henning cradles all the junk from the table. I can't read his expression at all. Maybe he's mad about what Dad said, or maybe he's relieved. I might be cracked, but I swear he looks like he feels guilty about something. "That's your call, Mr. Hartwick."

Voices rise in the hallway, and there's knocking on the door, some actual yelling, then the door gets unlocked and shoved open. I see another detective for about two seconds before Cory's parents come busting in, all red in the face.

My heart slams into high gear and I cover my head on the table and wait for Mr. Wentworth to grab me and start killing me.

Cory's mom is the one who starts talking first. "What's going on here? Why are you doing all of this?"

I peek out from under my own armpit. Mrs. Wentworth really does look like an older version of Cory, and this would be Cory in totally pissed, hide-the-softball-bats mode.

Mr. Wentworth's got on smudged jeans and a dark T-shirt, and his big plumber's hands are clenched into sledgehammer-sized fists. "Why are you holding Del?"

Detective Henning stands by the table with his arms still loaded down, saying nothing. He nods to the detective at the door, who gives him a shrug, then pulls the door closed again.

Cory's mom is hugging my mom, and Mr. Wentworth's shaking hands with my dad, and I'm still alive, so I figure Mr. Wentworth must not know what I told the detective.

"Cory told us everything," Mrs. Wentworth says to my mom. "Well, what little *everything* there is. I have no idea what these people have told you, but we don't have any problem with this. It's an issue for us, for their parents, not the police."

At this, she looks at Detective Henning again, and so does Mr. Wentworth. My parents are looking at him, too.

Um, so am I.

She told them everything?

I glance at Mr. Wentworth's hands, then back to the detective. I'm not sure who to be scared of, so I decide to be scared of both of them.

"Your daughter is under the age of consent," Detective Henning says to the Wentworths. "Cory isn't in trouble. You don't need to be here—none of this will involve her."

"None of what will involve her?" Mom asks as Mrs. Wentworth folds her arms, looking as confused as I feel.

Detective Henning's expression turns flat, then sad. "Del admitted to having sexual contact with Cory."

"I didn't have sex with her!" I'm out of my seat before I even think what I'm doing, eyes on Mr. Wentworth, ready to move in case he comes after me. "We just touched each other! Just touching!"

And finally, *finally*, Detective Henning starts talking to

me instead of questioning me. "By law, putting your hands on or in her private areas—that's sex, son. You're over the age of consent and she isn't."

"I don't like how this is sounding." Dad comes over to where I'm standing and puts his hands on my shoulders.

"Are you kidding me?" Cory's father sounds furious, but not with me. "They're the same age."

Sex? I had sex with her according to the law? Makes no sense. We didn't have sex.

"He's older, and over the age of consent," Detective Henning tells Mr. Wentworth. "She's not. That's all the law cares about."

For a long few seconds, nobody says anything, and my heart's still banging, and my brain's still repeating *I didn't have sex with Cory. We were waiting.*

"Well, if that's illegal, we don't want any charges filed," Mrs. Wentworth says, and stays close to my mother, who has gone wicked ghost pale. "This is ridiculous."

"No charges," Mr. Wentworth agrees, maybe so he can kill me himself, but maybe he's actually being a nice guy. I don't know. I can't figure it out.

"It's not up to you," Detective Henning says. "I'm sorry. None of you have any say in this. Really, you haven't since the coaches found the pictures on their cell phones."

"What are you talking about?" Dad's starting to lose it. I can tell because he's talking through his teeth. "What the hell is going on here?"

Detective Henning glances at the table like he's considering putting the tapes and notebooks down, but then he seems to think better of it. "Once the coaches found the pictures, the law mandates that they turn them over to law enforcement. And once we get information like this, we're obligated to turn it over to the district attorney, William Kaison."

Mr. Wentworth's jaw comes unhinged. He laughs. Shakes his head. Gets himself together enough to say, "You're turning over a report of two kids making out to the DA. Are you serious?"

"It'll be up to him how to proceed," Detective Henning says.

Mom's not shaking, but her voice trembles when she whispers, "There's not even a year's difference in their age."

I'm hardly keeping up with anything the detective's saying, but I see that guilty look on his face again when he speaks back to my mother. "Ma'am, it doesn't matter in the eyes of the law in this state if it's just one day."

Mr. Wentworth's not finished. He's between the detective and the door. "But they're our kids."

"Like I've been telling you, your daughter is under the age of consent." Detective Henning definitely seems unhappy now. "She's considered a victim. She won't even be charged for the sexting picture."

"The what?" Mr. Wentworth asks.

Oh God. I'm dead. I'm so dead. My breath chokes away

again, leaving me swallowing, only I can't swallow because my throat's so dry.

"The pornography," the detective says, and now I'm really waiting to get hit or die. I'm sweating everywhere, even behind my knees.

"What pornography?" Mrs. Wentworth asks, and now she looks a little guilty. "You mean—that picture Cory took of herself? I found that and had her delete it. We talked about it."

Mr. Wentworth stays quiet, glaring at his wife, but he doesn't say anything. Neither does the detective or my parents.

"We went over why it was a bad idea, and she heard me," Mrs. Wentworth keeps going, talking mostly to the detective. "She understands—but how on earth could you call that pornography?"

"When Del and Cory took pictures of themselves, in the eyes of the law, that's creating child pornography." Detective Henning shifts his attention to my parents. "When your son accepted the picture, he received and remained in possession of child pornography, as did Cory, but she's too young to be charged."

I'm staring at the phone in all the junk in his arms, feeling like I need to explain, not that anybody will listen to me. "She sent me a picture of herself," I mumble. "It was just a picture. We thought—we thought it was safer than having sex. Better than having sex."

Dad gets hold of my shoulder. "Did you show it to any-body else?"

"No!" I pull away from Dad's grip, furious at that thought, even madder that Detective Henning and his buddies probably took a good long look at Cory and the rest of the girls, too. "I just—I just sent her a picture back." I wish I could die. "She asked me to."

"For God's sake, the kids took pictures of themselves—nobody did this to them," Mrs. Wentworth says while Mom tries to get me to sit down. "They wanted to and they did. They aren't selling this stuff."

Detective Henning sighs. "Money doesn't have to be involved."

I sit down at the table again to make Mom happy, and she grabs my wrist, sort of holding my hand.

"Curiosity is natural," Mr. Wentworth says, even though he's still glaring at everybody. "Didn't you ever play doctor when you were little? How old were you when you made out with your girlfriend for the first time?"

For a second or two, Detective Henning just looks at him, then at Dad, then at me, and finally at Mom and Mrs. Wentworth. He seems to be sagging a little, maybe from holding on to the tape player and phone and notebook. "It's out of my hands. Everything goes to William Kaison, the DA, for review and he decides what charges get filed."

"What's he like?" Mom asks, still hanging onto my wrist

and pulling, but stopping as she finishes her question. Her voice has changed, and I know she's really upset.

For the first time tonight, Detective Henning looks outright unhappy, then completely uncomfortable. He faces my crying mother and Cory's mom, who's holding on to my mom, and he rubs his chin like he's trying to give himself time to figure out exactly the right thing to say.

Then, like he's speaking in some kind of ancient code, he says, "District Attorney Kaison . . . doesn't have children."

My parents and Cory's parents jerk like they've been slapped, and everything in the room changes. They pull in around me like a legion defending me from Detective Henning and the world, and my mother grabs me from behind, her arms around my neck so tight she's almost choking me.

"Del's through talking," my father says to Detective Henning. "We want a lawyer, and we want one right now."

Now

(I'm not sure I've got music for now. Maybe I should try harder to break the whole music addiction.)

The past is over. The story of my fourteenth year ends with Dad demanding a lawyer, and the lawyer giving us the facts on what I could be charged with and how many years of prison I'd be facing. Plea agreements got worked out, and I stood in court and told a judge I understood everything, and it was over. I went to juvenile, survived, got out on probation, and here I am, sitting in Branson's office.

Who am I?

I'm that guy. I'm that kid from the papers. I'm the one who—you know. Got convicted for pornography making and receiving pornography and other even worse stuff.

Why am I here?

I'm here because Christmas break is over and the court

says I have to show up, and I need Branson's recommendation to get off probation. I know the question is bigger than that, but right now in my life, it's hard to think past the moment.

What's the point?

I don't have an answer for that and I don't want to think about it too much.

Branson's big hands grip each rejection letter as he reads them, checking that college off on his grid.

His office is the opposite of Dr. Mote's. It's in a small office complex, not an old house. It's always cool, never warm. And it's not at all built for comfort or familiarity. Everything in Branson's world is made out of wood and leather. Everything feels stiff. He's got pictures of cops and officers hanging everywhere, and a big portrait of the president under a snapshot of a waving flag on the wall behind his head. He has a nameplate on his desk, with his credentials as a juvenile probation officer.

This place smells like polish and cleanser and paper and ink. At least it doesn't smell like piss samples. Thank God I've never seen any of those sitting around. He's even got his holiday decorations all put away, and it's barely even January.

"What about Community?" Branson sounds gruff when he's working, but I don't let it bother me. Much.

I sit on the edge of the wooden chair in front of his big desk. "They didn't answer by mail."

When I glance at his grid, I notice it looks a lot like the one I keep on my little desk at home, but Branson's writing is bigger and bolder. He doesn't look up from his papers. "Did you follow up with a telephone call?"

"Yes, sir. The lady who answered told me no answer means no."

"Her name?"

I give him the woman's name, her phone number, the time I called, and the date I called.

"Did you ask to speak to her supervisor?" Now he looks up, silver eyebrows raised.

My guts sink. Is he kidding? But his dark eyes look way past serious. "I didn't think about that," I tell him, and hear the hint of a whimper in my tone.

"You should. You should try everything, Del." He smacks the papers down on his desk. "Don't let them off easily. Don't let them off at all."

"So . . . you're going to make me get arrested all over again for stalking or harassment?" I'm not being sarcastic. I really am nervous about that. The flag behind his head looks gigantic, and like it's growing out of his silver hair. Sideways red and white flames shooting out of a blue star field. I can't be assertive like he's wanting. I'm a criminal. A kid convict. An absolute nothing, and something less than nobody. How am I supposed to demand anything from anybody—least of all the people who have all the power?

Branson frowns. Narrows his eyes at me like he's

reading my thoughts. I'm used to this with Dr. Mote, but it's not so intense with her most of the time.

"You've got a point," he finally admits. "Let me make a call or two and get back to you."

For a second I just sit there, shocked, then squeak out, "Thanks."

Branson has done tons to help me in his own way, but this is the first time he's offered to do any of my "work" for me. He looks . . . different. Worried, maybe?

For the first time, it occurs to me that Branson's pushing me so hard on this college-and-future-plans thing because he has no idea what I'm supposed to do, either. My nerves jangle so loud I start hearing music in my brain, and it's "Space Oddity" by David Bowie, about an astronaut who launches off toward the moon. Something goes wrong with the spacecraft and he goes out to repair it, then gets lost forever.

Lost in space.

Back to that, because it's the best metaphor I can find. I'm holding on to my chair arms like I'm that astronaut, Major Tom, trying to keep my bearings thousands of miles away from anything that's familiar and makes sense.

Here am I sitting in a tin can, far above the world . . .

Branson's supposed to be Ground Control, like in the song. The guy's talking to the astronaut, trying to bring him home. But in the song, the astronaut never makes it back, and there's nothing Ground Control can do.

That couldn't be true, right? Branson's better than Ground Control. He knows the way back to Earth.

Doesn't he?

The clock in the back of my head, the one counting down to my eighteenth birthday, keeps right on ticking. How am I supposed to come up with some genius plan or set of options when Branson can't think of anything, either? There is no Ground Control anymore, is there? I'm just floating away, farther away, and I've been kidding myself that I'd ever make it home.

I am so totally screwed.

"Here's what I'm going to do," I say as Branson's fingers tap on his grid. He looks determined in that don't-you-dare-talk-back-to-me way, but also interested. "No more messing around. I'm going to write another request and send it to Community. Will that be a good start?"

Branson considers, then nods. "I'm going to call. Send them another letter."

"Yes, sir." That's what I say, but I have less than no idea how to make it work.

Branson shuffles his papers into a stack and asks, "Is Cherie Blankenship still giving you plenty of space?"

"She's keeping her distance." Like a dark thundercloud trying to figure out how to get close enough to hit me with lightning. "She hasn't been at the graveyard lately, not since before the holiday break when I told her I had a girlfriend."

"Hmm." He keeps looking at his papers.

Hmm is better than *hmph*, I guess.

"And how is the girlfriend?"

"Livia's fine." I try not to get tense even though I know he's about to hit me with—

"Does she know?"

I look at my sneakers, which seem absurdly battered and filthy against his shiny, polished wooden floor. "Part of it. That I got in trouble, that I've got a felony conviction and I'm on probation and have to see a therapist, that I'm working in a graveyard because nobody else would hire me, and that I might have trouble going to college."

"And the rest?"

"I put it off for a long time. The last three times I tried, she put it off."

I expect Branson to be like Dr. Mote and tell me to quit making excuses and get it done, but he goes quiet. After a while he says, "She really is a pretty thing. You just—you be careful."

And this time I'm sure I see worry on his face. For a second I get ticked, thinking he's worrying about how I'm treating her, then I realize I'm an idiot. He's worrying about what will happen to me when she knows everything and walks away without a second look back.

"You're close to the finish line," he tells me, confirming this.

"I know."

"Don't screw it up."

"I won't."

Branson gestures to the little restroom at the back of his office. "Leave me a sample before you go."

Sometimes stories get on my nerves—especially the ones where unfair things keep happening to the hero over and over, for no reason at all, and he valiantly overcomes it all.

Life isn't like that.

Not every hero can stay valiant. Sometimes, they can't even stay a hero, so what does that make them? A failure? A pussy? A total failure jerkwad with no hope on the horizon save finding a cemetery and digging rectangles in the ground for the town drunk?

I suppose I could go über-religious. I could say I sinned and God punished me, but most days, I try to believe in God, and I try to believe in a God who wouldn't want somebody done and finished with life before they're old enough to have hair in all the right places. Now that I've got hair—mostly in the right places, though I'm not saying a word about amounts or anything—I keep letting myself hope there's a way to put my life back together.

Other than the whole court-ordered thing, that's a big part of the reason why I keep showing up at Dr. Mote's office and sitting on her couch, which is still familiar, and still comfortable, and sometimes I get kind of scared, wondering what it'll be like to turn eighteen and not have to sit here anymore, wrapped in the pine paneling and the mountain pictures and tree pictures and beach pictures, staring across at her while she stares across at me. She's got on a skirt today, a long denim one, and it almost hides the top of her clogs—red, a light shade that looks funny against the green area rug.

Dr. Mote's leaning forward, and she knows I was just spaced out, so she asks her question again, never frowning or looking annoyed because I tapped out on her. "Did you have any idea how it would affect your life when you went to court and pleaded guilty?"

I can't really smell the pine paneling and the trees and mountains and beaches when I breathe, but I can smell the carpet and the couch. Kind of old and musty, but Dr. Mote burns vanilla candles, so it's vanilla-y old must, at least.

<Answer her.>

It's easier to focus on the vanilla must. On how the couch feels saggy and soft.

<I don't want to.>

I'm being stupid and I know it, but I can't make myself open my mouth.

<God, I'm worse than Clarence the rescued rooster, running from the people being good to me.>

"It didn't really matter whether I pleaded guilty or not." I'm kind of touching fourteen way back in my mind, so it's weird. "Cory told them the truth and so did I, because we thought we were supposed to. We thought it was the right thing to do, and so did our parents, and even after we got a lawyer, that's what he said to do, too. Now my mom and dad just feel like shit because they think they made me cooperate with the police that night."

Dr. Mote waits, not matching her green rug with her blue skirt and red shoes. She always knows when to talk and when to just sit there in her vanilla-smelling barrel chair and wait.

"We all thought we were doing the right thing," I say.

"Did you have any idea, one single clue, how it would affect your life?" She shifts in her chair a little, relaxing more, and I realize I didn't exactly answer what she asked me the first time.

I shake my head.

"Answer me out loud," Dr. Mote says.

We've talked about this before—how I push away feelings by going quiet, by not speaking out loud, or by saying "you" and "people" and "anyone" instead of "I" and "me."

Like, *You can't help wanting to beat the crap out of lawyers and police officers and people who keep telling you everything will be fine, when everyone knows it'll never be fine again.*

I can't help it. My fingers dig into the worn couch cushions. "I had no idea." I'm clenching my fists, wanting to stop, but can't—just can't, and I know Dr. Mote doesn't want me to stop. She'll be fine if I beat the living hell out of her ancient couch, or throw myself on her floor and pound on the boards until I brain-damage every spider in the basement.

"Maybe I deserved it." Whispering now, but I want to be shouting. "Somehow. Some way. Maybe I'm paying for doing stuff wrong in the eyes of God, if there is a God."

Dr. Mote shakes her head like I did a minute ago, cheating. "I'm not here to tell you you did anything wrong, Del."

She stays quiet for a time after that, and I don't think she's waiting. More like . . . considering, or finding her way. It usually makes me feel better when she has to do that, too, like maybe I'm not an idiot, but today, after the whole Branson incident, I start worrying that she has no idea how to help me, either. That maybe all our sessions have been her and me, both trying to find a way through a maze with no exit when all along I thought she knew the way.

When I can't take the silence anymore, I ask, "If God's there, do you think he forgives me?"

"Yes."

Dr. Mote's answer comes so fast, so certain, it makes me twitch on my comfortable couch cushion. She keeps on with, "The thought of God forgiving you—how did that make you feel?"

I could blow this off. I could blow her off, and therapy, too. I could just show up and sit here and not do any real work. Lots of people do, I guess.

"Good," I say. "Shit, are you going to start going on about me forgiving myself again?"

"No." Dr. Mote smiles even though I can tell she really didn't mean to. "I'm going to start going on about the fact

I'm not sure you did anything that needs forgiving. The whole sex before marriage issue I'll leave between you and your God. But what happened with you and Cory, in my opinion, it was natural."

She waits.

"It was understandable," she says after a while. "It was predictable. Cory didn't think it was wrong. You didn't think it was wrong. Neither of you was hurt by the natural, understandable choices you both made until a jacked-up district attorney made a big deal out of everything."

I can't say anything.

Dr. Mote's been direct about her opinion before, but not this direct. Calling William Kaison, Esquire, *jacked-up*—now, that's special.

"It wasn't wrong, Del." Another shrug, but it doesn't seem casual. "I don't think you and Cory were wrong at all."

She's tiptoed in this direction before, but never gone there. I'm not sure she should have. I spent all that time in Juvenile, and all these months in therapy, and all my time on probation accepting responsibility, and now, what's she saying?

I shouldn't have accepted it?

Christ, why am I getting pissed? What am I pissed at— which thing? What's she trying to do? "You aren't supposed to say stuff like that, that it wasn't wrong or my fault. This is court ordered. You're supposed to rehabilitate me."

Dr. Mote's whole body tightens as she leans forward, drilling me with those therapist eyes. I can almost smell the smoke as her brain tries to bore straight into mine. "I'm supposed to treat you, and we're running out of time. *You're* my patient, not the judge or that unbelievable bastard Kaison who did this to you. To Cory. To all of your poor friends."

Jacked-up.

Bastard.

I'm mature enough not to snicker when people older than me use bad language, but hearing it fly out of my therapist seems a little strange. Kaison deserves it, though, for sure.

"Thanks."

I think.

And I'm also thinking, *Maybe she does know the way home, but she's just been too hesitant and "professional" to show me.*

Dr. Mote waits while the wheels grind in my drilled-into brain, and what churns out is, "But if I decide that being with Cory wasn't wrong, that I've been completely screwed, what keeps me from making more mistakes? From doing something else that gets me arrested when I don't even know it's wrong?"

"Nothing."

My breath wheezes out like Dr. Mote just punched me in the stomach.

I . . . didn't expect that answer. At all. I didn't want to hear it. And I can't get my breath back. Everything my dad said a while ago comes whizzing back.

No control . . . Sometimes the bad stuff just shows up knocking and we have to answer the door . . .

"Nothing's keeping bad things from happening right now, Del—to you, to me, to the world." Dr. Mote leans forward again, letting me know I really, really need to listen. "None of us can see nightmares like William Kaison barreling down on our lives, or we'd run like hell and never, ever get hit. Avoiding life, avoiding making any concrete plans for your life—that's just one way you're pretending you can keep bad things from happening to you again."

The nervousness claws up my belly and into my throat, and suddenly, all I can think about is digging graves. My breath comes so short I wonder if I'm going to pass out. Dr. Mote just sits there and lets me flip out even though I'm not really sure why I'm flipping out.

"It's possible you were a victim in this, just like Cory. It's more than possible." She puts her hands together, and I have a weird thought that if I were sitting next to her, she would have put her fingers over mine, light, not intrusive, just enough to bring me out of airless space. "You're the real victim here, Del. All of you were, and I'm sorry."

"Therapy kind of sucked," I tell Fred, who sits on my chest looking at me with her yellow eyes with the big black dots in the center, like she really doesn't believe me. She makes a barking noise, so I know she's listening.

My headphones are off, lying beside me out of Fred's reach. She can snip through a headphone wire with one neat click of the beak, so I'm careful about that. I sit up slowly, shifting Fred to my shoulder, and I grab my notebook off the floor beside the bed.

I'm supposed to be writing a new letter to Community College, which is about thirty miles from my house. Branson knows I've got absolutely no chance with those people. They probably have the newspapers with all the headlines about me on file in their library, for God's sake.

"Fred," Fred says, sounding confident as she marches down my arm and locates herself on the bedspread.

"Fred," I say right back to her.

She deposits a little Fred gift on my floor just to make me have to bend over and wipe it up with the paper towel wad I always carry when I've got her out in the house.

I wish I could call Marvin, but he's at work. I wish I could call Livia, but she can't talk after seven at night due to "family time." Mom and Dad are at the Humane Society with their cage cleaning volunteer brigade. It's just me, and the sleeping rooster outside in his coop, and the rescue cats and dogs sacked out in various locations all over the house, Gertrude asleep on the couch because she's full of the tuna I slipped her after dinner, and Fred, who's trying to pick at my notebook pages.

"Fred," Fred says again between assault attempts, like she's trying to help me.

"Fred is a good bird." I ooch her away from the pages and she scoots down my leg to my ankle and starts picking at my sock. That's okay. I let her eat my socks. It's one of her favorite activities.

The notebook paper just sits in front of me, looking blank. If I called Branson, I might tell him to stuff this whole letter thing in his ear.

I need to make myself real. Make my situation real.

Okay, fine. How do I get real?

I imagine myself in this big bubble of immunity, able to say anything or do anything without being afraid. I imagine myself before all of this happened. I even picture myself talking to a whole bunch of waxy-looking big-shot types at the special legislative session. If I could still be me, the real me way down deep inside, I'd write stuff that didn't make anybody feel happy or comfortable. I'd write . . .

Dear Ms. Johnston:

My name is Del Hartwick and I have a felony conviction. In the eyes of the law, I am a criminal. I can't tell you I didn't do it, because I did. I can't tell you it was right, but I'm not sure it was wrong.

I was fourteen years old, and my girlfriend was thirteen, just a few months younger than me. Neither of us understood about age of consent laws, or that sending each other pictures of ourselves wasn't legal. We both wanted to be together, and we thought we were being responsible. The law says it was wrong, so I have to accept that, but I would like you to know the rest of the truth.

I'm not what those charges say about me. I'm not anything like that.

I'm Del.

I'm seventeen.

I have a parrot and a best friend and a girlfriend and a job digging graves. I have good grades and I want to be an avian vet, and maybe help my folks with the Humane Society and all their animal rescue operations.

My life got stolen from me, and I want it back. This application means a lot to me. I'm lost in space and I want to find a way home. Nobody else can get me back to the planet, so I have to do it myself. That's why I'm writing to you, to ask permission to apply, and to ask your help in getting a fair chance at going to college.

My name is Cain Delano Hartwick, and I want a future. Let me apply, judge me on what I can do, and give me a chance. Please.

I sign the letter with a big, scrawled *DEL*. Then I take off my sock and give it to Fred, get off the bed and go to my desk, fold up the letter, seal it in an envelope, address it, stamp it, and mark Community College off my grid for the second time. Tomorrow, I'll let Mom mail it because it doesn't matter, and I'm sure now that Branson knows this.

Fred makes a fluttering noise. I brace myself. She takes off from the bed and lands easily on my shoulder a second later.

She says, "*Cerote*," then lowers her beak and neck, begging for a scratch.

I rub one finger across the top of her head. "Turd. Yep. A great big stinky one."

Now

(Now can exist without background music. I think.)

There's something eerie and beautiful about a campfire in a graveyard. Harper's passed out in his house. It's freezing outside, and it's already dark way too early in the evening. I've finished my one grave, and Livia's got the blaze built high out in the back section of the graveyard next to the house, burning up some of the wood Harper and I had stacked in big piles. Fred's travel cage is hanging on a low branch near enough to the fire to keep her warm, but far enough away to keep her safe. She's staring at the fire and making crazy whistles.

Livia's wearing a black sweater and jeans and black gloves. Her hair's loose around her shoulders to keep her ears warm.

She's eating the last of the hot dogs she brought us, and she's already pushed the little picnic basket off of our quilt so there's nothing between us.

"Isn't the moon beautiful tonight?" She wipes her gloves on a paper towel, balls up the towel and pitches it into the fire to make a flare, then stares at the star-filled sky again. "It looks like a round piece of ice."

Her breath ribbons into the darkness when she talks, joining the fire's smoke. I could stare at her forever.

You're all I've ever wanted, but I'm terrified of you. . . .

A line from "Dracula's Wedding," by Outkast. I make myself quit thinking about it because I'm trying not to hide in my music.

Still, here in front of all the crackling flames and smoke, under the ice moon, those words seem perfect, and Livia's perfect, but I have to stop it all, stop everything tonight, even though I'm not sure why—just instinct that I've let it go on long enough. I'm feeling numb from all the digging and the cold, even though I'm sitting a few feet from the fire and right next to the smartest, prettiest, nicest girl in history. Maybe I'm just getting ready for what it's going to feel like when she's done with me, when I have to watch her walk away, get in her car, and drive down the dark road.

"I have to keep track of the time." She glances at her watch. "Dad's coming home from work early because of a staff meeting. I want to get to the house before he does."

She reaches out one gloved hand. I take it, feeling the

warm leather against my cold skin. "Okay. This probably won't take long, anyway."

Her smile fixes on her face, then it slides away, and I know she knows I'm going to try, and that tonight, she has to listen.

Terrified of you . . .

My insides try to lock up, but I make myself keep breathing. No panicking. No backing out. It's only words. I need to say them and be done with it.

"What happened when I was fourteen, it wasn't ugly, but it sounds ugly." I look away from Livia and into the fire. Fred whistles at the flames, then she whistles at me, and I can feel her getting nervous because I'm so nervous. "People made it ugly, anyway."

Livia squeezes my fingers. "You don't have to do this."

"I do. You know I do. It's way past time."

She stops talking. Closes her eyes and breathes. Then she leans toward me and kisses me just once, fast, and for a second, her face is an inch from mine and she's the only thing in the universe. I can't believe I ever got to have her, even for this long minute in my life.

Fred fire-alarm shrills, and we both jump.

When my pulse slows back down to normal, or as normal as it's going to get talking about all this mess, I try to get started. "I had a girlfriend named Cory, and she was younger than me. Just a few months."

Livia counts out loud. "You told me your birthday.

I'm four weeks and two days younger. September thirtieth
for me."

"Cory's birthday was October eighteenth."

"Virgo and Libra." Livia's face seems to glow in the
orange firelight. She has to be nervous because she never
talks about stuff like zodiac signs. "Are we a lot different,
Cory and me?"

"Well, yeah, in lots of ways." Why didn't it occur to me
that Livia would want to know about Cory? Stupid. I should
have thought more about this. "She was pretty. You . . .
you're beautiful." I don't like the comparing, but Livia seems
to need to know, so I keep trying. "She was into sports and
singing, and you're into art and writing. I liked her, but we
were, you know, really young and stuff. I like you in different ways. With you and me, everything's deeper."

I think I love you.

That's probably a line from a song, or a lot of songs, but
tonight, it's all mine. I just wrote it in my own head, and
I mean it. I told Cory that, but I didn't know, not then. I
didn't know about feeling like this.

Livia stands up in one fast, fluid motion, like a dancer
about to run across the stage and leap into the air.

I get up, too, ignoring Fred's alarm screech.

The change makes my brain spin for a second, and I
have to take a few seconds to get a grip. Fred and the fire on
my left, Livia on my right, and not far away, Harper's house,
dark in all the windows. The graveyard stretches in all

directions from our quilt. The moon's still one big round piece of ice over our heads.

Livia clenches her hands together, but when I move toward her, she steps back. "No. Go on. Tell me and get it over with so we can both stop worrying about it, okay?"

I spend a little time fishing around for phrases and descriptions, since I don't have any of this rehearsed. I should have rehearsed a thousand times, but I couldn't, so I'm just standing here being a giant jackass about it all again.

Get. Over. It.

"Cory and I were getting serious with each other, and we—you know, we did some stuff together."

"How much stuff?" Livia's frown mixes in with the shadows from the night and the fire.

"She texted me a picture of herself naked, and I sent her one of me." Shit, this is embarrassing, and right this second I hate all the coaches from Good-bye Night and all the detectives at the police station and every lawyer and especially William Kaison for making me have to tell anybody this. Ever. Stuff like this should be private for always, unless a person wants to share it.

Share, Del. Share it all.

My shrug muscle's trying to fire but I'm holding it back for now. "We kissed and made out a few times."

Livia's waiting for the bad stuff, and I'm trying to figure out how to explain that she just heard the bad stuff, as far as Kaison and the law were concerned.

Before I get hold of what to say next, a quiet voice behind me says, "Why her, Del? Is it because she's older?"

I spin so fast I get goofy in the head again, and suddenly I'm face-to-face with Cherie, only that's disorienting, too, because she's got on jeans and a white sweater and no weird makeup, and she looks . . . normal.

"She's definitely prettier." Cherie looks past me at Livia. "Livia, right? I asked around until I figured out your name. Too bad about your sister and all that. That must have been total hell."

I hear Livia's quick breath, but I can't see her, and I can't imagine what she's thinking. "Cherie—"

"Del's a convicted rapist." Cherie's too-black hair looks like night shadows clinging to her head. "Did you know that, Livia?"

The words fall out of Cherie's mouth like a body dumped from a casket, thumping on the ground, still and cold and too horrible to look at.

I manage to turn until I can see Livia, too, but she's gone frozen. She can't talk or say anything or do anything but blink. I can't say anything, either. I feel like my heart's getting staked and I'll be a dead body, too, and maybe that's better than trying to stay alive through the rest of this, because Cherie's not finished.

"You're not from here, so you probably don't know, but Del went to jail for three counts of rape of a child, and for making and receiving child pornography."

Cherie glances at me, and I think I'm expecting all this rage, but she looks scared. Sort of confused. I wish I could be mad. I know I should be furious; I know I should want to punch her right in the face, but really, I just want to find my jacket, wrap it around her, and send her home.

"I see." Livia's voice has turned to stone. Her face has turned into a marble monument of the fairy girl she used to be. Her words come out steady, but her hands are shaking, and she's not looking at me.

Does she want to scrub me off her, to shower and run water in her ears until even the memory of talking to me is gone? This is my fault for not just wearing a damned sign around my neck to get the labeling over with. Rapist. Pornographer. Worse than any graveyard or dead body. I feel numb and cold, and I know for sure now, I'm the biggest chickenshit in the entire universe.

"It's not like it sounds," I say to Cherie. "You know it's not."

"It is what it is," Cherie shoots back. "You should have told Livia what she was getting into. She didn't know. I did, and I liked you, anyway."

"I'm sorry I don't have feelings for you." Am I really saying this in front of Livia? Shit. "I'm sorry I hurt you and got you in trouble with your parents. This isn't the way to handle it."

Cherie just glares. "Piss off."

"May I speak to you?" Livia's question cuts through

everything, each word a silent silver blade flashing through the darkness. "Inside?"

Before I can answer her, she says to Cherie, "Thanks for doing what you thought was right, if that's what you just did."

Cherie tries to give her the same piss-off look she gave me, but the expression dies halfway formed. Something in Livia's steady gaze killed it, just like it's killing Cherie's temper and her mouth and whatever part of my heart's still left alive.

"Whatever!" Cherie storms away from us into the grave-yard, kicking divots of grass with each thumping step.

I think about telling her that the road's back the other way, but she knows her way around this place well enough, and Livia's walking toward Harper's dark house.

I follow her.

It's not locked, and a few seconds later, we're in Harper's living room with a single lamp making the only light between us. Harper's probably out cold in the bedroom. I don't know because the door's shut, and for now, Livia and I are alone and she's looking at me.

Not yelling.

Not crying.

Not reaching out for me or touching me or giving me any hint this is going to be okay, but she's . . . here. In front of me.

She's giving me a chance.

I'm melting.

Maybe numb and cold were better, because melting

makes me start to shake. It makes hot dogs flood back up my throat, bitter in my mouth as I fumble around, getting back to where I left off before this chance goes poof and Livia goes poof, too.

"Cory and I made out three times and sent each other naked pictures of ourselves—just one each, I mean. It was right before high school started."

Livia keeps very still, like she's waiting for the really bad thing, how I lost it, how I held down my girlfriend and forced her to have sex against her will and beat her. Or maybe how I got it on with her little sister or some other baby or kid—I mean, rape of a child, right? It's horrible. It's got to be horrible.

"In this state, the official age of consent is sixteen, but it's not that simple. If teenagers have sex, they both have to be at least fourteen." I keep my eyes on hers, watching for any change or flicker. "So when Cory and I made out and I touched her in a sexual way, by law, I committed rape of a child. Three times. The law doesn't care that I was only a few months older than her, or that she wanted me to touch her."

Nothing from Livia.

Nothing at all.

She's still waiting, then she latches onto everything I just said. Her eyebrows lift, breaking that awful stone expression. "You . . . never had actual sex?"

I shake my head.

"Oral?" Livia's arms have loosened up despite the question she just asked.

"No. Just touching. Fingers. That's it." God, I can't believe we're having this discussion, but thanks to Kaison, this is my life now. All about sex one way or another, even if it's something I've never gotten to enjoy.

Livia's fallen into Kaison's sex mud-puddle with me, because she's still asking questions. "And she wanted it? Cory. She wanted what you did?"

My face turns red-hot, but I manage to nod. "It was her idea. So were the pictures. We thought they were okay because they weren't really sex—we thought they were better. But because we were under eighteen when we took the pictures, the law says we made child pornography. When we sent them to each other, we distributed child pornography. Because I kept the picture she sent, I was in possession of child pornography. She didn't get charged, since she wasn't old enough to agree to anything. I'm kind of glad about that."

Now she remembers the news stories. Now she knows. I can tell by the fast switch on her face, the jaw loosening, the way she's looking at me now. I've seen that look before, a lot of times. "The Duke's Ridge Eight. You had some friends—"

"Yeah. They took some pictures, too." I fold my arms and shiver. Harper's house is cold, probably because he gets drunk and forgets to turn on the heat. "We got caught with them at a city league sleepover, and the coaches turned them in to the police. Nobody else admitted to having sex or doing sexual stuff, so they're just stuck with the porn charges."

Livia seems to be winding down as I crank to the extreme, wanting to crawl out of my own skin and bones and just . . . leave. Jump up and down. Yell and bang my head on the wall.

"Did you really go to jail, Del?" Like she's ticking down a list of what's real and what's Cherie's bullshit. The sad thing is, it's all real, and it's all bullshit, too.

"The lawyer my parents hired advised us to sign the confession to keep it in Juvenile and cut my sentence." I keep staring at Livia, but her face doesn't change. For a wild second or two, I feel like I'm writing to the colleges, putting mechanical words on paper that nobody will bother reading, not once they see what kind of convictions I have.

"You didn't know about the rest. About what would come later." Livia says this with sympathy shining in her face like the ice moon glowing in the dark sky outside.

"With all the craziness, my parents and I didn't realize that even though my record will get sealed when I turn eighteen, I'll still have to register as a sex offender forever, at least in this state. In most states. So it won't be over." Now I have to look away from her at the stack of beer cans taking up the far right corner of Harper's little living room. "It'll never really be over."

"You—" Livia starts. Stops. Her voice snatches my attention right back from the beer cans. "Forever." She shakes her head. "For making out with your girlfriend and getting a sext from her?"

"And sexting her once." Yes, Del, by all means, let's get every detail correct.

This time, the silence goes on for a while. Livia's throat works without making any words, and her dark eyes just keep studying me like she's about to find some major clue or answer that'll make everything I told her make sense.

"That's the stupidest thing I've ever heard in my life." She's smiling as she says this, and I can't tell if she's serious, or seriously pissed. "I can't believe it's true."

My heart stutters. "I can get you the court documents, or let you talk to my folks so you know I'm not lying." *Desperate* doesn't quite cover what's happening in my brain. More like *nuclear panic*. It's real. It wrecked my life. And now I need to prove it to have a shot with my girl?

"No, no, not what you're saying." Livia waves both hands in front of her. "What happened—what they did to you. Are you serious? You got convicted of all that awful stuff for touching your girlfriend and looking at a naked picture of her?"

She's . . . not freaked out. She's confused and angry, but all of a sudden her expression's reminding me of Mom when she's trying to work out a puzzle. Livia's thinking. But she's accepting and she's believing, and she's still right here in front of me, talking. That might be the best part of all.

All the power drains out of my knees and I take the few steps to Harper's dirty counter so I can lean on it. "I may be the world's only virgin rapist," I hear myself mutter, then wish I could roll that little confession right back into my mouth. I'm such an idiot.

Livia comes over to the counter, not up close, but close enough for me to know she's not totally disgusted. "And you didn't even rape her, and she told them."

"Yeah. And her folks told the police, and my parents did, and her mom and dad didn't want to press charges, but it was up to the DA, and he took it to court."

"I feel sick."

I go back to studying her face, trying to figure out, sick about what—me? Everything she just heard?

From somewhere a million miles away, a smoke alarm screeches.

Instinct makes me glance toward the other end of the counter—where Fred's cage isn't.

"I didn't bring her in," I mumble.

The alarm-screech echoes through the graveyard outside the house over and over and over again.

"Fred?" Livia asks. She's looking around, too.

Cold dread stabs into every muscle in my body.

The fire . . .

Oh God.

No more thought. No more breath. I bolt for the door as Fred screeches and screeches.

Livia beats me to the front of the house. She throws the

door wide open, and we both charge into Rock Hill, beating it toward the fire and the blanket and the tree where I
left Fred's cage hanging on the bottom branch.

Cherie's already there.

She has Fred's cage in her hands, and the door's open,
and she's just standing there, crying, and Fred . . .

Fred's not in the cage.

Heat blasts all over me, not fire, not outside fire. "Where
is she?" I shout, my voice so loud it hurts my ears. "What
did you do to her?"

"She was alone—I thought . . . I . . ." Cherie holds out
the cage. "The door came open and she flew. She flew
away."

I snatch the cage away from her and throw it on the
ground. "You're lying! I heard her screeching."

"I let her out. I didn't mean to!" She starts wailing, but
I block her out. My heart rips and pounds in my throat, my
mouth.

"Fred!" I yell, trying to turn in every direction at the
same time. "Fred? Hello?"

"Fred," Livia calls, and starts walking in the direction
Cherie's pointing. Away, like she said. Into the sky. Into the
thick woods bordering Harper's property.

God, it's so cold. It's so damned cold!

The darkness seems to get even darker.

"Fred!" I grab her cage off the ground. "Fred!"

Not loud now, because I'm crying and hugging the cage

and not wanting to let myself know that my bird is gone. My Fred. My bird. Gone forever into the woods. Gone.

Cherie rushes past me bawling about it being an accident and I don't listen to her, and she never stops running. I feel like I'm completely losing my shit as an engine turns over in the distance and tires squeal out of the cemetery and away, away, gone like Fred.

I want to run into the woods and climb every tree. I have to. Fred's in there somewhere, maybe still alive, at least for now, at least for a few hours. If she gets high enough to avoid raccoons and foxes and coyotes and opossums, if no owl sees her, then maybe I can find her and bring her home before she freezes to death or starves to death or dies of dehydration.

It's over, idiot.

It can't be over. Not just like that, because of an accident. A split second of Cherie being stupid or mad or mean.

It's over.

"Fred." I sit down, hugging the cage, feeling how totally and completely empty it is, not sure what to do next or how to do it.

My bird, my best little friend.

Harper's got flashlights somewhere. I have to find them. I have to stop blubbering like a frigging idiot and get moving.

"It'll be okay, Del." Livia's voice floats down to me, way too much like the sort-of lie I told Marvin the night we all got arrested. "We'll find her. Come on. Get up. We'll find her, and she'll be okay."

Now

NOW is frozen.

NOW is too hard for words.

"Do you have any idea what time it is?" Mom's yelling before I even shut the door. She looks wild, her hair sticking out in all directions and her green SPCA shirt smudged with brown streaks that look suspiciously like graveyard dirt. She's storming toward us from around the corner in the living room, which is why she doesn't see Livia.

Dad, who is standing in the hallway between us and the living room, does. Which is why he's not saying anything. He's got on jeans and his SPCA shirt, the blue one, and his shirt is dirty, too.

Mom roars up beside him and spots Livia standing

beside me, and her sneakers squeak like brakes on the hard-wood. I know they're taking in my scratched hands and torn jeans, the cut on Livia's face where she got hit with a pine branch, and the fact she's holding my hand. I'm so cold I'm numb. Livia's face is tear streaked and we're both red eyed and hoarse from yelling.

I feel empty. I can't even talk, and Livia's teeth are chattering.

Dad looks like he's trying to work up a reasonable set of questions because the clock on the wall says fifteen past eleven. After curfew. Way too late.

"Where's Fred?" Mom asks, zeroing in on the problem and already raising her hand to her chest. "We came to the graveyard looking—your blanket, we found it and the fire, but you two weren't anywhere around."

"Harper wasn't much help," Dad mutters. "We were thinking about calling the police, but . . ."

But all of us would let each other freeze to death on a cold winter night before we'd ask the police for anything. I get that. I think Livia probably does, too.

"Honey, where's Fred?" Mom's voice sounds worried and high-pitched.

She's gone.

I can't say it, but my eyes are telling Mom, and her eyes are filling up with tears.

Fred's gone.

"There was an accident," Livia squeezes my hand as she

talks. "Cherie Blankenship let Fred out of her travel cage and she flew away into the woods."

Mom's hugging me before Livia finishes talking, and then she's hugging both of us and Dad's there, too, both of his hands on my shoulders.

"We looked"—my voice chokes out, sputters back into motion—"for hours. And we called. Nothing." My mother still smells like raspberries under all the Humane Society and graveyard-searching stink. Raspberries. Sweet and fresh and momlike. With her arms around me and Livia beside me and dad behind me, I feel stupid and small but not like I'm floating away, because my mother still smells like raspberries.

"I'm sorry, son," Dad tells me, and I know he means it. "She's roosting by now because it's dark. We'll go with you in the morning before school at first light to look again. Maybe we'll have better luck."

She's roosting. Not, she's been eaten by an owl or she's freezing to death or she's out in the pitch-black night all alone.

Fred's roosting.

It sounds better.

"You're both freezing," Mom's saying as she lets us go. "Come to the kitchen and let me make you something warm to drink—and oh, honey, that cut on your forehead." To my dad, she says, "Go get the first-aid kit. We need to clean that up."

.   .   .

Mom and Livia seem to like each other, talking nervously but fast back and forth, sometimes finishing each other's sentences as Mom peroxides Livia's cut and dabs on antibiotic ointment.

Dad and I have our second cup of cocoa, and I'm not blubbering like a baby, so we've made a little progress. My fingers are thawing. It feels warm in our small kitchen at our antique wooden table with its wooden chairs and Mom's decorative horn of plenty spilling out apples and pears and oranges on the spring-green table runner. Mom always puts out spring decorations in February. Dad calls it wishful thinking, but she insists it's "hopeful thinking."

I watch Mom and Livia, and catch, "Cherie Blankenship, that girl's been such a problem for Del. . . ."

"I don't think she meant any harm. . . ."

"Maybe not, but therapy could help that child. . . ."

My insides ache, watching them, watching how frenetic Mom is as she helps Livia and talks to her and listens to her.

It hurts because it could have been like this. My life. It could have been about baseball and school and dating and pretty girls my mom approves of sitting in my kitchen while Dad grins into his cocoa. This could have been my world, my planet.

"Livia's nice," Dad says, still more to his cocoa than to me. "I knew—well. She's even prettier than—well, she's—she's nice."

He's struggling not to be weirded out by the whole situation, me with a girl after more than three years.

The banging on the front door makes everybody look up at the same time. Livia takes hold of Mom's wrist, and her dark eyes get really, really big.

"Oh my God," she whispers. "What time is it?"

"Late," Mom tells her, then her eyes get big, too. "Did you call your family and let them know you'd be late?"

"I forgot my cell phone." Livia gets up from her chair as Dad heads down the hallway and the banging on the door gets louder. She pushes past Mom and me to get out of the kitchen, hurrying to catch up with Dad as he reaches the door and pulls it open.

The front porch light lights up the big man outside, a dark-haired mountain in jeans and a heavy flannel shirt. He's got huge hands that make huge fists, and he's breathing fast, sending up jets like smoke signals.

"My daughter's car is in your driveway," he says, part worry and part accusation.

"Yes," Dad starts, but Livia interrupts him with, "I'm here. I'm fine."

Dad steps out of the way to let Mr. Mason inside, and then ushers everyone into the living room. It's the biggest space in the house, with two couches and two recliners and a big television and hardwood floors—but Mr. Mason seems to take up a lot of the room. He stops with Livia in front of

the far couch, and Mom and I join Dad near the living room
door.

"This was the first house after the graveyard," Mr.
Mason says to Livia. He sounds furious, but also worried. "I
didn't know where to start looking after I searched the cemetery, but your car was here."

Livia faces her father. There's no hint of whine or anger
or defensiveness when she says, "I'm sorry, Dad. It's been a
bad night and I got really distracted. I just realized what time
it was."

Mr. Mason's cheeks look red, like they've been scrubbed
by the cold and all of his emotion. He squares off with his
daughter, and now he seems to be towering over her with
those fists still clenched. "What the hell happened?"

I feel his question in my gut, because it's accusation now
that his worry's ratcheting up. I'm doing *tense-wary*, getting
ready to help Livia if he gets much louder. Dad gets hold of
my right forearm and clamps down hard, shaking his head
slowly.

"Bullet and a target," he murmurs so that I can hear
him, and that image keeps me still.

For the moment.

Livia doesn't seem afraid of her father. It's more like
she's upset with herself. "Del works at the graveyard." She
tips her hand toward me. "His parrot flew away and got lost.
We were trying to find her."

Mr. Mason glares at Livia, but his attention shifts in my direction.

I have no idea if I'm supposed to say anything or not, and Mom and Dad don't seem any more certain than me. In a fit of not knowing what else to do, my parents introduce themselves and they introduce me, too, using my whole name. My very weird and recognizable name.

Mr. Mason's face tightens, and a narrow-eyed scowl slowly creeps over his face, and I realize he knows. He remembers my name from the news.

"You. You're . . ." He points at me and takes a step, then Dad gets between us before Mr. Mason can say anything else.

"Del's parrot escaped her cage," Dad repeats, like the truth will make any difference. "Your daughter was kind enough to help him search for the poor bird, and we appreciate her help."

"Go get in the car, Livia," Mr. Mason says without taking his eyes off me.

"Dad—"

"Now."

Livia gives me a look that tells me she doesn't care what he says or does. I gaze back at her, grateful but worried and still not sure about anything. It's me breathing fast now, and Mom, too. Seeing her scared digs deep, and I try to think of something to make this all okay.

"You move or I'm calling the cops right now," Mr. Mason tells Livia.

Her mouth comes open. "For what?"

Now she sounds angry. Defiant.

Mr. Mason doesn't react to her at all because he's still staring over Dad's shoulder, right into my face. "He's not allowed to be around you. I know he's not."

That's not true, but Livia doesn't know it. I see worry cloud her ticked-off expression, softening it to concern and confusion.

"It's okay," I tell her because I don't want her in any more trouble. "You can go. Mom and Dad will help me look for Fred in the morning."

For some reason, she looks hurt instead of relieved.

"Don't you talk to her." Mr. Mason points his finger at me. "Don't you say another word to my daughter."

Livia's staring at me and her eyes are telling me *No, I'm not going just because he tells me to. I don't care. You matter to me.*

She matters to me a lot, too. I want her to stay until she's ready to go, but her dad's big and pissed and in my living room, and I'm not sure what's about to happen. I feel myself going limp, like when pinhead Jonas gets in my face, because he might hit me and I can't hit back.

If Mr. Mason hits me, it might be the only punch I ever take. I'm scared, but I'm more mad. I don't know what Dad is, other than in front of me, where he's likely to get hit first. Mom's beside me, saying something about *calming down and talking like rational people.*

"Go to the car," Mr. Mason tells Livia again, this time

through his teeth. His glare never lets up and I feel it like lasers on my face, but it's Livia I'm looking at.

Ask me to stay, her face pleads. *Ask me to stay and I will. Let him do whatever—we can handle it.*

"You—ah, you probably should go," I tell her. "That would be best."

The words hit her. Wound her.

Cherie's laughter sounds in my head, along with her favorite insult.

Pussy.

Livia slips out of the living room without looking at me or my parents and heads out our front door, letting it bang shut behind her.

I want to run right after her, but my father and Livia's father are standing inches apart. Livia's father becomes Clarence the rooster in my head, and I'm sure he's going to jump at Dad, spurs out.

Dad's not trying to talk Mr. Mason down. This is one rooster he's not trying to tame and save. He's got his fists clenched like Mr. Mason's, and I've never seen that from my dad, not ever.

Pussy, Cherie's voice says again, this time with no laughing, but maybe it's my voice. I'm still limp. Just standing there. I'm doing nothing. I feel the weight of it, the not moving, in my hair and teeth and skin and bones. Helpless. Useless.

"Go to your room, Del." Mom's voice is quiet but insistent.

I should argue. I should stand with my father or at least go after my girl, but I hear her engine gunning, and her tires spin on the gravel. I'm moving before I think about arguing with Mom, doing what she told me to do instead of going after Livia.

Piece of dirt. Useless. That's all I am.

I have no options, no way of doing anything without facing more trouble, and I can't stand that, not for Livia or Dad or anybody.

What kind of person am I?

I keep moving even when I hear Mr. Mason say, "You stay away from my daughter, you little bastard. You keep your hands off her."

"That's enough," Dad tells him in a voice like his clenched fists, hard and strange and dangerous. "I don't know what you've heard or read, but obviously you don't know the whole story about my son. He only—"

"I don't give a damn!" Mr. Mason cuts Dad off, looking three times more furious. "Nothing you say or *explain* will make it okay for that pervert to go *near* my daughter, understand?"

Mom heads for the kitchen phone as I reach the stairs, and I know she's pretending to go call the police.

Mr. Mason probably doesn't know she's pretending, and

after everything that happened to his family, I bet he's as scared of cops as we are.

I take the stairs two at a time, then turn at the landing to see him backing out of the living room toward the door, refusing to turn his back on my father. He glances in my direction. "If you touch her, I'll break your neck."

Mom makes it to the kitchen and picks up the telephone.

Mr. Mason goes out the door and slams it behind him.

Dad stays where he is and so does Mom and so do I until we all hear the grumble of a second car's engine and see headlights sweep across the front window.

"You okay?" Dad asks. I'm not sure who he means. The house has gone so still and quiet he might have been talking to the rooster out back.

Mom sighs and I hear the faint beep of her punching off the receiver. "I'm good. Del?"

I stay on the landing and can't say anything. I'm cold inside, and empty and numb. Fred's gone. Livia's gone.

Livia's gone.

Livia . . .

Nothing, absolutely nothing seems real, except it all seems too real at the same time. That eighteen inches of dirt I piled on my past, it's all swept away, and there's nothing inside me but coffins and sewn-shut eyes and things that shouldn't see the light again. The dead zone is back. It's probably going to stay forever this time.

"You didn't do anything wrong, Del," Mom says from

the kitchen, though she doesn't sound totally convinced. Then, "I'm so sorry about Fred, honey."

"And the girl," Dad says.

His voice echoes in my head.

Livia.

My parents don't have to tell me I can't see her again. They don't have to fight with me or argue with me or watch me vow to love her forever or storm out of the house or any other stupid shit. Livia and I aren't eighteen, and I'm totally clear who's in charge—and that Mr. Mason is too much of a risk to me and my family and even Livia, depending on what kind of person he is.

Dead zone. Everything inside me, it's going underground. The air feels chilled as I climb the rest of the steps like a badly oiled robot, jerking at the joints.

I imagine Fred out in the dark woods, huddled in some tree, scared and alone with no hope of getting home. I'd give anything to hear her little birdie *hello.*

"Del?" Mom's calling after me from downstairs, but I can't answer. I just don't want to talk anymore, at all.

Now

"Not a lot of use in this." Harper's bloodshot eyes look like red puddles in the gray light. His chapped, stubbly cheeks are even darker red as he switches off his flashlight near the edge of the woods. "It's going on three days. That bird's frozen solid or long gone. She's probably winging it back to Mexico."

"She's an African parrot, but she was probably born in captivity in the States." I search all the low-hanging branches I can see for the third time this morning, and I think about how Fred blew into that man's garage. Was this how it happened? Did somebody who adored her look away for five minutes and just let her get lost forever?

"Your—uh—that girl, she didn't come by this week-end," Harper says, casually, but fishing.

The words gig me worse than any hook.

I clamp my jaw shut for a second and keep looking at the trees, trying not to think about Livia's face or her eyes or the way it felt to hold her hand—but, of course, I do. When I finally unlock my mouth, I manage, "Her dad got pissed because she stayed out late looking for Fred. Looking for Fred with *me*, I mean."

"He knows about the trouble?"

"Everybody knows." Why did he have to bring up Livia? It's not like I'm not already thinking about her myself, every five seconds in between worrying about Fred.

"Haven't seen Marvin much, either," Harper says.

I shut off my flashlight, too, because there's too much light to use it now. "He's busy with his job and this girl named Lee Ann, and getting ready for Notre Dame."

"He backed off when you had that girl here all the time," Harper mutters. "I think it made him nervous."

I don't answer him.

He keeps quiet as we cover the last of the path back to Rock Hill, until we get right to the edge of the woods. That's when he comes up with, "You don't act like a shit head and start blowing everything off and kicking doors and punching holes in walls like lots of kids in your situation. One day that's gonna mean a lot."

"Yeah?" I turn back to the woods and call Fred one more time, looking at each tree, straining my ears for any hint of a word or a whistle or a fire-alarm screech. "When?"

All I hear is the wind and Harper's wheezy breathing.

"Sooner or later, hard work pays off, kid," he says. He coughs, and the wet noise makes my skin crawl. "And you work hard."

I shrug, feeling another flicker of the anger Dr. Mote and Branson stay on my ass about expressing. "I've always worked hard, and it got me arrested and kicked off planet Earth."

"It's getting you good grades and you're keeping your job here." Harper coughs again, and this time he spits off to the side. Yellow with red flecks. I try not to look.

So, I'm keeping my grades and my job. But not my parrot. Not my girlfriend. Not my best friend. What about my sanity? Guess the jury's still out on that one, because I really want to beat up the nearest pine tree.

And, of course, that pine tree is just as empty as the rest of the trees. It's bird free, and I wish it wasn't with my entire being. I pray to see a splash of gray or red or to hear some swearing in Spanish in Fred's tight little bird voice.

As for the rest of what Harper's trying to tell me, I don't think I want to hear that, either. He's trying to make stuff better, but he's not very good at it.

It's all gone, Harper. Everything in my life got blown up again, and you're what's left. You and the graveyard. Congratulations. You win the prize, and too bad for you.

When we get back to the section near Harper's house, I hang Fred's cage in the spot where it was when Cherie let her out. "I'm going to keep food and water in here, okay?"

Harper laughs. "Why? To feed every squirrel and raccoon and rat in Rock Hill?"

"Just in case." I touch the cage. Seeing it hanging there all stocked and ready for Fred makes me feel better enough to think about facing G. W. on a Monday morning, even when I'm sure I won't see Livia tonight, or tomorrow night, or any other night.

When she left the house, she seemed mad at me, or maybe disappointed. Can't blame her for that. She thought she'd found out the worst about me, but now she knows the rest and so do I.

I'm a coward.

Harper shakes his head like I'm being totally stupid about the cage in the tree, but as I'm walking toward the road to meet Dad and get to school, he shouts, "I'll look a little bit longer. What should I do if I find her?"

I turn long enough to tell him, "If she's on the ground or a low branch, throw a blanket or a towel over her, wrap her up, and get her in her cage. Or just call Dad, okay?"

He waves once and heads back into the woods.

"You really need to stay clear of trouble." Marvin's being that new version of himself again. The one who's started to wear classy khakis instead of jeans. The one who frowns. The one who's probably leaving Duke's Ridge as soon as he can and maybe doesn't care anymore. "Livia's dad could have busted out your teeth. I knew it would end badly."

Today of all days, I wish Marvin could just be old Marvin, smiling and laid-back and happy and not in my face. If Harper hadn't said something about me not knocking holes in walls—and if the walls at G. W. weren't made out of concrete—I'd be tempted. "I lost my frigging bird. Livia was just helping me look, and neither one of us took time out to look at a stupid clock."

"Curfew's curfew. Branson could be harsh." Marvin's expression gets even more grim as we elbow toward Advanced Math. "You're lucky Mr. Mason didn't kick your ass. Del, it's like five minutes until you're eighteen and your probation ends. Keep your shit together until then, and stuff will get a whole lot safer."

"Yeah." Short. Cop-out. But the best I can do. I grip my pack as cold air whips through the hall and about a zillion more people cram into the space, trying to get to class.

Marvin has to lift his right arm to let two freshmen get past him. "If Livia does show up, you be sure to tell her to stay away until her dad can't make trouble."

"I got it, okay? Can we just let this—oh, great." I stop walking and Marvin does, too, because Jonas Blankenship is standing outside the door to Advanced Math.

Jonas doesn't take Advanced Math.

He doesn't have his gigantic shadows with him. It's just him in his jeans and long-sleeved jersey, and he looks stressed. When he sees me, his mouth straightens into a line. Now he looks like a guy on a mission. I can smell his overdone cologne from where I'm standing, and the stuff makes my eyes water.

"Hartwick," he yells over the crowd and movement and noise. "Back door, now. I need to talk to you."

Marvin and I get a little closer. I use the few seconds to think, but I keep winding down to, *Whatever. It's not like it matters.*

When Marvin sees I'm not going to try to bolt around the pinhead and get into the classroom, he wheels on me, his brown eyes big. "Are you frigging nuts? You're not going with him."

I don't feel anything at all as I stare back at Marvin. I should, but I don't. Maybe I'm finally starting to crack. "It'll be okay," I say, even though I know he hates it, or maybe because he hates it. "Just go on to class."

A crowd of girls jostles Marvin as they scoot past him, but he doesn't give an inch. "Del, you're being stupid."

What's new?

Out loud I tell him, "Probably. But at least I'm not being a coward for once."

He shakes his head so hard I wonder if he's giving himself a headache, and for about one second, he looks like old Marvin, nervous and worried and like he really gives a damn what I do one way or the other. "I'm not going to just stand here playing lookout while you get your ass whipped or do something that'll get you more charges."

I glance at Jonas, who's stepped away from the door. "I'm not asking you to. Get to math before you're late."

Marvin's face goes still. He studies me, then shakes his head again—not hard this time, and only once. A second or two later, he lugs his pack into class and I shoulder mine, following Jonas through the hall. At least Jonas is big enough to clear a path.

When we get outside, he motions me into the greenhouse the school keeps to grow flowers to sell at holiday fundraisers. Nobody's supposed to be in the greenhouse except during assigned class or volunteer periods, but apparently that rule doesn't apply to Jonas and the football crowd, because he's got a key.

He opens the door, and when I go in behind him and close it, it's hot and it smells like the graveyard. I see that the wooden benches usually full of plants are empty, dotted with pots and dirt. I guess there's no holiday flower to take over after Christmas poinsettias, but I wish there were. There's something sad and devastated about a greenhouse with no plants.

Great. I'm finally having an emotion, and it's feeling sorry for an empty greenhouse. "What can I do for you, Jonas?"

Jonas positions himself in the middle of the greenhouse,

between the two biggest benches. I move to the same aisle so I'm facing him. He's already sweating, and so am I.

"You don't have brothers and sisters, do you, Hartwick?" Jonas asks me his question with a weird look on his face, not one I've seen before. It reminds me of Gertrude the cat stuck between two cans of tuna and confused about which one to pounce on—only without all the drooling.

"No siblings." My dad has a one-eyed rooster, but I don't think that counts. "I'm an only."

He scratches his wet blond hair with one big hand. "Yeah, see, I know you don't get this, but I'm a brother and Cherie's my little sister."

This again. For God's sake. "I haven't had anything to do with Cherie. She showed up at the graveyard Friday night, and—"

"And whatever happened, she came home hysterical, and she cried all weekend." Jonas's hand moves away from his head, and he's making a fist, and suddenly I'm not liking where this is going at all. "She didn't even come to school today."

My eyes dart to the greenhouse windows, which are covered with steam from the heat and moisture inside. We're invisible to the world outside.

"I didn't do anything to Cherie, Jonas. Never have, never do, never will." This needs to be over, this whole Cherie-Jonas-me crap. I've done everything I can to end it. What's it going to take?

"Then why won't she tell me what's wrong?" Jonas stares at me like he's actually waiting for an answer, but he's also walking toward me, and he pushes one of the dirty benches farther out of the way as he comes.

I hitch my pack and make myself not back away from him. "She accidentally let my parrot go. That's probably what she's upset about, that or seeing me with my girlfriend."

Ouch. That made me think of Livia, so now I'm frowning as bad as Jonas.

Stay loose. Don't let him get to you with this junk. Just don't make any sudden moves. My heart's starting to beat fast and I'm beginning to think Marvin was right, that I was totally stupid to do this.

"I'd like to believe you." He's close now and he still looks confused, but he also still has his fists clenched. "It's just—she's my baby sister, Hartwick."

What the hell? Is he pissed or just nuts? I can't figure out what he wants.

He moves so fast I barely see it coming. The punch catches me just under the left eye. A crack. Agony blasts through my head and I'm seeing stars from one eye and misty windowpanes with the other eye, not matching up, not together, like two separate bizarre worlds as I fall backward and hit the concrete floor, saved from a total smash by my backpack. The corners of my books stab into my back as I bounce. Then I shrug out of the pack and come up on my knees.

My whole face hurts like hell, and I'm sucking for air. When I touch my skin under my eye, it feels numb and slick. Blood. Not a lot, but enough to keep me focused on Jonas and his fists.

"Get up," he tells me, and I get up, but I keep my arms at my sides. My heart's beating so hard I can hear it, rush-rush-rush in my ears, and my throat's too tight to swallow.

Jonas comes toward me again and I don't move. He raises his fist slower this time, and I still don't move. My teeth grind as I wait for the blow, hoping it won't be my eye this time.

Jonas keeps standing there with his fist up.

I keep waiting, getting a headache from his first punch and from how hard I'm clenching my jaw.

"Why aren't you fighting back?" Jonas's gaze moves from the blood on my face to my hands, which aren't moving.

"Because I'm on probation." God, talking hurts. "I don't want to go back to jail. As long as I'm not the one hitting you, I think I'm okay."

Jonas still has his fist in the air, but it sinks a little lower. "That's . . . not right."

I laugh. I actually laugh in Jonas's face with him standing there waiting to bash my lights out completely. "That's my life. It sucks."

"Is that why my sister makes you nuts?" His fist goes down. "You afraid she'll do something or say something to get you locked up again?"

"Part of it, yeah." I risk rubbing my face. Pain stabs into

my skull with every touch. I can't even see Jonas through the bad eye, because it's swelling shut. "And part of it—well, she just does."

He smiles, which looks almost scary through the blurry eye. "I guess she makes you nuts because she's a nut."

I edge away from him. "Will you hit me if I agree with that?"

"Nah. I don't hit people who can't hit back." He's looking relaxed now, and I think he's relieved.

"Okay. Well." I try to lean down to pick up my pack. "If you're through beating me up, I need to go see my probation officer and explain why I got marked absent for Advanced Math."

Now Jonas looks guilty, and I have a gut-kicking memory of Cherie's face as she held Fred's empty cage and tried to explain what happened.

"Guess even missing a class would be serious for you," he says.

"Yeah."

Jonas glances at the greenhouse door. "Last period's a freebie for me. Need a ride?"

Jonas's year-old pickup has an iPod plug-in, and we listen to Citizen Cope's "Appetite (For Lightin' Dynamite)" all the way to Branson's office. We talk about Fred and a little about parrots in general, and how I used to play baseball and how I didn't say crap-all to Mr. Mason when he barged into my house and made Livia walk away from me.

"I wouldn't have opened my mouth," Jonas admits as he parks the truck at the curb. "Not with what's hanging over your head. I would have wanted to, though." He bobs his head to the music. "What album does that come from?"

"*Citizen Cope*." I'm watching Jonas, surprised that he said he wouldn't have done anything to Mr. Mason. His sister would have called me a—well, we all know what word goes in that blank.

"I'm looking this guy up." Jonas lets the song finish, then pulls the plug and hands my iPod back to me. "You should be a deejay or something, you know that?"

Deejay. Does that require a college degree or a background check? It's the first moment of genuine hopefulness I've felt in a while.

Then Jonas is driving away and I'm standing alone out on the sidewalk in front of my probation officer's building during school hours, with a brand-new swollen-shut eye and blood smeared down the side of my face and neck.

Darren got an appetite for lightin' dynamite and letting it blow up in his hands . . .

The song echoes through my brain, and the building looks like it's frowning at me. I quit staring at it, get my ass inside, and get up the stairs, wondering if school's already sent Branson an e-mail about the missed class.

Branson's door has his name and credentials stenciled

on the frosted glass windowpane like some old-style private investigator. I knock on the first letter of his last name, and he answers the door before I finish banging.

He's got on slacks and a white shirt, but his tie is off and his collar's open, and for a second, so is his mouth. Then it's, "You're supposed to be in school," and, "Get in here right now."

An ice bag and a few explanations later, Branson says, "I'm calling the police to report this."

I crush the frozen blue freezer bag against my throbbing eye and feel pins and needles all up and down my back and neck. "I'll be in just as much trouble as him. I'm the one with the record."

Branson walks around to his desk and puts his hand on the receiver. "You're allowed to defend yourself. He's got you by what, a hundred pounds?"

"It was no big deal." The heat climbing through me feels bad and good at the same time. It makes me smell the office's leather and polish too sharply. It makes me see the sweat on Branson's dark skin at the edges of his short silver hair, and the way he's watching me like he's not sure what's happening, but he's interested.

I'm not smiling.

I don't know why that occurs to me, but it does. There's no smile because I'm not holding back inside because I just can't, not with what I've lost and my eye trying to fall off my damned face.

"It was a crime," Branson says slowly.

"It was a fight!" I shove myself out of the chair. The ice bag goes flying and smashes against the wall beside me. I kick the leg of Branson's desk. "Don't you get it? Jonas brought it to me over his sister, I handled it, and we're fine. Why would you wreck his life for no reason?"

Branson stands on the other side of his desk staring at me. All the lamps in his office make him seem like he's glowing in the otherwise dark room.

"And his parents' lives," I yell. "You want to ruin his parents' lives, too? And Cherie's? What if some prick-minded DA figures out a way to charge Marvin for knowing we might fight and not telling anybody?"

I'm yelling at my probation officer, but I can't shut up and I don't even want to stop. "I don't want anything to do with cops or attorneys, now or ever again. I'm dealing with *you*. I'm doing everything I'm supposed to do. I've been frigging perfect with all of it, even all the stupid colleges you know won't take me, so cut me a damned break, would you?"

Branson gives it a few seconds. He points to my eye. "Your parents are gonna lose it."

I stare at him, wanting to scream, but I'm a guy and guys don't scream. I'm sick of crap going wrong and getting harder instead of easier. I'm sick of working so hard when nothing matters. I hate this shit. All of it. Every bit of it. I'd hate Branson, too, if he'd ever once act enough like a dick to give me a reason.

"Finally you're wanting to beat the snot out of something." The man actually sounds happy. "Like, maybe me?"

Right about now, I'm wishing I had the freezer pack back, so I go get it off the floor. When I come back to my chair, I sit down and say, "You never act like an asshole. I don't have an excuse."

"If you ever need to go a few rounds, we'll put on the gloves and let you have at it." He stays on his feet and gestures to a pair of boxing gloves on one of his shelves. "I'm not bad and I won't let you win. You'll have to earn it."

"I don't want to fight anybody." I push the freezer pack against my eye, shivering from the cold and the relief.

Branson sits down, still studying me like he's waiting for the alien to pop out of my brain and start screeching. "I think you would like to fight a lot of people, but you've already learned fists won't solve your problems." He picks up his pencil and points at me with the tip. "I think you need to keep letting that anger out in safe ways and in safe places, with safe people. There's no way you're not pissed off—and don't tell me that what you feel doesn't matter."

"But it doesn't, and you know it." I wish I had two ice packs so I could hide both of my eyes.

"Things can change, Del. If you keep doing the next right thing, stuff can get better."

"Look. I've got a black eye, and I lost my bird, and I can't see my girl, and my best friend's hostage to a cookie bar all night long, where I can't even go visit with him, and—and he's about to walk away from me and never look back. I don't want to talk about things getting better. I just can't believe that right now."

Branson doesn't blink once at my pessimism. "If you make a future for yourself, things *will* get better."

"I don't have a future." I'm pushing the ice pack into my swollen face so hard it's what's hurting me now. "Not the kind you want for me."

And it's there in the glowing, leather-polish silence between us.

You could testify at the juvenile sex offender hearings next month.

You could try to get them to change the laws.

You could do something to make your life better, even if you're not really the one who screwed it up.

You could forget about yourself for a while and testify just to help other people. How novel would that be?

I've got no answer for this, and I can't even come up with a smart-ass expression or solid refusal. I don't want him to say anything about all of that, not out loud, because it's not fair today. Not today. Today I can't fight back about anything.

What Branson says is, "Come on. I'll take you home. We'll call your folks on the way, and I'll get in touch with the school about that class." He fumbles in his pocket for his Jeep keys. "But don't think I'll be making excuses for you twice."

Now

After rape and pornography convictions, a job digging graves, losing a parrot, and provoking my girlfriend's psychotic father into threatening to kill me, my parents take the black eye in stride. Almost. They do call the Blankenships, but when Jonas apologizes on the phone, they accept. Life moves along again, or crawls along. I spend my days going to school, working, writing college letters nobody answers, and staring into Fred's cage.

The emptiness inside the big bronze-coated space hurts every time I look at it, but I don't think I'll ever be able to take the cage apart and put it away. It's hers. It's what I have left of her. It feels like when I didn't save Fred, I let part of myself fly away into the night. Everything's tied up with that—Livia and Marvin and everything.

Livia's still gone, too, and Fred's travel cage at Rock Hill is still hanging right where I left it. The food gets eaten down to dust every two or three days. February ticks away, and March comes with so much rain Harper and I have to fight to keep the dirt from washing back into the freshly dug graves.

Marvin barely comes to Rock Hill anymore. We don't talk much at school except about Lee Ann and Notre Dame and other things that make me feel like shit.

Of all the people in the universe, Harper seems to get stuff more than anybody right now. He keeps up the occasional search for my long-lost and definitely probably dead parrot, determined to at least find her little bird skeleton so we can give her a funeral, and a few times, he drives me past Livia's house.

It's a small place, white with black shutters and a small garage. No cars sit in the driveway. Harper goes slow so I can see every detail, then he takes a different way back to Rock Hill so there's no way anybody could say he was going by just to let me look.

If I had e-mail or a website or a way to get text messages, maybe Livia could say something to me, but I don't know if she even wants to. It's a long time until her eighteenth birthday on September thirtieth, and she might be mad at me, or she might be trying to protect me. Whatever she's doing, I have to let her because I can't risk pissing off her father again.

"You getting ready for graduation yet?" Harper asks as his truck rattles away from Rock Hill, taking me to town for my appointments.

"It's just another day." I watch Livia's house pass by and wonder why the curtains are always pulled and the place looks like nobody's ever home. I've got the truck window down even though it's cold, because the breeze keeps my brain awake.

Harper glances at me fast, then turns his bloodshot eyes back to the road. "Not going to walk with your class?"

"Nah. I'd just get booed right off the stage and people might throw shit."

"Damned small towns." He shakes his head. "People ought not to judge other people."

He smells like alcohol all the time now. It's like he bathes in it even when I know he's not drinking, or that he hasn't since the night before. I wonder if it gets in his skin like some kind of invisible dye, coating him everywhere.

We've passed Livia's house, but Harper glances into the rearview at the stop sign just before he turns. "I think she's lying low until her eighteenth birthday so she doesn't get you in trouble."

"Yeah." Nice thought. Love to believe it. Maybe I'll find out in what, six months? I can't think that far ahead. It's hard to believe I'll even be alive in six months, much less waiting for a girl who might or might not be thinking about me.

"I think she likes you a lot," Harper's saying as he steers us toward town. "I think she might be a keeper."

"But." I stare straight ahead as Duke's Ridge streams into focus on either side of the truck.

"But what?"

"I can't tie somebody to my non-future."

Harper's laugh sounds like a wet, wheezy cough. "You're both too young to worry about that. Just enjoy each other. After she's eighteen and her father can't yank her chain or yours, I mean."

The truck's bangity-bounce movement and the thick scent of stale alcohol make my stomach a little queasy. "Are you giving me that live-in-today shit? Shame on you. My therapist and PO are working so hard to get me to make plans for the future."

"The future's overrated." Harper takes a hand off the wheel long enough to wave it once in the air, like he's brushing off my comment. "When I used to go to AA and other twelve-step meetings, they told me if I put one foot in the past and one foot in the future, all I can do is piss on today."

"That's . . . graphic." I hold on as he slows on the main road and makes the last turn. "Ever think about going back to Alcoholics Anonymous, like you mentioned?"

Harper snorts. "Yeah. About as much as you think about all your rosy options for tomorrow."

The truck's gears grind as he pulls to a stop at the curb in front of Dr. Mote's office. He gives me a nod before he drives away, and for a while, I'm caught up in feeling like I should have said more to him about AA and drinking and pissing on the future, but what would that be?

How can I say anything to him when he knows the problem and he knows the solution, and he just won't do it?

It's still on my mind later, long after Dr. Mote and I start our session. Today, we're on the floor on the green rug, with the chairs and beanbags and sofa and pine paneling rising like a strange forest around us.

We've beaten the Livia and Fred and Marvin issues to death, so Dr. Mote's back to the cards today, but different cards. I don't see *tense* or *wary* or any of the old ones spread out on the thick piling between us. Today we've got a lot of adjectives, like *strong* and *cruel* and *handsome* and *kind*, and maybe thirty more.

"What do you think about yourself?" she asks me, gesturing to the array. "Pick some cards that describe you."

I go over each word, feeling nothing about any of them except a twinge in my chest when I get to *quiet*. I pick that and hand it to her.

She rests it on her jeans for a second, then places it off to her left. "What else?"

I choose *smart*. "Not as smart as a lot of people, though."

She points out a few, starting with *strong*. "What about these?"

"I'd probably go for that one first." I point to *fearful*.

She picks it up and moves it into my group. "Fearful's reasonable. Bad things have happened to you and you've had some tough losses lately. I'd be fearful, too, if I were you."

"It's not that." I put my chin on my knee, keeping my eyes fixed on the word. "I'm fearful about saying anything to Harper about his drinking."

Dr. Mote doesn't frown or look startled because she hardly ever does, about anything. "What are you scared of, that he'll fire you?"

"No, not really. I'm scared—I'm scared of judging him or making him feel less than and like I don't respect him."

Dr. Mote nods. "You're scared of making him feel like you do almost every day."

My fingers twitch, and I reach out and pick up *angry*. Dr. Mote doesn't challenge me. She just waits.

"It doesn't matter what I did or didn't do." I add *frustrated*. "My convictions are just there. They just are—like you and Branson. A part of my life. I can't change my record, so what am I supposed to do about it other than work hard, stay out of trouble, and have patience and all that other bullshit you and everybody else tell me?"

Dr. Mote gazes at me for a time, then picks out *strong* and *brave* and puts them in a line at the top of my group. She adds *funny* and *tough*. Then she looks at me. "You're a good person, Del."

Who am I? Why am I here? What's the point? The

questions come back like echoes through my heart and soul. Her choice of words—it's sweet, but I don't feel it. I got confused about the whole coward-not-coward thing until Jonas smashed my face, but other than that, I don't have answers to those three questions that fill up the room every time I come to Dr. Mote's office.

I pick out *cautious* and add it to my group. *Cautious* feels better than *cowardly*, which is one of the choices. "My dad said sometimes bad stuff just comes knocking, and you have to answer the door."

Dr. Mote matches my *cautious* with a *serious*. "Good stuff can come knocking, too. I hope you don't forget that."

I jam my shovel into the wet earth and start the grave. This one's for an eight-year-old kid, so it's a small one. I've never dug a kid grave before. Harper's always done those, but I haven't seen him at all this afternoon. I found the grave list on his kitchen counter along with a note that a funeral director's stopping by after six tonight to get his signature on some papers.

Harper's handwriting looked bad, like he was way drunk when he wrote all of this down. His bedroom door was shut, so I figured that's where he was, passed out until further notice. Being in his cluttered little house creeped me out. I didn't linger.

Outside, it's not raining, but almost. It's not dark, but

almost. Everything feels . . . edgy in ways I can't explain. Mainly, it's so quiet the place feels spooky, but maybe that's just because I'm digging a grave for some poor little kid who didn't wear his bike helmet and hit a speed bump at his apartment building. I've got Fred's cage sitting next to the grave like I used to when she was in it. Fresh food. Fresh water. I'm still at it. I miss her. I miss them all. With no Fred, no Harper, no Marvin, no Livia—even Gertrude the cat gave up on finding Marvin and tuna, and she usually stays at home now. Most of the time, it's just me and my thoughts and too much thinking, especially since I don't let myself hide in my music anymore.

I mess up the grave's corner and have to start back again. There's barely enough room to move in this one. It's so small. If I were God, I'd make sure no kid ever had to die. If I were God, I'd change a lot of things, starting with the huge ones like war and famine and crime and hatred and racism, and I'd get down to the medium things fast—hurricanes, earthquakes, tornados, and tsunamis, stuff like that. Then I'd tackle diseases and stupidity, and we can't forget hypocrisy.

My shovel moves faster and faster.

Good things can come knocking. Who did Dr. Mote think she was fooling with that? I mean, I know good things do happen, but this is me we're talking about. I focus on the grave for a few seconds, then glance at the gray sky as a bird crosses in front of the setting sun.

"Just give me something," I mutter. Then, just in case

there is a God, and just in case He/She happens to be listening, I add, "It doesn't have to be much. I'm just trying to understand. I just want to find my way."

Nothing happens.

After a minute or so, I start digging again, listening to the chop and swish and plop of making a grave for a little kid.

"Feeling sorry for yourself is probably a lot like being a coward," I say to nobody, because there's nobody to talk to anymore. "Don't need to go there."

But I do for a while, long enough to get the grave almost finished. It seems to take forever, but as light drains from the sky, I count my last few shovelfuls with, "Three, two, one."

And as the dirt drops to the ground beside me, somebody says, "Four." Then, "Four, four, four!"

I'm hearing things. I have to be.

But when I spin around to see where the sound came from, I know right away I'm not crazy. Not that way, anyway.

Fred is sitting on her travel cage.

"Four," she says again, then whistles.

I stop breathing. I want to smile, but I'm afraid to move. I don't even twitch because I might make her fly away. I don't let myself shout like I want to, or jump out of the grave and grab for her—nothing. She looks a little skinny, maybe minus a few more feathers on her belly, but there she is just standing in front of me and giving me her mysterious little parrot smile.

Then she lowers her beak, grips the bars, and swings her gray and red body inside the cage. Now I'm jumping out of the grave and grabbing and shouting, closing the door, hugging the travel cage while she gives off fire-alarm screeches and whistles and loud cries of, "Four! Four!" and "*Cerote!*"

I have never finished a grave so fast in my life. It takes force of will to make myself stay long enough to cover the dirt and get everything neat and perfect for the little boy's funeral. Then I grab Fred's cage, make sure it's secure, and I jog out of Rock Hill, almost getting run over flat by Harper's late-evening appointment.

I don't even look back. I just keep jogging, moving as fast as I can all the way home, carrying Fred as carefully as I can, making sure I don't rattle her around too much.

"Mom! Dad!" I bang through the front door, barely remembering to pop off my muddy shoes on the front porch. "Can somebody call the Pet Emergency Clinic? Can somebody take me?"

My house seems as quiet as the graveyard. "Mom!" I call again, knowing I saw both cars in the drive. The wild joy riding shifts to irritation and a little worry. "I've got her. I've got Fred! Can we get her to the vet to be sure she's okay?"

I see them then, coming toward me from the living room side by side. My parents have on matching jeans and matching Adopt Pets T-shirts, and they're wearing the same sad, stunned expressions.

Didn't they hear me? I hold up the cage. "She's not dead. Fred's right here and she's alive."

Tears slip out of Mom's eyes as she gets to us. She puts one arm around my shoulders and with her free hand, she touches the cage bars, careful not to let Fred take a chunk out of her fingertips.

I don't get it. Mom should be happy, like me—and Dad's putting his hand on my face, my head, ignoring the cage and the bird.

Before I can go ballistic with confusion and frustration, Dad makes me look at him, and his simple statement blows up everything in my world all over again, one more time.

"Son, I'm sorry," he says, looking more miserable than I've ever seen him look. "It's Harper."

Now

What do you say at a funeral, when you're talking about one of your only real friends in the world, and he's lots older than you, and he died in a bad way?

After all he did for me, helping me keep my shit together and giving me a job and warning me about Cherie every chance he got and searching for Fred and driving me past Livia's and never once judging me for my past, Harper died alone. He bled to death in his little house at the back of the graveyard from esophageal varices—some horror-movie condition that happens to people who drink too much. One of the funeral home reps found him when he didn't come to the door to sign off on a burial plan, and he'd been dead for a while, probably since that morning, just after he wrote the grave list and note for me.

We got the preacher from the church where Harper was baptized, where his father and his grandfather went, and he's talked already, and now he's standing in the newly opened Dogwood Section of Rock Hill with his Bible, smiling like preachers do at funerals, and he's waiting.

He's waiting for me because I'm supposed to say something now.

"I . . ." I look down at the pine box, which is what Harper bought for himself a long time ago, through Johnston's Mortuary in Duke's Ridge, according to the papers I found in the envelope on his fridge. The envelope was marked *Open this when I croak*, so that was easy enough. It had all his burial information inside, and a lawyer to notify, and that's how we found out that the cemetery, his house, and his piece-of-shit truck are mine when I turn eighteen, and how we knew he wanted a pine box, and which church to go to for a preacher.

The pine box is closed, and I can't see Harper, and I didn't get to see him after he died. It wasn't pretty, according to the doctors.

"I . . . you . . ."

My parents stand around the open grave that I dug by myself, and Dr. Mote's there, and Branson, too. Marvin and his mom came, and Cherie and pinhead and their folks. It's Tuesday, but everybody's dressed Sunday-nice.

I keep choking up. My words don't want to come out at all. Everybody looks as sad as I feel, and I know I'm smiling, and that's wrong, but that's what happens to my face when I feel like this. Angry. Alone. Helpless. Made of paper and cut away from the rest of the world. Only the smell of dirt and pines and the first hint of spring dogwoods keeps me anchored to the planet.

I put my hand on the smooth pine, imagining Harper's beer-soaked peanut butter breath. "If I'd been there, I would have done something."

There. That's something. Better than nothing. It's stupid but true. I keep imagining I could have grabbed him and stopped the bleeding, maybe got him to a hospital in time to save his life. People always think that, right? When bad stuff happens. *If only I'd done this*, or *Maybe if I'd tried that*—but it's all dumb.

Harper's dead, and that's reality, and I have to live with it.

I close my eyes, then open them and try again, keeping my hand on the pine box. "Maybe I should have done a lot more to save you even though you didn't think you needed saving."

My mother makes a funny little noise, and my father pulls her closer. I'm not sure what she's thinking or why she'd feel guilty about Harper, who was my problem and responsibility if he was anybody's. Marvin's mom reaches out and takes her hand, and they share a look that tells me I have no idea what Mom's really thinking and maybe it's better that way. I can't even handle my own thoughts, much less somebody else's.

For a long time, seconds, then minutes, which seem endless when it's quiet, I can't think of anything else to say to Harper. It sucks that he's dead. It sucks that I lost him. It sucks that he lost himself.

Before I start blubbering, the right words come to me, and my hand makes a fist on the pine box lid. I bang it once and the sound's so loud it's like a gunshot in the graveyard, startling birds out of trees and making Fred sit up straight and whistle in her travel cage that I draped with a black cloth. She's hanging in the closest tree and I don't even care if she calls Harper names. Right now, I'd like to call him a few.

"You deserve better than this," I tell Harper. I bang his pine box again, and again, and I tell him that, and it's louder each time I'm saying it, and I feel like something in my gut is unclenching and turning loose, flying at the sky like the scared birds. "You gave me a chance, and you deserve better than this. Why didn't you give yourself a chance?"

Bang!

Bang!

The crowd's jumping each time I hit the pine box, but nobody's running forward to stop me. The minister's backing away, giving me more room.

"I don't know what I'm going to do now. What am I going to do?"

Bang!

Because I don't know. No college wants me and I've got a graveyard and an old truck, and all that's doing is pissing me off and scaring me in weird ways and making me sure about one thing.

Bang!

"I know this much." *Bang!* "Whatever I do, I'm not going to live your life. I'm not going to be you."

Bang!

The last blow almost knocks the pine box off its stand, but I'm through now. I'm breathing hard and sweating and feeling like I finally, finally said the right thing.

I back away from the pine box and have a weird thought that maybe banging on coffins is illegal and I'm going to be in trouble, but I shove that right out of my brain. My folks and Branson and Dr. Mote are probably swapping looks and murmuring about how to have me carted away.

The preacher doesn't seem able to move even though he's supposed to finish the ceremony now so Harper can be lowered into the ground he's tended since he was a little boy.

My hand hurts.

I finally make myself look at my parents—and I start feeling like the preacher, all frozen with surprise at exactly the wrong moment.

They're crying. They're all crying, even Branson and Marvin and Cherie. Pinhead's the only one giving me *you're-a-freak* eyes, but that's because out of everyone present, Jonas

Blankenship is probably the most normal person in the whole bunch.

That's sad. And it's funny.

Thank God I manage not to start laughing—or crying—until I've got Fred and we're walking home, leaving everyone else to watch Harper's pine box slowly disappear under the dirt I piled neatly beside his grave.

Now

I've read about how different types of parrots can be—well, different. South American parrots like macaws and Amazons have to find a lot of food in not a lot of space, so even though they look really different, they tolerate each other and sometimes form "multispecies flocks."

Bet that's noisy. And colorful. And probably crazy as hell.

African parrots like Fred, though, have plenty of room to eat, but they spend time eating on the ground, which makes them vulnerable to predators from the air. Some bigger bird could just dive down and snatch them up and eat them whole. The thing is, African Greys all look alike, with their gray feathers and red tails, so if I were a big, mean parrot-eating bird in the air looking down on a flock of African Greys, all

I would see would be like a moving carpet of gray. I wouldn't be able to pick out a parrot to eat, so I'd blow it off rather than risk diving when I can't tell what I'm grabbing.

This is why Fred doesn't usually accept new people into her "flock," because she's not sure if they'll get her eaten or killed or something. It's also why she grieves if she perceives somebody in her flock has gotten lost.

I'm sure I'm in for shit when Marvin and I start arguing in my bedroom, because Fred's in her big cage listening. Her eyes look weirdly wide and her wings are drooping, and I know she's sad.

Marvin isn't sad or tense or wary or anything simple like that. He's pissed.

"I have to do it," I tell him. "It's the only thing that makes sense. It's the only way out I see."

My already quiet bedroom gets that much quieter. Marvin's got his cookie uniform on without the big rubber hat, and he makes the room smell sweet and chocolatey as he stares at me. Just about everything from the goofball manga books on my little computer desk to the retro Cocoa Puffs sheets and bedspread on my bed seems stupid, especially me. I feel like I'm sticking out to Marvin or like I've changed into something he doesn't recognize, because that's how he's looking at me—sort of new Marvin, but mostly old Marvin, and his face is saying a bunch of things.

I've stuck by you.

I've been the best friend I could be.

I don't ask you for anything, and you can't give me this?

"I have to do it." The words pop out of me again. "I know you don't want me to, and I'm sorry, but—please."

"Please what, Del?" He shakes his head. "Shit, man. I'm finally eighteen. You're finally eighteen. It's finally as over as it can get. Why would you crack it all open again?"

I glance down at my sneakers, at the faint brown stains from graveyard dirt, marks that never clean all the way out no matter how much I scrub and rinse. "I think it's the right thing to do for my future, like Notre Dame's right for you."

Marvin's voice gets hard, and it seems deeper as he raises both hands sideways, like he's about to karate-chop the world. "Because Dr. Mote says it is? Because Branson says so? People haven't exactly given you great advice through this, have they?"

His brown eyes seem like they're on fire. I don't like what he just said because it gives me the sick butterflies like I felt back then, in court, when I was listening to my sentence. When I think I can talk without my voice cracking, I say, "Somebody's got to stop this. The system's out of control."

Marvin lets his hands drop back to his sides. "It'll be new publicity. News shows and papers and blogs—they'll print stuff about us—about you—all over again, Del." He turns away from me, staring at Fred's cage, and at Fred. She's drooping big-time now. "I can't go through it a second time, all the reporters, the stories, the calls and letters, watching your life flush down the toilet—no way."

"I'm not asking you to go with me." Maybe that'll help. Something needs to. His turned back and Fred's sagging wings are making me too jumpy for words.

"Good, because I won't have anything to do with it." Marvin tilts his head back. His eyes are closed, but that's about all I can make out from behind him. "I'm leaving for South Bend in two weeks. I can't be there for something like that. It'll be in the papers. It'll be on television. You know how that'll look."

Ouch.

Yeah. I know.

Marvin doesn't want to be there because it might look like he was supporting sex offenders. Some of the people at Notre Dame probably wouldn't approve.

Absolutely nothing at all to say to that.

He turns slowly to face me, and his expression goes through a lot of funny changes, old Marvin, new Marvin. He looks like he wants to take back what he just said, like he knows how it probably sounded to me. Then his eyes shift off to nowhere, and I'm not sure he's seeing me anymore. Or, he's seeing me, but I'm like a motorcycle rider in his rear-view mirror, getting smaller and thinner as he drives hard and fast away from me.

New Marvin wins out, and new Marvin doesn't have anything else left to say because he just might be thinking, *Finally. Let that image in the rearview go ahead and fade.*

I think . . .

I think Marvin's done.

With the past. With everything we went through. With me.

He's done because he *can* be done, and I'm getting that, even if he doesn't understand it yet, even if he may never put what's happening today into exactly those words.

It's stupid, but I have to try one more time. I have to see if I'm right, to find out if there's any way for us to stay in the same flock. "Don't make me pick between you and doing what I think is right."

Old Marvin would have frowned, maybe sat down, and at least given this some serious thought. Old Marvin would have considered my side and his side, but maybe I've been asking Marvin to look away from his own side too long, without even knowing it.

"I have to," I tell Marvin again, and maybe my own voice is different.

New Marvin says, "You're grown, Del. Do what you want."

Then he's out the door, and he's gone, and the sound of my front door slamming feels as final as my fist on Harper's pine box.

For a long time after Marvin leaves, Fred and I sit in our cages looking at the door with our wings drooping.

Now, Also Known as the Day I Pull My Head Out of My Ass

When people testify before Congress in the movies, it's always in Washington DC, and everything's made out of marble and tile, the ceilings stretch to the sky, and everybody listening looks stern and interested and intelligent. People whisk down the shiny halls, have a moment of angst outside the heavy doors, then walk courageously into the echoing chamber and valiantly say everything that needs to be said.

In real life, there's nothing shiny. There's carpet. Bad carpet. It's old and frayed with multicolored squares. If I look at it too long, it'll blind me. The walls are done in heavy, dark paneling instead of marble, and I have no idea about the legislative people listening to everybody, because Mom and Dad and Branson and I have been waiting six hours for my part, and I've run through the snacks we bought, and I keep going over my notes even though I know I can't memorize them because I've been trying for weeks. I'm not courageous or valiant or anything else. I'm hungry, I'm alternating between roasting and freezing, depending on whether anything's blowing out of the rattling vent over my head; my butt hurts from sitting on a wooden bench with no cushions in the hallway; and I'm nervous.

I'm sad, too. I miss Marvin and I keep thinking I shouldn't be doing this, but then I think about Harper and the rescue rooster and my life, and I get back to believing that I'm doing the right thing. That I'm doing the only thing I can do, even though it'll get me nothing but more trouble.

"They won't vote for it, not when the other party will accuse them of being soft on sex offenders." Mom rubs her eyes with her fingers, shifting her butt around on the bench next to mine. She's not really talking to any of us, so none of us answer her.

Dad's sitting beside Mom, butt firmly in place, and as people stream past us in the hallway, he says, "They're sticklers for the time limit. They keep a little timer running like it's some kind of swim meet or track race. When it's over, they ask you questions, then say thank you and you're done."

"Ten minutes goes by fast," Branson agrees from the bench on the other side of mine. He's holding a black CD player he carried in for me, since I couldn't have walked it through the metal detector. "But the questions can take some time."

I look at my rumpled, Fred-chewed fistful of notes, then drop them on the bench beside my leg and close my eyes. I'll never be able to say anything I wrote down. It all sounds as lame as the college letters I wrote. How could I be so stupid?

Why did I ever agree to do this?

I should have let Branson or Mom or Dad or all of them read over what I was thinking about and give me pointers. Maybe they should have written my speech for me.

Dad wiggles closer to Mom. "The audience is good sized for us."

So casual, like he's wanting to make conversation.

Gee, thanks, Dad; that helps so much.

I wonder if I spur him or peck him in the face, will he give me quiet space like he gives Clarence the rooster?

The doors to the chamber aren't heavy wood. More like leather or vinyl-covered metal. Big and not in sync with the paneled walls or the bad carpet. Nothing matches.

WHAT AM I DOING HERE?

About an hour later, when those doors finally open for me, I'm still asking that question. Then I'm walking down the mismatched carpet, trying not to notice the audience to my left or my right, or all along the back walls on either side of the doors. Reporters. People. Cherie and some other chicks in black. Those things I catch. Everything else I shut out.

Cherie being there makes me feel weird, but also happy, like maybe somebody other than my parents, PO, and therapist actually gives a shit. She gives me a thumbs-up, and I mouth, *Thanks*. I called Jonas when I found Fred, and he let her know everything was okay—even though I still didn't want her coming back to the graveyard. She hasn't, except to attend Harper's funeral.

If I could have brought Fred, I would have, but at least I have her beak marks on my notes.

Um, no I don't. The notes are still on the bench outside.

Oh, wonderful.

I'm a few feet from a long table with a microphone. In front of the long table, more seats line the left and right of the room, sweeping around to center. Most of these seats are filled with men and women with suits and very, very bored or irritated expressions.

My audience.

And I don't have my notes.

I don't even bother glancing over my shoulder at the door behind me, because people are all I'll see. All of them probably hate me or disagree with me, or they're busy making assumptions. Well, not all of them. Cherie's there with her posse.

Branson comes up beside me for a second, but he stops to speak with a sharp-looking woman in a dark suit. She's got dark, angry eyes, and her face kind of reminds me of

Fred's—fixed and hard, yet with a secret smile only a few people will ever learn to notice.

Seconds later, I'm seated with Branson and Mom and Dad behind me, and Branson's CD player at my feet. No notes, but there's music even though I'm not sure I'm allowed to play it. Branson thought it was unusual, but he also thought it was "me," so he helped me out on that part.

The clock is moving.

I'm not talking.

Get off your ass, Del.

Tick. Tick. Tick.

I focus on the bored, irritated people, pretending nobody else is in the room. "I . . ."

All the faces looking at me from the front. From the sides. From the back. I feel them even though I'm trying to ignore them. From somewhere, I smell french fries, of all things. That's just absurd enough to help me choke out the first sentence.

"I didn't want to come here today."

The bored, irritated people in front of me, the ones in the suits, the ones with the votes—they wait. I think they're assuming I'm about to tell them who forced me to come.

Run, my brain informs me, but I ignore that and try again.

"I didn't want to come here today because I've never known how to talk about this, and I still don't. I don't know how to find the words to tell you what happened to me because of the laws, and how the laws are written, and how they affect people my age."

I smile.

My audience doesn't.

Pick out somebody friendly. That was Dr. Mote's advice.

Right.

I'm staring at the zombie legislature from hell. Some of these people look so old they might have died last week and somebody forgot to wheel them out. Two of them are sleeping. One's scratching his nose. The nine or ten women, most of them pucker like they ate lemons just to get ready for me.

I pick out the meanest-looking lemon sucker, the one right up front with the flat face and black skirt and jacket, and the black hair pulled back so tight her eyes slant toward the ceiling. She feels enough like Kaison to do the trick.

"When I was fourteen," I tell her, only I'm really talking to Kaison—or at least a version of him with his hands cuffed and his mouth gagged, duct taped to his chair so he can't do anything to stop me or hurt me, "I had a girlfriend a few months younger than me, and we thought about sex and made decisions we thought were responsible. We didn't take chances with pregnancy or diseases, and we tried to stay within what we thought was right, in our parents' opinions, and in our God's opinion, and in the end, in our opinion."

Just not in yours, right, lemon sucker?

I'm sweating, and she's still got a flat face with absolutely no expression at all. Maybe she's related to Kaison.

"We found out later that it wasn't right in the law's opinion," I tell her, determined if nobody else hears me, at least she will. "Because I was over fourteen and my girlfriend wasn't, everything we did was wrong. Or it got made wrong. That part's hard to keep up with. It's never made any sense to me."

Lemon sucker goes even more sour, and my heart starts bumping the bottom of my throat. I think about my notes outside. Did I say it better in the thousand sentences I scribbled?

Probably.

"What does make sense is this: I was a straight-A student and an athlete, and I had a great girlfriend and a lot of friends. I wanted to be a doctor or a lawyer or a soldier. I never broke any laws, not that I knew about, and I still don't. Now, I can't be any of the things I planned to be. Since I've gotten older, I started wanting to be an avian vet, and I can't do that, either."

Now I look at my hands, because lemon sucker and all the other sleeping, nose-scratching sour faces are getting to be too much for me. I can't believe these people have control of my future.

"I've applied to twenty-seven colleges, community colleges, and even some night schools. Even though I'm eighth in my class with all As and Bs, I've got a steady job, and I scored in the ninety-fifth percentile on my entrance exams, all of my applications have been turned down. I have to register as a sex offender for the rest of my life, in most states. I'm not allowed to play on sports teams or go anywhere kids might hang out—even though I'm not that old. I haven't used a cell phone or the computer unsupervised in three years. Some parts of normal life—a lot of parts—are closed off to me, maybe forever. All I've had for three years is time and uncertainty and music. Music helped me relax and believe. It helped me keep dreaming."

I think about my iPod and my music, and now I'm talking to that and maybe to Dr. Mote in my head, and the sour-faced lemon suckers don't even exist anymore.

"Music helped me keep dreaming even though I'm a weight on my family and my best friend, and on any girl who might be nice enough to give me a chance. I don't know how I'm going to stop being a weight. I don't know how I'm going to make it without food stamps and public assistance, because the only job I've been able to get doesn't pay enough to live in today's world."

Deep breath. Don't stop now.

"All of this happened because I was fourteen and did some things with my girlfriend who was a few months younger than me and who wanted to do them, too. Because of that, my personhood got revoked. I got kicked out of society. It felt like getting kicked off the world."

The clock's ticking down, and when I look up, my audience looks bored.

Are they even listening?

"When you are lost in space, the world seems bright and vibrant and magical, but too far away to touch."

Done. Thank God. I did it. I talked to them even if they didn't care.

My knees feel weak as I stand and pick up the CD player Branson brought in for me. I put it on the table beside me, and my finger hovers over the button, and I almost press it. I check the lights to be sure the battery's working.

Why am I not pushing the button?

This was my big plan. Say what I had to say, then screw their question-and-answer session. Just leave them with the music.

Somebody on the zombie panel clears their throat.

Push the button.

It doesn't feel right.

I still listen to music. I still want my music. But I'm not sure I want it like this.

I put the CD player back down. From behind me, I hear Branson shift in his seat, surprised, but I don't look at him. I make myself face the zombies again.

"When you are lost in space, it's like living in an alternative rock song, in the soundtrack of some cheesy artsy movie that makes people wonder about the point of life. I was going to play you a song so you could hear how I've felt, and I was going to leave before the question-and-answer, but I don't think that's the way to go now. It seems too much like the guy I used to be, not the guy I'm trying to become."

Lemon sucker's looking at the CD player like it's a bomb, but a few of them seem mildly surprised.

"I need a chance," I tell these people who aren't listening. "I need a future. More than anything, I need the past to be over."

I hear Mom make a noise. It's just a little sniff, but I know it's her.

I give my state legislature one last look, and I sit back down and put the CD player on the floor. "If you have questions for me, that's why I'm here. I want to answer, so maybe you can change the laws and never let the state or a DA or anybody else do this to somebody else's life."

There's silence. A lot of silence.

Then lemon face asks, "You say this girl was only thirteen?"

I keep my hands folded in my lap and sit up straight, chin out, eyes focused directly on her wrinkly puckered cheeks. "Yes, ma'am, and I was only fourteen."

"And you touched her. And she wanted you to touch her."

"It was mutual, ma'am. We planned everything we did together."

This is about as much fun as a strip-search, but I think about Fred and everything she must have gone through out in the icy cold by herself. I can be as strong as my parrot, right?

The questions keep coming.

Did your parents know?

Did her parents know?

Tell us what happened with the phone.

Naked pictures?

What part of your anatomy did you photograph?

I answer everything without being sarcastic or asking if any of these people ever really were fourteen, or if they got hatched all ancient and stuck-up from alien eggs or something. Thinking about Livia helps. Her "strong" look. The way she always smiled at me, like *We'll see*, whenever I tried to put her off. She could do this. I can do this, too.

Why did you keep the girl's picture on your phone?

Did you look at it often?

Did you get sexual gratification from looking at the picture?

It goes on and on. They comb through every word, every whisper, every photo and embarrassing detail, even more than the police did. It's being recorded. It'll probably be on television or the Internet. Livia might see it. Cory might see it, or Marvin, or any of my old friends, and I hope I'm telling it like they'd want it told. No matter, I'm telling the truth, all of it, because it makes me feel better about myself even if it doesn't get me anything else.

An hour later, my brain's turning to oatmeal and my words are coming out hoarse, but I keep answering every question, no matter how small or stupid or humiliating, until lemon face says, "Thank you, young man. That'll be all."

"Thank you, ma'am." I get up, step away from the table, and head for the aisle.

Branson makes a move, and I hear the clatter of the CD player as he picks it up and pulls it to him. As I draw even with him, he lifts the player almost like a salute, and he pushes play.

A quiet Cat Stevens song fills the chamber.

Trouble

They probably won't get it, I think as I walk slowly down the aisle toward the exit, hearing the rustle of my parents moving behind me. A glance to my left tells me Cherie gets it. She gives me a giant, genuine smile and thumbs-up as the song plays:

I have paid my debt
Now won't you leave me in my misery

I'm sweating and shaking as I shove through the leather- (or vinyl-) covered doors into the hot-cold hallway. If I'd eaten anything in the last three hours, I'd puke it up.

I can't believe the questions they asked me. I really can't believe I answered them in front of God, everybody, and my parents. I can't believe Branson actually turned on that CD player in our state's legislature.

My notes are still sitting on the bench, so I gather them up without turning around. When I do finally manage to face two of my biggest supporters, Dad's got his arms folded.

I wait.

He stares at me.

Then he says, "I'm hungry. Want to hit the first burger joint we pass?"

My smile hits fast, because that's Dad for, *I'm fine with you,* and it's the most normal moment I've had in months.

Mom can't let it go at that. She has to wrap me up in both arms and say, "I'm proud of you. That had to be—I'm just—I'm proud."

Great.

Now, instead of burgers, I have to think about not crying like a little kid, because I don't think I've heard her say that since I was fourteen years old and still playing baseball and kissing Cory Wentworth.

I hold it together. Barely. And she finally lets me go, but she touches my face like she's measuring me and noticing, all of a sudden, how much I've grown since I was five or six or eight years old. She has tears in her eyes, and I have zero idea what she's about to say. Please don't let it be something sappy and sob yanking. Please.

She opts for nothing, and nothing is fine.

Dad follows behind, and I swear I can still hear Branson playing my music somewhere in the depths of the state-house hearing room.

Chapter One

If I'd known beating up a dead guy in a pine box, then talk-ing to a bunch of even more dead-looking people from the government would earn me a good recommendation from my probation officer and get me discharged from psycho-therapy, I might have tried all that sooner.

Okay, no. Not really. But it was still weird, saying good-bye to Dr. Mote and to Branson, too. I got my walking papers from probation two weeks after my birthday, about three months after graduation.

Who am I?

I'm Del Hartwick, high school graduate, graveyard owner, and guy still looking for a way to keep this little foot-hold I've managed to gain on planet Earth.

Why am I here?

Because this is my graveyard and I've got a grave to dig, already in progress. All right, all right, and because it's September thirtieth, and I'm . . . hoping. Stupid as it sounds, I'm hoping.

What's the point?

I'm starting to think I'll get the answer to this one when I'm eighty or one hundred. I'll let you know.

Fred gives me a fire-alarm screech from her cage on the tree branch just as somebody says, "You're still really good at that grave-digging thing."

Deep voice. Not the voice I wanted to hear.

"Thanks," I tell Branson as I put down my shovel. "I think."

I'm about to ask him if he wants a piss sample just for old time's sake, but when I turn around, I realize he's got somebody with him. A woman. A woman holding a battered piece of paper. She looks familiar and sort of intense, with her dark eyes and the way her face has no expression at all.

Was she at the legislative hearings? Did I see her there—and was it before or after I had to talk about exactly how my penis looked in the photo I took?

Heat creeps up my neck, threatening to turn my cheeks an even deeper shade of red than the digging already accomplished. I get out of the grave I'm hollowing out in Harper's Dogwood Section, too far from the main drive to hear cars. Behind Branson and the woman he brought to Rock Hill, I see funeral home staff taking up chair drapes from the service this morning. I'll need to finish filling in Mrs. Ammonson's grave, making it perfectly even and flat, so I can lay the turf back down with no ripples. Some of the ferns and other stuff Mr. Ammonson left at the plot, I'll plant around the headstone after Mom tells me which ones will survive in our climate. The ones that won't survive, I'll send over to Duke's Ridge Nursing Home, because a lot of the patients there love having plants to tend in their rooms. The flowers I'll move on top of the grave and leave them until they die, then clean them up and mail Mr. Ammonson any angels or doves or permanent parts of the arrangements.

There's nobody else around. Nobody at all, even though it's September thirtieth. I can't help the sadness growing way down deep, but I can put it off a while to be polite. I hope.

I dust off my hands, expecting Branson to introduce me to his friend, but he opens with, "It passed, Del."

Dust forms a thin brown cloud in the sunlight between us. I stop moving my hands. I think I heard him correctly, but I'm not letting myself believe it or even trying to understand what it means.

"Romeo and Juliet passed—and it's retroactive." Branson's words come out fast and happy, and then he does something I've rarely seen him do.

He smiles.

And just like that, half the nightmare of Good-bye

Night finally comes to an end. What happened between me and Cory—not illegal, since we were more or less the same age and both of us wanted to do what we did.

It's real but it doesn't feel real. Not yet.

"I'm not a rapist anymore?" I know the question sounds stupid, but I ask Branson, anyway, because my heart's speeding up and my breath's coming fast, and I just need to hear it directly, and from him.

His smile never fades as he reaches out and claps one big, strong hand on my shoulder. "You never were a rapist, Del. Now the law agrees with me."

I look at the woman with him, the woman I don't even know, and I tell her, "I'm not a rapist."

My head feels like a balloon, detaching from my neck and lifting toward the blue sky on a string.

"The sexting's still a problem," Branson says, letting go of my shoulder. "There's another law pending to turn that into a misdemeanor instead of a felony, but right now it's on hold because it conflicts with federal child porn laws, and nobody knows how that's going to work out."

I'm still Mr. Happy Balloon, way above the graveyard looking down. "So I still have to register as a sex offender for the pornography convictions."

Should be a downer, but it's not because I'm high on *I am* not *a rapist.*

"Yes. I'm sorry." Branson's smile falters. "Until you're forty-five years old in this state, and some other states, forever—but give it a year, maybe two, and maybe that'll change."

"You're an optimist." *I'm not a rapist. I'm not a rapist!*

"Somebody has to be." Branson finally notices how I keep looking at his lady friend, and he does the gentleman thing with, "Del Hartwick, I'd like you to meet Danita Johnston. Ms. Johnston, Del Hartwick."

Ms. Johnston grips her piece of paper in her left hand and shakes with her right. Firm grip. Very direct stare. "Congratulations on the law passing, Mr. Hartwick. That does make things easier."

I'm giddy, but I'm with it enough to wonder, *Easier for who? How?* "I think I saw you at the hearings." Remembering now. I thought she had a secret parrot smile. "You were there, weren't you?"

"I was." And she does have a secret parrot smile. It's so small nobody but a parrot nut would even notice it on her otherwise hard, immobile face. "I'm with Community College, Mr. Hartwick. I'm director of Admissions, and I went to those hearings to see if this boy was for real."

She holds up the battered piece of paper.

When I stare at it, not comprehending, she opens the paper along its worn creases and reads, "Dear Ms. Johnston." At this, she gives me a look over the top of the paper. "That would be me."

I'm turning red now, and losing my natural high over hearing about the law passing, and feeling like I can get in trouble with Branson even though I'm over eighteen and off probation.

His expression's not any lighter than Ms. Johnston's as she continues quoting the smart-ass letter I wrote what seems like a thousand years ago. "My name is Del Hartwick and I have a felony conviction. In the eyes of the law, I am a criminal. I can't tell you I didn't do it, because I did. I can't tell you it was right, but I'm not sure it was wrong."

She looks at me again. "Yes, ma'am" I say, because, *Sorry I was kind of sarcastic* seems lame, and *oh, shit* might get me slapped. Man, it's hot in the graveyard (even though fall's here) as she reads through the next part, and goes on to the next.

"I'm not what those charges say about me. I'm not anything like that. I'm Del. I'm seventeen. I have a parrot and a best friend and a girlfriend and a job digging graves. I have good grades and I want to be an avian vet, and maybe help my folks with the Humane Society and all their animal rescue operations.

"My life got stolen from me, and I want it back. This application means a lot to me. I'm lost in space and I want to find a way home. Nobody else can get me back to the planet, so I have to do it myself."

She pauses again.

I can't quite believe I wrote any of that. I could have been more respectful. Polite, maybe?

Ms. Johnston glances toward the tree holding Fred's cage. "This would be the parrot?"

"Yes, ma'am. Her name is Fred. Nobody knew she was a girl until she laid an egg, and it was too late to change her name."

"Fred," Fred says, tentatively, like she's testing the waters.

"I see," Ms. Johnston says, then she goes straight back to the letter. "That's why I'm writing to you, to ask permission to apply, and to ask your help in getting a fair chance at going to college. My name is Cain Delano Hartwick, and I want a future. Let me apply, judge me on what I can do, and give me a chance. Please."

Still looking at me, she finishes by saying my name emphatically, just like I wrote it.

DEL.

"Fred," Fred says from her cage, with almost the same emphasis.

Ms. Johnston gives Fred a look, and I'm thinking I see the parrot smile, but I'm probably crazy.

"And all this time," Branson says, "Dr. Mote and I were worried you didn't know who you were and what you wanted."

I don't know if I'm supposed to apologize or run. Both seem like viable options, but I go for what comes to my mind instead. "I know what I want. I just don't know how I'm ever going to get it."

Branson nods at this and looks back at Ms. Johnston.

"I've been following your progress since I got this let-ter," she says. "First with Mr. Branson, then later on my own. I've checked your grades. I've talked to the teachers who wrote recommendations for you. A little while ago, I even spoke to your parents."

Fred whistles, then drops a bomb, and I start hoping she doesn't start with the fart and burp noises. I fidget with my fingers, but make myself meet Ms. Johnston's gaze. "Why?"

Fred farts, and it's really, really, really loud.

Ms. Johnston shuts her eyes, but otherwise, she doesn't react to the fart noise. "Because I've gone out on a limb so far I can hear people sawing the branch behind me. I wanted to be sure I wasn't as crazy as everyone thinks I am."

"That sounds like something I'd say," I tell her as Fred follows the fart with a winning burp, an *excuse me,* and some witchy-sounding laughter.

Ms. Johnston's mouth twitches as she looks at the par-rot. Fred goes quiet and poofs out her feathers, one domi-nant female recognizing another—and maybe surrendering. For now.

When Ms. Johnston turns back to me, she says, "We're too late for this semester, because I had some board mem-bers still fence-sitting and putting up objections. With the passage of the law, that'll end. A little arm-twisting—how does January sound?"

"January," I repeat, beginning to understand, but like

before when Branson told me about the law passing, not quite able to believe it's true.

"To start classes." She nods. "We're solid in the sciences and I assure you, if you're aiming for premed or preveterinary, your scores from Community will get respect at any four-year that takes you."

She waits, like I'm supposed to say something, but my brain is a total blank.

Ms. Johnston fills in the silence. "Mr. Branson tells me your future might ultimately lie in broadcasting or the music industry, and Community also has a good communications program to give you a start in those areas. Does that interest you?"

I turn to Branson because I know him better and I trust him more. "Is she serious?"

He gives it straight back to me just like he's always done. "Are you?"

That's when I know it's true.

My head buzzes so loud it's hard to hear Ms. Johnston when she's handing me the full application to Community, along with a letter giving me permission to apply, and explaining that I need to fill in every single blank. It's hard to hear Branson, too, when he says he'll help me if I run into any problems on the application questions.

I stand there holding the application, thinking I should make twenty copies of it in case Fred eats a few or I get dirty fingerprints on the pages or something. I don't have a computer in Harper's old house, where I'm living now. A computer would probably fry his decrepit fuse box and burn the place to the ground—plus, it just felt weird to even consider. I don't have a cell yet, either, but that's because I can't afford one on my own and I don't want my parents paying for it. I think I'll start small with the cell. It's less intimidating.

Ms. Johnston steps over to admire some of the flowers on Mrs. Ammonson's grave, obviously giving Branson a moment alone with me.

"How are you, really?" he asks me, the familiar worry lines returning to his forehead. "Holding your own?"

"I'm doing okay so far." I gesture to the graveyard. "It's a lot of responsibility, but I like being busy. I just—I miss Harper. A lot."

"Whatever happened with your girl, with Livia?" Branson glances down at his watch, and I know he's checking the date.

My wild excitement about the law and Community College fizzles down to a quiet sort of background joy, and what comes to the front is that sadness again. That deep-down ache that doesn't have an antidote even if I know its name.

Livia.

"Today's her birthday, but she's not here," I tell Branson. "That's all I know, and I guess that kind of says it all."

He grumbles agreement and looks unhappy on my behalf. Then he makes it a little worse. "How's Marvin?"

"Gone. But he did send me a postcard from a cookie shop near Notre Dame." I point in the general direction of Indiana, or at least I think it's the right direction.

"What happened to Lee Ann?"

That makes me laugh. "He ended up with a harem those last few months. He was just waiting to turn eighteen, and all the girls he's dating have to prove they're eighteen. He said some of them think he's a dork for being so careful, but he doesn't care."

"Good for him. I know that whole mess took a toll on all of you. I'm glad you're moving past it." Branson's smile is back, and he glances toward Ms. Johnston, who's sniffing roses.

"His postcard said he'll pick me up for a visit, but I don't want him to." I turn back to the grave I was working on so I'm not looking right at Branson. "I don't know how Notre Dame will feel about having me on campus."

"We'll get the rest of this mess straightened out," Branson says. "Give it time, Del."

"Time's all I've got. Time and a graveyard." Jeez. Am I sounding like Harper? "And a lot of graves to dig. This place really is huge, and it serves a ton of counties."

Branson laughs. "Well, good luck to you. I'm not helping you dig."

"I will," says somebody from behind Branson, and I jump from the shock-tingle of hearing that voice, her voice, again after all these months.

From her cage in the tree, Fred cranks up with whistles and bombs and then a delighted chorus of, "Four, four, four, four, one, two, THREE, four!"

Branson and I turn around, and there she is, standing there just like a vision in her jeans and a blue shirt that hangs loose around her waist and stirs in the breeze. Her dark brown eyes look wide and hopeful, but also scared, and she's wearing her hair loose around her shoulders. It looks so soft my fingers flex because I want to touch it.

"Well," Branson says, gesturing toward Ms. Johnston, who has stopped sniffing roses and started making her way toward Fred's cage for a closer look. "I should go get her before your bird chews off her nose."

"Good idea," I tell him, and manage a "Thanks" before he moves off and leaves me alone in the sunshine, staring at Livia. The sun makes golden patterns in her hair, and her skin's turning pink from the heat and whatever's scaring her. I realize she's got a single suitcase, a black one, and it's sitting on the ground beside her.

She looks down at the suitcase, then back up at me. "Hi." Her lips work like she's running through a lot of things she could say. She settles on, "I've been waiting a long time for my birthday."

"Me, too."

She smiles, and I smile—the real kind of smile—and for right now, we don't have to say any of the rest of it, about why she waited, and how I know why she waited, and how we missed each other.

"I . . . ," she whispers. I wait, ready for anything, not even caring what she says as long as it has to do with her seeing me whenever she wants now, whenever we both want. I'm hearing five different songs in my head at once, but the loudest one is probably the corniest, "Brown Eyed Girl" by Van Morrison.

"I need a job," Livia says, and the fear's back on her face again.

I blink.

Not what I expected.

But the suitcase . . .

And I think I'm starting to get it. She didn't just come here to see me today. She left home to do it. Maybe she would have left home anyway the day she turned eighteen, to get away from her father and the cloud over her family after what her sister did—but she packed her suitcase and she came here.

"This is a dead-end place, in case you haven't noticed." I keep my eyes on hers and try to do the right thing. "You want out of Duke's Ridge and you want to go to college."

"Someday. But for now, I need a job. And I need a place to live." She's talking fast and she barely slows down for a breath. "I hope you say yes, but if you say no, I have some other options—an aunt in Reno and my cousin in New Jersey."

I eye her suitcase. "It's a long way to those places. You on foot?"

"The car was in Dad's name. So was almost everything else I owned." She lifts the suitcase. "This is it. I'm starting light. We'll call it Zen for now, if you don't mind."

Wow.

Now I'm happy and scared all at the same time.

"My car sucks." I jerk my thumb toward the ancient Ford truck I inherited from Harper. I parked it under the tree next to Fred's cage when I drove out to this spot to start digging. "Definitely not eco-friendly. Neither is the house. I'm still finding beer cans, and Gertrude came with me. She's drooling everywhere because I can't afford tuna."

"Fred," Fred shouts, and she drops some more bombs, and she farts for good measure, then laughs about it.

"I can take it," Livia says. I'm pretty sure she means the truck and the house and Gertrude's drool, even though Fred immediately launches through fresh burps and some Spanish swear words.

"If you keep hanging around here, you'll be lost in space just like me." I reach out and touch Livia's face with my fingers. She's close, and she's warm, and she's real even though I'm sure I'm dreaming. "It'll take a lot more than eighteen inches of dirt to cover up the history you'll be making if you're with me—and everybody will treat you like you're made of paper or invisible."

"You won't treat me like that, or your folks, or Marvin

and his mother whenever he's in town. Fred doesn't think I'm made of paper and Gertrude doesn't care." She glances toward Oak Section, where her sister's buried. "And my mom can see me whenever she visits Claudia. As for the eighteen inches of dirt"—she shrugs—"I don't think I'll be needing to cover anything up or hide anything at all. Not here. Not with you."

I trace her cheekbone, needing to know she's still right there and not about to vanish in a puff of smoke and broken sunlight the first second a cloud passes across the sky.

She frowns for a second, then smiles—almost a parrot smile, but a little better. "I'm not asking you to marry me, Del."

"If you did, I might say yes." I slip my fingers into her hair and pull her toward me.

Her kiss feels . . . like being on Earth, like being right here, right now, right where I'm supposed to be.

"Well," she murmurs in my ear, "maybe I'll ask you in three or four years."

"Deal. I need to finish school, anyway, and so do you."

"Nag, nag." She pulls away from me and picks up her suitcase before I can do it, and she heads toward Harper's house, which is my house now. And Fred's. And Livia's. It's our house until we figure out what's up, what's down, and what we're going to do on Earth now that we've all found our way back to the planet.

As I watch her go, Fred says "Livia" in my voice, or it might have been Dad's. I can't really tell.

"Livia," I agree in my voice, thinking Mom and Dad will probably show up any minute with burgers and cupcakes and balloons to celebrate the law passing.

A few minutes later, Livia comes back from Harper's in older jeans and a darker shirt, with her fairy hair pulled back.

She's smiling . . . and she's carrying a shovel.

Acknowledgments

Everyone I've ever known is braver than me. No, seriously. It's hard to tell the truth, just let it spill out, and there are lots of people who tell the truth better than I do. My daughter, Gynni, is one of them, and Gisele, and my son, JB, and my friend and agent, Erin, and my friend Judy. I have to thank them for being so brave.

Everyone I've ever known is gentler than I am, in so many ways. My editor is so very gentle, and her kindness and unassuming intelligence make me wish I could be her if it's even possible for me to grow up. Thank you, Victoria. On this piece, because Victoria was busy adding to the beauty of the world, I worked with Margaret Miller, who proved to be gentle, too, and waded right in with courage and determination, even when I was being stubborn. Thank you, Margaret.

Everyone I know is more loyal and better at sticking it out than I am. My friend Debbie, my friend Susan, my dogs Alfred and Katie, the guy who sold us our wonderful house, Ralph—these people face real adversity and keep on going, and they inspire me. Thanks, all of you.

And just as important, I thank every reader who has ever written me or e-mailed me with thoughts about my books. You're why I tick and why I type.